# DEAD CAT BOUNCE

# DEAD CAT BOUNCE

## NIC BENNETT

razOr
bill

An Imprint of Penguin Group (USA) Inc.

Dead Cat Bounce

RAZORBILL

Published by the Penguin Group
Penguin Young Readers Group
345 Hudson Street, New York, New York 10014, U.S.A.
Penguin Group (USA) Inc., 375 Hudson Street, New York, New York 10014, U.S.A.
Penguin Group (Canada), 90 Eglinton Avenue East, Suite 700, Toronto, Ontario, Canada
M4P 2Y3 (a division of Pearson Penguin Canada Inc.)
Penguin Books Ltd, 80 Strand, London WC2R 0RL, England
Penguin Ireland, 25 St Stephen's Green, Dublin 2, Ireland (a division of Penguin Books Ltd)
Penguin Group (Australia), 250 Camberwell Road, Camberwell, Victoria 3124, Australia
(a division of Pearson Australia Group Pty Ltd)
Penguin Books India Pvt Ltd, 11 Community Centre, Panchsheel Park,
New Delhi – 110 017, India
Penguin Group (NZ), 67 Apollo Drive, Rosedale, Auckland 0632, New Zealand
(a division of Pearson New Zealand Ltd)
Penguin Books (South Africa) (Pty) Ltd, 24 Sturdee Avenue, Rosebank, Johannesburg
2196, South Africa

Penguin Books Ltd, Registered Offices: 80 Strand, London WC2R 0RL, England

10 9 8 7 6 5 4 3 2 1

Copyright © 2012 Nic Bennett

ISBN 978-1-59514-469-0

Library of Congress Cataloging-in-Publication Data is available

Printed in the United States of America

*For Jo, Jake, Ty, and Izzy*

# Prologue

# AMSTERDAM

## SEPTEMBER 20

**The boy sat** in the hotel room weighing the gun in the palm of his right hand. He had never held a gun before, not till four minutes ago when his father had handed the nine-millimeter automatic pistol to him. "For your protection," he'd said. Jonah curled his fingers around the matte black handle and ran the middle finger of his left hand along the barrel. His right forefinger slipped behind the trigger guard and gently touched the trigger. The gun was colder and heavier than he had expected. It provided no reassurance to him, only fear.

He glanced at the laptop on the desk next to him. One-third of the files were safely installed. Seven minutes of download time remained.

He looked at the gun again. His father had told him to aim for the chest, the biggest target. He had grabbed him by the shoulders, his face only inches away from his own, his fingers and thumbs inflicting pain where they dug into his flesh. "Head shots are only for the movies. Take the target down first, and give yourself the chance of a second shot. Do you understand, Jonah? Do you understand? He will kill you if you don't kill him." His father had said this. His father who worked in a bank.

Jonah had nodded.

Five minutes of download time remained.

"And then you run. Bring the gun and the computer, even if it hasn't completed the download. Get out while you can. Do you understand?" His father's fingers had dug deeper, and Jonah had nodded again, more numbly this time.

"Now put on your coat. Hopefully it will be me coming through the door, not him. Just don't shoot me if it is. Even if you want to." This was not a joke, not an attempt at dark humor to lighten the situation. It was a statement of fact. "It will take eleven minutes to download the files and ten minutes to collect the car. I'll be back."

Then David Lightbody had departed, leaving his sixteen-year-old son alone in a dark hotel room in a foreign country, holding a gun.

Three minutes.

A floorboard creaked and Jonah's breath caught in his throat. His entire body seemed to tremble. A shadow had appeared at the bottom of the hotel room door. Jonah stared at it, forcing the shaking to stop. He raised the gun, adrenaline pumping through his lean frame. *Crunch!* There was a splintering of wood as the door crashed open.

Jonah could make out a black leather coat, a mustache, and a gun. He saw the intruder's familiar eyes lock on to him, the gun swinging his way. *He will kill you,* his father had said. Jonah squeezed his right forefinger on the trigger. For a short moment it was as if the world had stopped. The room was filled with complete silence. And then a deafening roar erupted. The intruder's head whipped back against the door frame. His body crumpled, his gun falling to the ground as his right leg twitched: once, twice, and then stillness.

Jonah's ears were ringing from the sound of the explosion. His hands began to shudder, the gun loosening in his grip. He squeezed his hands tighter to avoid dropping his one means of protection, the muscles on his forearms standing out with the effort. Slowly he lowered his shaking hands, his eyes still fixed on the body, and put the gun carefully down on the desk. Then he vomited three times, the bile flowing through his fingers. Shock was taking over.

He had just killed a man.

Jonah wanted to close his eyes, to pretend that he was somewhere, anywhere else. He retched again, emptily this time.

*No!* His brain was sending him a signal. He had been here before. He knew how to recover from this. Yes, he had finished a race. He was through the finish line, on his knees, shaking, vomiting. Someone would put a blanket around him, congratulate him on his victory, his record-breaking effort. He had pushed himself to his limit, and his body was now fighting back. The shaking would slow. The vomiting would end. He would feel the warmth of his achievement and hear the applause of his success. He would look up, and there would be his housemaster or coach. They would be looking concerned, only relaxing when he smiled at them.

Jonah brought his head up, but there was no noise, no warmth, no comfort. Only silence and the laptop, the bar of the download indicator nearly full.

Two minutes.

Jonah snapped upright, adrenaline again coursing through his body. There were still two minutes of download time left! He wouldn't get another chance to access these files. "And then you run," his father had told him. But Jonah wasn't so sure. He might lose the information they needed if he shut the download down now. He had to wait.

He turned and reached for the damp towel on the bed. The smell of his vomit was strong. He wiped his hands and threw the towel back.

Ninety seconds.

He put the gun in his coat pocket and placed one hand on the cable at the rear of the laptop, his thumb on the release. He'd be ready to run as soon as the download completed.

Eighty seconds.

*Clunk!* A mechanical noise invaded the silence in the room. Jonah recognized it as the sound of the elevator. It was them! The other men were coming. Jonah looked back at the download bar. Sixty seconds remained. How long until the men reached him? The elevator was old and slow. Jonah had timed it. Forty-eight seconds from the ground floor to the eighth floor. Next there were the double doors to open—first the automatic door, and then the manual one.

It would take Jonah ten seconds to reach the fire escape.

There was another clunk, and the whirring of the elevator machinery ceased. Jonah exhaled. His heart seemed to be trying to force its way out of his chest. They'd stopped on another floor. That gave him ten seconds extra . . . if he'd gotten the calculations right.

*Clunk!* The elevator started again.

The computer was now counting down the download by the second. Fifteen, fourteen, thirteen. Jonah had to leave at two seconds. Eleven, ten, nine. He was about to press down on the release when he heard another noise: a human noise. Jonah's hand jumped. It was the sound of a man groaning.

Jonah looked over at the body in the doorway. It was moving. The intruder wasn't dead!

Eight, seven, six.

There was another heavy clunk as the elevator stopped on Jonah's floor. Still he waited. He *had* to retrieve all the files. Five, four, three. The man groaned again.

Two seconds.

Jonah pulled the computer cable, his right hand closing the laptop, his left hand scooping it up under his arm. He looked at the now animated body, seeing that the man's head was coming up, his eyes beginning to open. It was now or never.

Jonah ran straight to the door, jumping over the man as he blasted through the doorway. He could make out the sound of feet pounding behind him as he sprinted down the corridor, transferring the laptop under his right arm.

"Oi!" someone shouted, but Jonah resisted the urge to look behind him. It didn't matter who was in pursuit. He'd been trained to focus on the finish line.

He reached the fire escape and slammed his right leg into the ground as a brake. He pivoted off the same leg, smashing his left shoulder into the fire escape door and dropping his left arm down so that it hit the bar and released the lock. It was a deft move, and by the time the heavy man behind him reached the door, Jonah was already down the first two flights of stairs. He took small, fast steps, projecting off the handrail with his left hand at the end of each flight, gaining vital seconds at every turn. The weight and strength of the man chasing him was no match for his speed and agility.

But now he could hear a second set of running footsteps, this time coming up the stairs toward him. His father had told him that there were three men watching their hotel room. One was coming down the stairs above him. One was in the getaway car outside. It was the third man! He must have guessed the escape route. Jonah was trapped.

He looked downward to see if he was close enough to jump down the stairwell to the bottom. Straining to make out the number of flights below, he missed the last step and stumbled, falling to his knees. His right elbow hit the ground, sending pain through the whole of his arm. The computer jolted out of his grasp.

"Got you!" a voice from above shouted. This time Jonah looked behind him. He saw a heavyset man bounce off the wall on the landing above, a gun in his hand. Jonah looked downward again toward the oncoming attacker, wondering if perhaps he could make it past him after all, and caught a brief glimpse of a familiar orange watchstrap. A feeling of warmth rushed through him at last. It was his father coming up the stairs! He still had a chance!

"Go! Go! Go!" Jonah's father shouted.

"Gun!" Jonah shouted back. Still on his knees, Jonah scooped up the computer and dive-rolled down the stairs past his father.

David Lightbody never paused. He propelled himself upward in a kind of Superman-flying pose, his right arm stretched outward, his fingers knifing into the attacker's throat. The man made a choking sound as David slammed him to the ground, forcing the gun from his hand so that it bounced down the stairs past Jonah. Jonah watched as his father swung his head back and drove it down hard into the man's face. He heard the sound of cracking bone and saw his father roll off the now immobilized attacker. Suddenly, his dad was back on his feet and running down the stairs, two steps at a time. He picked up the fallen gun without breaking his stride and grabbed Jonah on his way past.

Together they made their way down the final flights of stairs and out of the hotel to a narrow street that ran along the east side of the building. Twenty yards to their left was an illegally parked, nondescript small car. Jonah's father unlocked the car remotely as they ran toward it, pushing Jonah toward the passenger side. As soon as they had both dived into their seats, David started the engine and accelerated south toward the main road, ignoring the red traffic light as he swung the car left into the traffic.

Behind them the man Jonah had shot appeared at the fire-escape door they had just exited. He gasped for breath, his right hand gripping the top of his left arm to apply pressure to the wound. The man's expression steeled as soon as he noticed the car's taillights in the distance. He reached into his right pocket and pulled out his cell phone. He tapped the touch screen and spoke, holding the phone a small distance from his mouth. "East side. Pick me up now. Fast."

He hit the screen a second time and looked at the image that appeared, a blinking dot overlaid onto a street map, moving away from him. The tracker was still live. He replaced the phone in his pocket and leaned against the wall, breathing deeply. For a moment he grimaced in pain, causing his mustache to turn upward at the ends. He looked at the blood on his right hand, tested it by rubbing his thumb against his fingers, and then wiped the whole of his hand on his black leather coat.

A motorcycle hurtled around the north corner onto the street, long blonde hair visible under the rider's helmet. She pulled up next to the man, and he climbed into the sidecar with surprising nimbleness.

"Straight ahead and turn left," he ordered. "He's cracked the security. They have the Apollyon files. We must not lose them."

# Part One

# *LONDON*
## FOUR YEARS EARLIER

# CHAPTER 1
## Monday, August 23

**Jonah Lightbody was** twelve years old when he discovered what he wanted to be when he grew up. He wanted to work on the trading floor of one of the big banks in London or New York. He wanted to make millions, wear a suit, and drive a fast car.

It all started during the summer holidays. He was home from boarding school, alone and bored. All his schoolmates were away with their families or playing with "homemates." Jonah didn't have homemates. And he might as well have not had a family. His parents were divorced and he lived with his father, a dour, distant figure who worked long hours and traveled a lot. As for as his mom, Jonah hadn't seen her since she'd fled to America to start her "new life" three years previously. The au pair was the nearest thing Jonah had to family or a homemate, and she was more interested in entertaining her new boyfriend than entertaining Jonah.

Then, two weeks before the end of the holidays, he found a memo from Helsby, Cattermole, & Partners sitting on the kitchen counter. His dad must have left it there when he had been angrily throwing the contents of his briefcase about the previous night trying to find his passport. Jonah knew that he probably shouldn't snoop, but the memo's subject line was "Re: Take Your Children to Work Day," so in a way he supposed that it was meant for him. After all, Helsby Cattermole was the bank where his dad worked, and Jonah was his only child. As soon as Jonah read the memo in full, the wheels of his mind began spinning. The opportunity to spend the day at his dad's office might be what he'd been looking for: If he visited him at work, the two of them might actually have something to talk about.

Of course his dad said no at first, but Jonah didn't let that stop him. He nagged and nagged until he got the answer he wanted.

Now the day had arrived, and Jonah was bouncing off the walls with anticipation. Even the ringing of his alarm clock at five thirty A.M. failed to dim his excitement. He was going to spend a whole day with his dad. Just the two of them. At his office!

He jumped out of bed, got himself dressed, ran downstairs to have breakfast and back upstairs to brush his teeth and grab his shoes. "Have you seen my other shoe, Dad?" he yelled, charging back down the stairs, holding a single black loafer up high in his left hand.

"No," said David Lightbody, standing by the front door, his foot tapping on the ground. It was now six fifteen, ten minutes later than he usually left for work.

"Urgh. I can't figure out where I left it," Jonah said, now rummaging through the pile of shoes that they left by the front door.

"Where did you find the other one?" The tone of David's voice was not sympathetic.

"By my bed," said Jonah, still rifling through the mountain of discarded footwear.

"Did you look *under* the bed?"

Jonah stopped searching, his stomach dropping. "No," he answered. His dad always had a way of making him feel foolish despite his continued efforts to impress him. Jonah swallowed. "I'll be really quick!" he said as he dashed back upstairs and returned seconds later with the other shoe to find that his dad had already exited the house.

"Shut the door after you and get a move on," David shouted over his shoulder.

Jonah slid on his shoe and chased after his father, slamming the front door behind him, his sandy blond hair dipping into his eyes. When he caught up, he still had to skip every few steps to keep pace. His recent growth spurt and forays onto the school track team were still no match for his father's broad, six-foot frame and long stride.

"Are we walking all the way to the tube station, Dad?" Jonah asked.

His father nodded without turning around, his gray trench coat swishing as he walked even faster.

"Do you always walk?" Jonah added.

"Yes," grunted David.

"Isn't it kind of far?"

"No," came the blunt reply.

"Oh, okay," Jonah answered, now trotting, and added timidly, "Err, could you slow down a bit?"

His father halted abruptly and looked down, his ice-blue eyes boring into Jonah. "We're late, Jonah. Thanks to you. It's you who wants to come to my work, so we move at my pace, not yours. Understand?" Without waiting for a reply, he marched on, once more staring straight ahead.

Jonah winced and resigned himself to trotting in silence all the way from their narrow three-story townhouse, along the River Thames to Hammersmith Bridge, and across the river to the underground station. *Not a great start*, he thought as he looked around. He'd never been out this early in the morning. The sun had only just risen but there were already a large number of cars and bicycles on the road, and he could taste the bitter flavor of pollution on his tongue as they streamed past. He felt very grown up; there were no other children outside at this hour.

At the station Jonah's mind again fizzed with curiosity: *Which line were they taking? Which station were they going to? How long would the trip take?* But when he opened his mouth to ask these questions, he was immediately discouraged by David's repeated tapping of his foot as they stood in the line to buy Jonah a ticket. He tried again when they eventually took their seats on the underground train,  but his father buried his head in his salmon-colored newspaper—the masthead read *Financial Times*—making Jonah worry that disturbing him might cause him to send him back home to the au pair.

Finally, as they emerged from the Cannon Street tube station and headed for a café opposite St. Paul's Cathedral, Jonah's father spoke. "I'm going to buy a coffee. Would you like something?" he asked, pushing open the door to the shop.

"Yes, I'll have a coffee too," Jonah said, grateful that the silence had at last been broken. He stepped behind his father in line, leaning away from the people surging past him with hot drinks in their hands.

"You don't drink coffee," said David, cocking his head.

"I do when I go to work," Jonah replied, pleased that his choice had commanded a response.

"Anything in particular?" his dad asked, his attention now on the apparently indecisive woman in front of them in line. He raised his finger, looking like he was about to tap her on the back and complain to her directly, but he decided the better of it, his foot drumming out its beat of irritation once more.

Nearly thirty seconds later, Jonah heard the woman finally order something along the lines of a "Venti skinny Caffè Misto extra hot." Whatever that was, it made no sense to Jonah. The chalk-written menu was no help either. Were these things even drinks? All of a sudden, an image came to Jonah's mind. He must have been no more than five years old in the memory, but he could clearly recall his father dipping his mouth into his coffee mug—so that his lips were covered with foam—and making faces that made him and Jonah giggle. It was probably the last time he had seen his dad laugh.

A few seconds later, the woman in front of them stepped away, having finally finished her order. It was David Lightbody's turn.

"I want a frothy one like you," Jonah announced.

David raised his eyebrows at Jonah and turned to the brunette behind the counter. "Two cappuccinos please."

"Cappuccino. Cappuccino," Jonah said to himself as they waited for their drinks to be made, enjoying the shapes his mouth made while forming the word. "Cap-ooo-chee-no. Cap-oooo-chino. Caaap . . ."

He was in mid-sentence when David handed him the coffee, gave him a withering look, and pointed outside. "Come on. We'll drink while we walk. We haven't got time to sit down."

*Shoot*, thought Jonah as he held the white cup by its cardboard holder and eyed the drink warily. Hot chocolate was as far as he'd gone on the hot beverage front, and then he usually only consumed the whipped cream that was squirted on top. He brought the cup slowly to his mouth as they marched off down a narrow lane, his tongue searching for the hole in its lid. There was no discernable odor. He began to tip the cup upward slowly. Suddenly his tongue was burning, then his bottom lip, and then the roof of his mouth. The coffee had come out much quicker and was much hotter than he had expected, and he tipped the cup back upright quickly to stop the flow. He checked to see that none had spilt on his white button-down shirt and only now began to get a sense of taste inside his mouth. Until today, everything he had drunk had been sweet: fruit juice, Coke, energy drinks, milkshakes. This was bitter and dry. It wasn't unpleasant, but it wasn't pleasant either. He took another sip, this time rolling the fluid around his mouth, cooling it, testing it. His tongue was working hard, savoring the sweetness of the chocolate that had been sprinkled on top.

Suddenly, he was intensely aware of his surroundings. Everything was louder than a minute ago. Images were sharper. Jonah noticed it all—a bus spat and hissed, a dog barked, a petite lady spoke with a foreign accent. There were people everywhere—crossing the road, striding along the pavement, staring out of the windows of the bus. It was a level of acute awareness like Jonah had never experienced. If this was what it was like to drink coffee, Jonah could understand why adults seemed to throw back one cup after another in a relentless stream.

"What do you think of the coffee?" his father inquired, seemingly shouting.

"Makes you buzzy," Jonah answered, and riding his caffeinated high followed up immediately with, "So why don't you tell me what we're going to do today?"

His father's eyes narrowed. "Look, I don't want you to get your hopes up. You're not going to be able to do much. There are rules, you know?"

"Uh-huh," Jonah grunted as a wailing police siren invaded his father's sermon-like drone. There were always rules.

"You will have to be quiet as there is a lot of money at stake."

"Yes, Dad," said Jonah, wanting to say that he'd asked what they *were* going to do, not what they *weren't* going to do. He took another swig of the coffee, practically stamping through the puddles that were still left on the street from the previous night's rainstorm.

"Just sit and watch and listen. You'll probably be the only kid there. I doubt anyone else will bring their children in. They haven't before."

*Enough!* thought Jonah and stopped mid-stride. "Dad, I get it. I'm twelve. I'm not a baby," he said, puffing his chest out. "I won't embarrass you. I only want to find out what you do all day. I think it might be interesting."

"I . . . umm . . . uh," Jonah's father stammered, obviously taken aback. "Yeah. Sorry. You're right. It will be a good . . . learning experience . . . for both of us." One side of his mouth tipped upward in a kind of half-smile, and the tension that had existed since they had left the house seemed to drain away. Jonah felt very pleased, if slightly surprised, with himself.

He looked at his cup of coffee. *Good stuff this*, he thought.

"Okay, let's start again," said David. "Let me tell you about the firm. We're not the biggest player, but we're very profitable. We do what we know, and we know how to do it well. Helsby, Cattermole, & Partners is . . ." Jonah tried to concentrate on what his father was saying, but the action around him was a constant intrusion: a man screaming on his cell phone, a newspaper salesman calling out the front-page headline.

". . . we make money for our clients by trading in the financial markets, stocks and shares mainly."

Jonah didn't want his father to think that he didn't care about what he was saying, especially after he had finally gone to the trouble of describing things to him. But when he saw a bright red Ferrari roaring into an underground parking garage, it was too much for him. "That's so coooool!" he exclaimed and immediately threw his hand over his mouth in embarrassment.

His father ceased talking and shook his head in apparent despair. "Hopefully, you'll be less distracted when we get inside," he said and pushed his way through a huge glass revolving door, muttering to himself, "It's only a bloody car."

Jonah stayed outside for a moment watching the red Ferrari disappear and noticing that it had driven into the garage of the same building he was about to enter. *Only a bloody car!* Their Volvo was only a bloody car; that red streak of speed was something else entirely.

He pushed his own way through the revolving doors and entered a cavernous reception area with a ceiling as tall as any he'd seen in a church. Ahead of him, his father was striding off to the left toward a turnstile. Jonah hurried after him, but before he had taken two steps, a burly man in a navy uniform stepped forward and reached his hand out, stopping Jonah in his tracks. "Hold on there little fella," he said gruffly. "We need to take your photograph and get you a pass."

Jonah saw his father halt and spin around. "He's my son," he snapped. "Does he really need a pass? I'm late enough as it is."

"Everyone needs a pass, sir," the security guard said firmly, turning Jonah around and propelling him toward a long, high desk with *HELSBY, CATTERMOLE, & PARTNERS* emblazoned on the front of it. "It won't take a second."

Jonah's mouth dropped open.

Above the reception desk was a huge fish tank built into the wall. And inside the fish tank were two sharks, circling menacingly. He gulped.

"Can we have a pass for this young man?" asked the security guard as Jonah continued to stare.

"Of course, Bill," said the female receptionist. "What's your name?" she asked, more to Jonah's back than to Jonah directly. He was still transfixed by the sharks.

Jonah felt a tap on his shoulder and tore his eyes away from the tank in front of him. "Tell the lady your name," said the security guard. "And smile for the camera."

Jonah looked up at the receptionist, still thinking about sharks, gave his name, and smiled as she took his photo with a webcam fixed to the top of her computer screen.

Almost immediately she was handing the security guard a badge, which he pinned on Jonah's chest. "There you go," he said. Jonah looked down at the photo on the badge, seeing his pale skin, dark brown eyes, and fair, straight hair. Next to his photo was printed his name and the word *VISITOR*.

"Welcome to Hellcat," said the security guard.

Jonah looked up at him. "Hellcat?" he asked quizzically.

The security guard furrowed his brow as if deciding whether he'd said something he wasn't supposed to. "You had better ask your dad about that one. Go on, I think he's in a hurry."

Jonah nodded and walked swiftly over to his father, who was standing on the other side of the entry turnstiles, tapping his foot once more. A glass gate next to the turnstiles magically opened for Jonah to join him, and David immediately started off toward some escalators as soon as his son was through. "What's Hellcat?" Jonah asked, once more scrambling to keep up with his father's relentless pace.

"It's the bank's nickname," his father replied. "It comes from the first letters of our real name: Helsby Cattermole."

Jonah broke it down in his head, H-e-l from Helsby. C-a-t from Cattermole. "You're missing an *l*," he said.

"Well, what would you have liked for us to have been called?" his father replied, throwing an arm up in exasperation.

"No, it's cool. I just wanted to check." Jonah answered promptly, stepping on the escalator. He decided to switch tactics. "Were those really sharks?" he asked.

"Yes," said David, three steps further up the escalator. "Bit silly if you ask me, but it's supposed to say something about the way we operate; supposed to impress our clients. We actually call the whole reception area the Shark Tank."

Jonah closed the gap on his father as they climbed upward. He didn't think the sharks were silly. Sharks were at the top of the food chain. Like lions. And Ferraris.

A fat man descending on the down escalator greeted Jonah's father. "Morning, Biff."

"Morning, Flash. Asia behaving?" David replied.

"Not too bad," said the fat man as he passed.

Jonah glanced behind him at the man and then back at his father as they reached the top and began marching down a long corridor. "Why did he call you Biff?" he asked.

"That's my nickname. Like the bank has a nickname, most of us here do as well."

Jonah thought for a second. "Isn't Biff the guy from *Back to the Future*?"

"Yes," replied David, marching on.

"Isn't he the bully who's always beating people up?"

David stopped suddenly and looked his son up and down as if deciding how much more he could take. "He is. But I'm called Biff because I refused to fight someone."

Jonah screwed up his face, puzzled. "But that doesn't make sense," he insisted.

"A lot of nicknames here are opposites. You get used to it." His father shrugged and started walking again.

"Would I get a nickname if I worked here?" Jonah asked.

"What?"

"Would I get a nickname?" He'd always wanted a nickname, but the nearest he'd gotten at school was some of the seniors calling him "Lighty."

"Probably," said David into space.

"Cool. Do you get to pick?" Jonah asked. He didn't wait for his father to respond. "Because I don't want a name like yours, the name of some huge jerk." As soon as he said it he knew it had been a stupid thing to say. His eyes caught his father's, and for a moment, Jonah and David stared at each other, the years of mutual pain and disappointment swimming beneath the surface.

David turned away. They had come to a halt in front of a set of huge double doors. He ran his ID card over a sensor on the right and glanced back at Jonah. "Good thing you don't work here then, isn't it?"

But Jonah wasn't listening.

The doors had opened.

## CHAPTER 2

*"Wow!" exclaimed Jonah,* his mouth agape. In front of him rows and rows of desks filled the biggest room he'd ever seen in his life, stretching away the length of a football field. The desks were jammed together in blocks of eight and sixteen, and on each desk were at least two computer screens. Some had four. The screens seemed to move with a life of their own, flashing and twinkling like hyperactive Christmas trees. Each desk had a chair with a jacket hung on the back, and in each chair there was a person. Some were sitting forward, hunkered down, their faces intent, voices low. Some were leaning back, relaxed, feet on the desk, maybe a smile on their faces. Many were standing, talking, hands waving, agitated, excited, urgent. Everyone was attached to a phone or two: clamped to the right ear, gripped in the right hand; clamped to the left ear, right arm curled over the head; held out in front like a cat grabbed by its scruff; or dangling by the cord like a condemned man.

"Wow!" said Jonah for a second time, still not moving. His skin tingled. There was electricity and tension in the air. He had the same feeling that he had before a race or an exam—that knot in his stomach, that feeling of stepping into the unknown with only his wits to carry him forward. His fingers twitched.

He breathed deeply through his nose. Something deep, deep down inside him was waking up. His nostrils flared and his pulse quickened. A multilayered scent pervaded the room. There was the cold smell of technology, of computers and metal and glass and air-conditioning. There was the warm smell of coffee and bacon and toast. But underneath these was a subtle odor that Jonah couldn't immediately identify. It was primeval and fundamental. It brought images of gladiators to his mind; knights on horses standing in a line, lances lowered; infantrymen charging over the top of a trench, bayonets fixed to their rifles, their faces contorted into screams of anger and terror. *Yes, that was it!* It was the smell of battle.

"Come along," said David. "It's hardly the Grand Canyon."

Jonah stood as tall as he could, pushing his shoulders back as if he were a soldier, and stepped out onto the trading floor for the first time.

He hoped it wouldn't be the last.

As they walked toward David's desk a third of the way down the second row from the left, Jonah became enveloped by the noise. The grumbling and shouting seemed to be sucked up into the cavernous space and then thrown back downward in a wall of white noise pierced by screams and yells: "Buy two thousand!" "Sell four thousand!" "Yours!" "Mine!" "GOTCHA!"

David shook his head. "The beginning of the day is usually the busiest," he said. "It'll calm down later."

26

Jonah wasn't so sure he wanted it to calm down.

They arrived at David's desk, which was in a block of eight, all of which were made out of artificial wood and separated by glass partitions. The men on either side were younger than his dad and were both talking on the phone. Jonah thought that they must be brothers as no two people could have had such prominent brows and such messy hair without being related. They stared unpleasantly at Jonah and his father, and the one on the left covered the mouthpiece on his phone and snarled, "Scrotycz is after you, Biff. Better jump to it." Then he looked directly at Jonah and said, "I didn't know we were going midget bowling later!" before bursting out laughing and returning to his telephone call without waiting for a response.

Jonah sensed his father tense up as he ushered Jonah to his desk. Jonah placed his half-empty coffee cup on top of the desk and glanced around, unsurprised to discover that there wasn't a single family photo or personal keepsake. In fact, the desk was completely bare save for three yellow Stickies. Jonah watched his father read each one before tearing them off the desk and throwing them in the trash, mumbling under his breath, "Bloody Scrotycz."

"Why is there a jacket on the back of your chair? Did you leave it behind?" Jonah asked.

"It's a tradition," said David as he pulled up a second chair for Jonah to sit in. "Once upon a time it was a trick to fool your boss that you were on the trading floor, making money, rather than out at lunch. Everyone had two jackets. One to wear and one for the chair." David took his jacket off and hung it on the back of Jonah's chair. "There you go. Now you've got one too," he said. He undid the buttons on the cuffs of his shirt and rolled up his sleeves.

"Who's Scrotycz?" Jonah asked, also rolling up his sleeves to match his dad and noticing that they were two of the only people on the floor who weren't wearing ties.

"He's one of my clients," David replied. "I'll call him in a minute."

"And your clients are the people whose money you look after?" asked Jonah, recalling the bits and pieces he'd gleaned from the phone calls his father often had to take over dinner.

"Yes, that's right. And I try to earn them extra money by trading in the financial markets." David rolled his chair around so that he was facing Jonah directly.

"Have all of your clients got such weird names?"

"Some do. Scrotycz is Russian, which is why his name seems so unusual."

Jonah sat up straighter. "You speak Russian, don't you?" he said quite loudly so that the other men would hear him. He bet *they* couldn't speak Russian.

"Correct," replied David, his voice much softer than Jonah's. "It's what got me into the City of London. You know I was brought up in Africa and only moved to England when I was twenty?"

Jonah nodded.

"Well, when I arrived, I first joined a shipping company that traded with Russia. After a couple of years I got a job with a bank and a few years later I moved here when Helsby Cattermole started doing business with Russia. Russia has some very rich people."

"Do you make them a lot of money?" Jonah asked, sucking down one last big gulp of coffee.

"No. My job is to make them some money, but mainly to make

sure they don't lose any." David threw his empty cappuccino cup into the trash.

"Oh. I thought you said you made more money than anyone else here." The disappointment was clear in Jonah's voice. He dropped his own empty drink into the waste bin.

"No, I said the *bank* earned more money," David corrected. "There are other traders here who try to make their clients huge amounts."

Jonah wondered if one of those people was the driver of the red Ferrari he'd seen earlier. His gaze drifted to a few of the other men on the floor.

David powered up his computer screens before continuing with his explanation. "But those traders also take a lot of risks, so they might actually end up losing their clients' money instead." He looked at Jonah to see if he had understood, but Jonah had already moved on to his next question.

"So why don't clients give all their money to those traders?"

David banged his fist against the desk and glared at Jonah. "What did I just say?" he snapped.

Jonah shuddered. He'd heard that tone of voice before. "Sorry, Dad," he said meekly.

The two cavemen-looking guys snickered.

"So pay attention. You came here to find out what I do, so do me the favor and listen when I'm telling you."

Jonah shrank back in his chair and watched David take out his wallet, count out a hundred pounds, and put the money on the desk.

"Ready," he demanded.

"Yes," said Jonah.

"Good. Say you had a hundred pounds to save. You could put it in a bank and get some interest, say five pounds." He added five pounds from his wallet to the notes on the desk. "You also wouldn't lose any of your money, and because of that, your investment strategy would be absolutely risk-free. Does that make sense?"

Jonah nodded. He had savings accounts and knew about interest from school.

"Good. But you might want to make a bit more money than that, and to make more money you'd have to do something that involves a bit more risk."

Jonah shivered in anticipation. What his father was describing sounded exciting. "So what would I do?" he asked.

"You'd go to the financial markets, the stock market being the most obvious one, and buy shares in a company. Then you'd earn a portion of the company profits, which we call a dividend. It's like interest, so let's say that it's the same as if you'd put your money in the bank." David motioned to the money already on the desk. "But—and here's where it gets interesting—if the price of that share you bought goes up, you'll make more money, say another twenty pounds." He added a twenty pound note.

Jonah quickly added the numbers together in his head. "So now I'd have a hundred and twenty-five pounds," he said, his eyes growing wide.

"That's right." David nodded and held up his forefinger while reaching for the money with his other hand. "The trouble is, the price might also go down, and you could lose some of your hundred pounds." He took forty-five pounds away and threw them in the garbage. "Understand?"

Jonah nodded, fighting the urge to reach into the bin and retrieve the forty-five pounds his father had thrown away. "So to make more money I have to risk actually losing some of the money I already have?"

"Very good," said David. He sounded impressed.

Jonah smiled. "Why would the price go up or down?" he asked.

"Excellent question," David answered, making Jonah's smile grow even wider. "The price goes up if people think a company is going to do well, and therefore they buy the shares. It goes down if they think it's going to do badly, and they sell the shares. Does that make sense?"

"Yeah. I think so," said Jonah. "It's like with trading cards at school. If you've got a really good card, you can swap it for loads of others because everyone wants it. If you've got a bad one, you can't swap it for anything because nobody wants it?"

"Spot on!" David exclaimed.

Jonah beamed and went to make a high five, before pulling back at the last second, knowing that his dad probably wouldn't reciprocate. All the same, coming to work with his father looked like it had been the right decision after all. They were finally talking—really talking! It was going to be a good day and maybe even the start of something more.

"Now," David continued. "You might be willing to take a lot of risk so that you could double your money and turn your one hundred pounds"—he reached into the trash bin and put twenty pounds back on the pile—"into two hundred pounds."

Jonah's eyes lit up. "Yes," he said, thinking again of the red Ferrari. "How do I do that?"

"Well, you might buy something called a derivative." David took more money out of his wallet and put it on the desk. "But," and here David paused, causing Jonah to take his eyes off the money, look at his father, and finish the sentence for him.

"I could lose it all?"

"Very good," David said, and once more Jonah smiled. "But . . . it could be worse than that." David picked all the money off the desk and threw it in the bin. "Because derivatives are very, very risky and"—he threw his wallet into the bin—"you might lose even more."

Jonah's face dropped. "No way! More money than you had in the first place?" He was on the edge of his seat.

"Yes, way," said David.

Jonah wrinkled his forehead. He had a hundred pounds in his savings. Maybe he should buy a derivative and turn it into two hundred pounds. "But you could *make* a hundred pounds," he said thoughtfully.

David shook his head and gave a patronizing smile. "Yes, you could make a hundred pounds. But that would be very unlikely."

Jonah was not to be dissuaded. "What *is* a derivative?" he asked.

"Well," said David thoughtfully, "it's kind of a piece of a piece of a piece of something."

Jonah's brow furrowed, and his father seemed to think again about his explanation.

"Actually it doesn't really matter what it is," he said briskly. "The only thing you need to know today is that derivatives are extremely risky." He gestured at his computer screen. "I don't deal in them myself."

Jonah's heart fell. Of course his dad didn't deal in the exciting stuff. "I'd still like to buy one," he said.

David shook his head again, this time unsmiling. "No, Jonah. You need a lot of money to buy derivatives, a lot more than you have."

Jonah's heart fell further, but before he could ask how much money he needed, the ugly man on the right screamed, "SCRO-TYCZ!" at the top of his voice, making Jonah jump. The man was leaning over the partition holding out his phone to David. "WANTS TO SPEAK TO YOU NOW!"

David looked up. "Can you ask him to hold for thirty seconds? I'm nearly done."

"FUCK OFF!" came the reply, making Jonah gasp. The man pointed at Jonah, and Jonah shrank backward. "Are you working to-day, Biff, or playing nanny? 'Cuz if you're playing nanny, get some-one else to answer your calls. Not me." The man made a sneering face at Jonah.

"Give it a break, Gravel," David retorted. "Do you think I want to be doing this? Ask him to hold."

"NO!" Gravel bellowed. "He's really pissed off. Why have you brought the midget in anyway? Nobody else has. It's not a play-ground. Do you see any other kids here? Nobody else would be so stupid."

The man on the left joined in. "Yeah, Biff. Why've you brought your kid in? Thicko!"

Jonah sat stock still, looking straight ahead, trying to avoid the eyes of the men, wondering whether he could hide under the desk, aware that his dad had said he didn't want to be doing this.

"Oh, for God's sake," snapped David, snatching his phone up. He punched a slow flashing light on the board in front of him, took a deep breath, and spoke calmly into the mouthpiece. "Good morning, Mr. Scrotycz, how can I help you?"

Jonah heard a voice shout something unintelligible back down the phone and watched his father close his eyes and move the handset away from his ear. When the voice stopped ranting, his dad brought the phone back, opened his eyes, and started speaking again, this time in Russian, which Jonah couldn't understand.

With his father's attention now elsewhere, Jonah looked surreptitiously around the trading floor to see if there were any other kids.

The ugly man was right. There weren't.

Now he felt really bad. He sat there, trying to be invisible, listening to his father speaking in Russian, watching him trying to rein back his temper, imagining the hateful eyes of the other traders on his back, imagining them talking about him.

Suddenly, a voice behind him boomed, "What have we here?"

Jonah hunched his shoulders in fear. *Oh, no*, he thought, *another horrible man about to tell me I shouldn't be here*.

"Are these Neanderthals being nasty to you?" the voice roared. "I heard some grunting as I was passing Drizzlers' Den and thought I'd come and find out what the commotion was about."

Jonah carefully spun his chair around and looked upward. All he could see was a huge mustache: thick, black, and waxed to a sharp point about three quarters of the way across each side of a broad face. There was more to the person, but beyond the fantastical mustache it was impossible to take in anything else at first glance. The mustache began to move as the voice boomed again. "And if your dad won't do anything about it, I will."

There were eyes too now, looking straight at him, dark and cold below a high forehead topped by an aggressive crew cut, also black.

"What would you like me to do? Shall I *biff* them?" The word "biff" was accentuated, and the man raised two very hairy fists and held them in front of his face like a boxer. "I will if you want. Trust me. My word is my bond. It's the only way to treat bullies, to fight back." He threw two fast punches into the air. "Biff, biff!" he exclaimed and dropped his hands back down. "You've probably been told that."

Jonah found that he was inadvertently nodding in agreement, although he'd actually been told the opposite over the years.

"But you normally don't have to. Just *look* like you will."

The mustachioed man turned away and raised his fists once more. "Oi! Rock. Gravel. Want to pick on someone your own size?" he growled.

Jonah looked up to see that it was now the two ugly men who were cowering, trying to hide behind the glass partitions.

"See what I mean? Drizzlers all the way through. Say boo to them and they'll run a mile. They're like a loud fart that doesn't smell. Noisy but nothing dangerous, eh?" The man paused for a second, apparently pleased with his analogy, humor in his eyes.

Jonah turned back to face his father, holding back a snicker, when all of a sudden he heard a loud "BOO!" from behind him.

He spun his chair quickly back around.

The large man was roaring with laughter and pointing at Rock and Gravel. "Did you see the looks on their faces?!"

Jonah glanced in the direction of his father's desk mates to discover that they were in fact visibly shaking. He gave up holding back his snicker, now impossible to contain, and burst out laughing himself.

"Very good, sonny," the man said, straight-faced once more. "You didn't even jump. Impressive. There aren't many lads of your age who wouldn't bat an eye at all the hubbub here. Certainly not anyone who would end up with this lot. Maybe you should come with me and join my band of Whistlers, eh?"

Jonah didn't know what a Whistler was, but if they were like this man, joining them sounded like fun. He shifted his eyes to see if his dad was paying attention, but he wasn't so Jonah took a closer look at the man who'd so easily silenced his tormenters. He now had a big grin on his face, and a set of teeth had appeared from beneath the mustache. They were immaculately white and straight at the front, and as the smile grew wider it revealed a glint of gold on the sides. Below the smile was a hairless chin and a huge tie knot framed by a white collar, framed in its turn by a dark blue jacket with broad chalk stripes running down it. His neck was thick, his shoulders wide, his chest powerful.

Jonah's insignificant twelve-year-old hand reached out of its own accord and shook the man's. As he pulled his hand back, he caught a glimpse of a skull-and-crossbones ring on the man's little finger. A pirate's ring! Jonah wanted to say as much, but before he knew it, he was introducing himself. "I'm Jonah. Lightbody. David's son."

"Hello, Jonah. Lightbody. David's son. I am the Baron," said the man.

"The Baron?" Jonah's voice sounded like the squeak of a trapped mouse against the deep, mellifluous growl of this extraordinary being in front of him. His eyes traveled back up toward the gold teeth, the mustache, and the dark eyes.

"It's only a nickname," interrupted David, his phone call now over. "What do you want, Baron?"

The Baron's eyes stayed on Jonah's and momentarily darkened even further. Then they lightened, and he drew his hand upward to stroke his mustache, his fingers snapping as they sharpened it at the ends.

He glanced at David. "That's right, Biff. 'Baron' is a nickname, like *Biff*." And again the "biff" was emphasized. "Only this one has been gained by action, not inaction." He turned back to Jonah. "Comes from the Bloody Red Baron, sonny. The greatest flying ace in the First World War. More kills than any other pilot."

The man's skull-and-crossbones ring was now fully visible in all its heavy, gold glory and his eyes twinkled as if to suggest that there was more to the story than what he was saying.

"You didn't kill anyone, did you?" Jonah asked breathlessly.

The Baron gave a knowing grin. "Trading killings, sonny. That's why the market calls me the Baron. More *trading killings* than anyone else in the market. Nothing violent. We don't like violence here, do we *Biff*?" Only now did he turn and really look at David, the challenge obvious in his eyes.

David opened his mouth to reply, but before he could say anything the Baron had continued.

"But enough of this bantaaaaaar, Biff. You asked what I wanted. Well, I saw your lad sitting, doing nothing, and I thought, *Well, maybe he'd like to do stuff that's a bit more interesting. Learn something about trading from the best.*" His eyes flicked back to Jonah and winked conspiratorially before returning to David. "My trading assistant's got a dental appointment, and I need someone to do some inputting for me and the lads. Straightforward stuff." He turned again to Jonah, and, sizing him up, he added, "Child's play in fact, with all due respect."

Jonah smiled in encouragement.

David snorted with derision. "You *are* joking, aren't you? Let you and your bunch of reprobate financial terrorists loose on my son?"

"No joking, Biff," countered the Baron, shaking his head. "Only trying to help. Sounds like you've got your work cut out filling orders for some Russkie. And my reprobates—who, I might add, make more money for this firm than the rest of this floor combined—will treat him much better than these two Neanderthals have been." He waved dismissively at the ugly traders on either side of David, and Jonah found himself willing his father to say yes.

"Go on, Dad," he pleaded, certain that doing anything with this Baron man would involve excitement and fun. Maybe it was even his Ferrari he'd seen earlier. "This way you can get your work done and maybe we can have lunch together later. And I promise I'll go home after that."

David hesitated, his eyes searching Jonah's to see if this was what he truly wanted. Jonah nodded. "All right then," David finally responded, and looking up at the Baron he added, "But no funny business, eh? He's only a kid."

"My word is my bond, Biff." The Baron smiled and flicked his head at Jonah. "Come on, sonny. To the Bunker!"

As Jonah stood up, feeling excited once again, David said to him, "If you get bored or don't like it, come and find me here, and we'll get you a taxi home."

"Yes, Dad," he replied, doubting that would happen, and, turning his back on his father, he followed the Baron across the trading floor. He didn't know it then, but it would be years before he ever turned back.

# CHAPTER 3

**Jonah followed the** Baron down the avenue of desks, fascinated as each new group of traders raised a hand in greeting. Clearly, everyone here knew the Baron and wanted him to know them. The Baron, for his part, acknowledged the fawning traders with a short nod of his head or a swift flick of the wrist. Words, however, were never exchanged. Jonah felt as if he were part of a royal procession, albeit one where he received quizzical looks as to what his involvement was in all of this. Some traders even went so far as to roll their eyes at him—a gesture that suggested the Baron was the king of their trading floor—and what right did he, Jonah, have to be taken under his protection instead of one of his long-loyal acolytes?

Jonah's stomach pained ever so slightly with guilt—he didn't want to usurp anyone's role—but mostly he was overwhelmed with a warm sense of pride that the Baron had selected him specifically.

As they approached the far corner of the floor, Jonah noticed a grouping of desks that was set apart from the rest. The desks were arranged as three opposite three with a double desk at the end, and above them hung four models of old airplanes, the largest of which was a six-foot-long red triplane marked with the German cross. Down the center partition was a huge castle made out of Lego bricks, and to the side there was a fish tank, which, as far as Jonah could tell, had no fish in it, only a model submarine, a sunken model battleship, and two fifty-pound notes stuck to the inside of the glass. On the wall behind the double desk, there was a massive TV screen showing CNBC News. This double desk stood in stark contrast to the others in the block. They all sprouted screens like satellite dishes on a telecom tower; the double desk had keyboards but no screens and was covered with figurines.

"Welcome to the Bunker!" the Baron pronounced.

There were five men and one woman gathered behind the desks, drinking coffee and talking animatedly. None of them were on the phone. They all had crew cuts, except the woman, whose platinum blonde hair was tied up in plaited bunches. As Jonah and the Baron arrived, this group stood to attention by clicking their heels together and raising their right hands in a flat-handed salute, palms forward much like policemen giving stop signals. The Baron stopped, returned the salute, and threw his briefcase onto the double desk. It landed with a thud, luck more than care ensuring that it avoided the endless figurines that dotted the surface.

Jonah's eyes expanded to the size of saucers—did that really just happen?

A piratical voice rang out from the other side of the desks. "What you got there, Baron? A new recruit?"

Jonah searched for the source and found a man with sallow

skin and a face like a weasel making a funny, leering expression.

"Something like that, Dog," said the Baron, guiding Jonah forward and around the desks so that they were on the same side as the traders. "This here is Jonah Lightbody, Biff's lad. I've rescued him from Drizzlers' Den to join us for some piracy on the high seas of finance."

The group sneered at that one. "Ooo arrrr Jim lad!" the man from before yelled out. Jonah tried not to laugh. This was more like the prefects' common room at school than his dad's work.

The Baron, however, wasn't as pleased. His eyes flashed with silent rage, daring the man—Dog he'd called him—to say more. He didn't. Seeing he'd won the battle, the Baron visibly relaxed, unclenching his jaw and wrapping his arm around Jonah like a kindly uncle. "Jonah is going to be helping me this morning, so keep the language down. We don't want him getting a bad impression, do we now?"

"No, we wouldn't want that," said a man in a pink shirt, a smirk playing at the edge of his lips.

"Good," replied the Baron, stone-faced. Then, apparently confident that Jonah would be at least reasonably well cared for, he added, "Settle him in, will you? I'll be back in ten minutes. Got to make some calls." And with that, he turned and strode off across the floor.

The area grew strangely silent with the Baron's departure. Whatever animation had existed while Jonah's protector was there disappeared once he was left to fend for himself.

A pen clicked. A chair swiveled.

Jonah searched for a friendly face, but the traders looked at him with a mixture of curiosity and disgust, as if unsure what to make of this newest entry into their gang.

A tall man looked like he might be a potential ally. That is, until he licked his lips as if Jonah were the latest delicacy to be chomped on and spat out. The woman also seemed promising—perhaps she'd be warm and supportive like Jonah's English teacher Mrs. Humphries? But as soon as Jonah's gaze darted in the woman's direction, she narrowed her eyes, and he realized that she was nothing like his teacher.

"Does he speak?" said a man in a bow tie.

"Nah, doesn't seem so," answered the man whom the Baron had called Dog.

Jonah glanced nervously back across the floor to where his dad sat with the two "Neanderthals." *That's what the Baron had said they were, right?* He wondered if perhaps he'd made a mistake leaving the Stone Age.

"Guess that's it then," said the man in the pink shirt. "The Baron's brought us a mute."

"Too bad," said the tall man. "I thought he might have been fun to have around here."

Jonah knew he had to do something quickly and recalled the way that these people had responded to the Baron. Even this man, who was a good foot taller than his boss, had stood at attention. Obviously, bravado triumphed around here. Jonah summoned all of his strength. "Hello," he said to the traders around him. It came out as "Lo" because his voice cracked on the first syllable. He steeled his nerves and tried again. "What's everyone looking at? I figured you'd all have work to do."

"Oooh frisky, isn't he?" said the woman with a slight French accent, a look of self-possessed shock on her face.

"Well," Jonah practically choked, "don't you?"

"Hah," guffawed the man called Dog. "What are we going to call you?" he said.

"My name's Jonah Lightbody," Jonah supplied, breathing a sigh of relief that his gamble had played off.

"We know what your name is," answered the same man—he was apparently the leader of the pack in the Baron's absence. "But you've got to have a nickname if you're going to come a-raping and a-pillaging with us Bunker Boys." He paused, once again making his weasel face. "I'm Dog by the way."

"Wasn't Jonah that bloke that got eaten by a whale?" asked the man with the pink shirt. He nodded at Jonah. "I'm Milkshake." Jonah wondered if the nickname had anything to do with the flavor-of-the-week shirts he appeared to prefer.

"What about 'Jaws'?" suggested the tall man.

"Jaws was a shark, you prat," sneered Dog. "Don't let Birdcage's height fool you, Jonah. He's so busy seeing into the clouds that he's got no idea what's going on here on Earth."

"Bloody big shark though. Killed a lot of people," Birdcage mumbled. Leaning over to shake Jonah's hand, he added, "They call me Birdcage because my surname is Avery. Like an aviary. Pleased to meet you."

"That and because he's got a birdbrain," chirped Dog, but Jonah noticed that the comment seemed to fall on deaf ears.

"Moby Dick. He was a whale," was the next suggestion, this time from the man with the bow tie. Jonah was about to ask him his name, even though his icy exterior hadn't completely melted, but before he could, the man simply said, "Jeeves" in a way that required no explanation. Given the name, Jonah wondered whose valet he was exactly—the Baron's or Dog's. . . .

"As in 'I feel a bit Moby Dick'? I don't think so," said Dog.

Jeeves scowled, then immediately reined himself in as Dog raised his eyebrows. Jonah smiled to himself—he supposed that answered his question.

"What's wrong with Jaws?" tried Birdcage for a second time.

"It's not a whale," Dog answered.

"There's that film *Free Willy* with the whale in it. What about Willy?" suggested the woman with the blonde hair. Looking at Jonah, she added, "I'm Françoise if you're curious."

"Françoise!" interjected Dog. "Only your mum calls you that. Your name is Franky." And then he leered, "Or sometimes Spanky, eh?"

"Get lost, Dog," said the woman, and, turning back to Jonah, she threatened, "It's Françoise or Franky, but never Spanky. Got it?"

Jonah nodded. *Scary woman*, he thought.

"Gentlemen, let's get back to the task at hand," Jeeves announced, waving his hand in a call for silence.

"How about Steamboat?" Milkshake now piped up, getting back in on the action.

"No. No. I got it. Orchid," said Birdcage.

"Orchid?" Jeeves echoed, as stone-faced as before.

"Yeah. You know. The name for a killer whale," said Birdcage. This time his voice took on a more nasal quality.

"Orca, you idiot. Orc—'ka, ka.' An orchid's a flower. Kind of thing Franky likes to receive from that doctor chap of hers," Dog explained, shaking his head.

"She wouldn't want some huge aquatic mammal arriving in the

post, would she?" Jeeves taunted, crossing his arms with an air of finality.

"Ten seconds on Birdcage!" shouted Dog, and to Jonah's amazement the whole of the Bunker fell on Birdcage, throwing him to the ground as they jumped on top of him.

Franky was the only one who stood to the side, and she rolled her eyes at Jonah before calling out "a one stupid trader, a two stupid traders, a three stupid traders" like one of the referees in WWF Wrestling.

Birdcage remained pinned down on the ground, and Jonah could see punches and knees being aimed at him. Milkshake stood to the side kicking him and chanting, "You're thick and you know you are, you're thick and you know you are . . ."

"A four stupid traders, a five stupid traders, a six stupid traders, a seven stupid traders . . ." counted Franky. As she yelled, the Bunker Boys continued to pummel Birdcage, who could be heard screaming, "Ow!" and "Get off!"

"An eight stupid traders, a nine stupid traders, a ten stupid traders. OFF!" she shouted, and instantly the fight broke up.

The traders returned to their seats, giggling like crazy while Birdcage stood up and straightened his clothes, also laughing. "All right, all right. I am a stupid trader. BUT AT LEAST I'M NOT POOR!" he screamed at the top of his voice.

"Yeah!" shouted the others in unison.

Jonah stood alone, stunned at what he had just witnessed. The Baron had said that the men who worked directly with his dad were cavemen. If so, what did that make the people who worked *for him*?

# CHAPTER 4

**Franky stared at** Jonah for a few seconds before saying, "So you're Biff's son." Now that she wasn't screaming, Jonah could detect more of a foreign accent. She had dark makeup around her eyes and a heavy gold necklace around her throat.

"Um yes," replied Jonah, glancing around to see if anyone else on the trading floor was behaving in a way that would suggest something unusual had occurred in the last twenty seconds. But nothing seemed to have changed: The murmuring and the shouting continued as before. Jonah looked back at Franky. "Yes. I've come to find out what he does at work," he continued.

"Oh. That's nice," replied Franky flatly.

Jonah couldn't help himself anymore. "What happened there?"

"What?" Franky seemed surprised at the question. "That pile-on? Don't you do that at school?"

"Kind of," said Jonah. "But we're kids. You're grown-ups."

"Ha!" laughed Franky. "Does that make a difference?"

Jonah tried to picture his father doing something like that. "My dad wouldn't do that."

Franky's face turned serious. "No. Your dad wouldn't do that, would he? He's very somber, isn't he?"

Jonah nodded. "But all the grown-ups I know are like that." He thought of his teachers. Not even Mr. Jagger, his science teacher, would allow a brawl like that, and he was pretty mad.

"Well," said Franky, smiling again, "we're not like that. We're Whistlers. They're all Drizzlers."

The Baron had also mentioned Whistlers and Drizzlers, but the distinction wasn't one Jonah had heard previously. "What are Whistlers and Drizzlers?" Jonah asked.

Franky laughed again. "It's a Baronism. He says the world is split into two kinds of people. There are the Whistlers, who like to have fun, break the rules, take risks, and if things go bad, they forget about it and move on to something else. And there are the Drizzlers, who complain all the time and stick to the rules and are scared to do anything out of the ordinary because it might go wrong."

"But that's not our style, is it?" boomed a voice. The Baron was back and—though Jonah couldn't be sure—it looked like his mustache had curled up even more definitively during his brief absence, as if it had been electrified by the excitement in the air.

Franky grinned at him admiringly. The others acknowledged him with a nod or another small salute.

"Here on the Prop desk it's Whistler wonderland! Now let's go to the Cockpit and get you settled in."

Jonah glanced around frantically. "I'm sorry, sir, I don't know what you mean." He grimaced, afraid that he was being a thicko.

The Baron gave a dismissive wave. "Why would you, sonny? We use a whole different language here: Whistlers, Drizzlers, longs, shorts, bulls, bears, dragons, tigers. You'll pick it up." The Baron paused. "They didn't come up with a nickname for you while I was gone, did they?"

Jonah shook his head. He couldn't be sure, but he thought he heard Birdcage whisper "orchid" under his breath.

"Good. Glad to see they waited for me to make the big decisions." The Baron placed his hand on Jonah's shoulder and led him to the double desk onto which he'd thrown his bag a few minutes earlier. "This here's my desk, but we call it the Cockpit. It's the control center for the entire Prop desk."

There was that phrase again. Jonah gazed up at the Baron quizzically. "I'm sorry, sir, but I don't know what a Prop desk is either."

The Baron pulled out a chair for Jonah and signaled for him to sit down. "Never apologize, sonny. You're better than that. And why should you know what I'm talking about anyway?"

Jonah did as he was instructed, mouthing, "I shouldn't?" and watched as the Baron took a seat next to him in what appeared to have been a specially designed chair, its contours molded to perfectly fit the Baron's hefty frame.

"Damn right, you shouldn't," the Baron answered, laughing heartily. "By 'Prop desk,' I mean Proprietary Trading Desk. That's what the Bunker is. We Whistlers trade Hellcat's money, not client money. It means we're allowed to take bigger risks than the other traders."

Jonah leapt at the mention of bigger risks. "Do you trade derivatives?" he blurted.

"Derivatives. You're a bit sharp, aren't you? But yes, we trade derivatives." The Baron turned to his troops. "We like derivatives here, don't we, boys?"

The whole of the Bunker whistled and yelled excitedly in response.

Jonah breathed deeply. "I think I'm a Whistler then," he said very seriously.

The Baron burst out laughing and punched Jonah on the shoulder. "That's why I brought you here, sonny. Now watch this. I know you're going to love it as much as I do." He motioned toward the double desk with his hand. "You will have noticed that I, unlike my faithful followers, have no screens on my desk."

Jonah nodded. The Baron grinned mischievously, reached under the desk, and pressed a button. Suddenly the desk partition in front of him began to rise, revealing four screens.

"Yeah!" Jonah cried out. "It's like on a spaceship!"

"Wait," said the Baron, his grin growing. "There's more."

Now the sides the desk began to rise to reveal four more screens so that each person sitting in the Cockpit had four screens of his own: two in front and two on the side.

"Voilà! Le Cockpit," said the Baron, pushing the side screens outward slightly so that it was possible to see all four at once, and pressing another button so that they all switched on.

"That is so cool!" exclaimed Jonah. "My dad only has two."

"Well, your dad doesn't exactly do the kind of work we do here. None of the Drizzlers do."

Jonah nodded sagely, suppressing the burgeoning sense that he was somehow betraying his father by being here. "What's that?" he asked, pointing to a screen that was now flashing at least five hundred lights.

"That, sonny," said the Baron, "is the comms board. The phone is everything here. It's our link to the markets and clients. To make a call we just hit the buttons on the comms board, and we're through."

Jonah remembered his dad had done something similar to retrieve that man Scrotycz's call.

The lights on the comms board blinked, beckoned, burned—refusing to let go of Jonah's attention as he tried to take in the other screens in front of him. One came to life with letters and numbers in different colors; another had an e-mail program on it; the last looked like it contained a list of some sort. All needed passwords to get in.

"Are those all computers?" Jonah asked.

"Yes," said the Baron reverentially.

"And what's that one?" Jonah pointed at the monitor that showed a colorful jumble of things.

"That's the Bloomberg terminal. It displays all the prices and market data."

"I can't believe you've got so many computers," Jonah marveled, his voice hushed but full of awe.

"Yes. We need them though. The financial markets never sleep, and London, or specifically the part we call the City, is probably the largest international financial center in the world. Trillions of pounds, dollars, euros, yen, you name it, change hands each day within a square mile of where we're sitting."

Jonah had no real idea what he was talking about, but the numbers were big. Trillions. That was millions of millions. That was seriously big.

"Okay," the Baron continued, "so this screen you won't need to worry about. It shows messages from other traders at Hellcat and other banks." The Baron pointed to the monitor that Jonah had assumed was used to display e-mail. "This screen on the left is the one you'll use today as it shows all our trades and trading positions."

Jonah stared up at the screen, stymied by the sheer awesomeness of the trading floor's inner workings.

"When a trader makes a trade, he writes out a ticket, which will go to you. You'll input it into the computer so that it comes up here." The Baron paused, checking to see that Jonah understood what he was saying.

Jonah nodded.

"Dog and the others will probably tell you that I'm a bit old fashioned—"

"Wouldn't say it if it weren't true!" Dog exclaimed, interrupting the Baron.

"Aren't you supposed to be working?" the Baron rejoined, his voice taking on a harsher tone. "This conversation is between me and young Mr. Lightbody."

Dog blanched and returned to his work.

"As I was saying, I don't like it when my traders just enter the trades into their own computers. That's not really owning a trade, is it?"

Jonah bobbed his head in agreement.

"Absolutely right, sonny. Only pressing a button makes it all a bit unreal, don't you think?"

Jonah nodded once more. He wasn't about to disagree with the Baron, given the way he'd just responded to Dog.

"So that's basically it," concluded the Baron. "You'll be helping me out a lot since my trading assistant Jammy is out getting his teeth cleaned."

"Yeah, right. Getting drunk is more like it," Franky murmured.

Jonah's eyes darted back and forth between her and the Baron. He couldn't tell if the Baron had heard Franky or not, but he didn't acknowledge the remark.

Instead, he said, "Think of yourself as my eyes and ears. It's you and me on the front line of battle, and you're the only one standing between me and enemy gunfire." The Baron gave Jonah a chance to absorb what he was saying.

Jonah's heart raced. "So I'm going to do some real work? Sitting next to you?"

"You sure are, boy," the Baron said in a cowboy-type voice. "I think you and I are going to do great things together."

"Not today, you're not," interjected a deep but familiar voice. Jonah looked up to see that his father had joined them, his clothes more crumpled than they were earlier. "It turns out that Scrotycz's people and I have to have a last-minute client meeting, so I'm taking you home."

"There's no need for that, Biff—"

But David was not to be swayed. "Stay out of this, Baron. I appreciate your taking care of my son, but it's now time for us to go." He cocked his head toward the exit and began striding in that direction, his gait as speedy and determined as ever.

Jonah stayed where he was. "Wait, Dad!" he called out. "We haven't even gotten to the good stuff yet."

Jonah's father didn't turn around.

Jonah looked earnestly at the Baron, silently pleading for his assistance.

"Hmm . . ." said the Baron. "Difficult times we live in. Very difficult. Why don't you see whether your father will let you come back tomorrow?"

Jonah felt the disbelief creeping into his expression. "You'd want me back?"

"Of course, sonny. Didn't I say that we were going to do great things together?"

# CHAPTER 5
## Tuesday, August 24

**The Baron and** his mysterious phone calls, eh?" said Franky the next day, nodding toward a closed door that Jonah now knew led to the Baron's office. Apparently, he had one area for private matters and the Cockpit for when he wanted to be immersed in the Bunker. He was inside the former now.

"Guess he has a lot of important stuff to deal with," offered Jonah.

"Hah!" Franky snorted. "Or maybe he's terrorizing traders at other firms. Do you know how he got his nickname?"

"It's something to do with a German fighter pilot, isn't it?" Jonah answered, still in total shock that Jammy was once again out and that the Baron had somehow managed to convince his father to let him come to work a second time.

"That's right," said Franky, her eyes wide. "He got the name from a trader at another bank whom he'd shafted with a brilliant trade. When the trader caught sight of his losses, he screamed,

'There's blood all over the place! This is what it must have been like facing the Bloody Red Baron in the First World War.' "

"Hahaha," Jonah chuckled. "Is that really what happened?"

"Yup," Franky replied, her mood far more cheerful than it had been the day prior. She pointed at the trading screen. It was covered in numbers, most of which were blue. A few red figures stuck out. "You see, a blue number is a gain, but a red number means you've lost money."

Jonah nodded along as Franky continued with her explanation. "That trader's screen would have been covered in red numbers, covered in blood." Franky paused for effect. Then she pointed at the model above them. "The original Red Baron—the German— flew a plane like the one up there—a Fokker triplane. Nowadays our Baron always sends a little model of one of those to traders he's stuffed, to remind them of what he's done. Sometimes he even sends one just for the hell of it to wind them up." Her eyes glimmered with the thrill of it all, and she tossed her hair, which she wore looser today.

Jonah felt a rush of pride that he had somehow ended up on the same side as a man who had that kind of nerve. But that sense of satisfaction disappeared as quickly as it came as his thoughts shifted to his father and the weakness implied by his nickname. Jonah took a deep breath. This wasn't the first time in the last twenty-four hours that he'd thought about how different the two men were.

Franky took Jonah's silence as her cue to continue. "This job is all about fear and greed. Greed in that everyone is trying to make money; fear in that we're all scared of losing money. The Baron is the most feared trader in London, and he plays on that fear."

"Is that why he's such a good trader?" Jonah wondered aloud.

"That's part of it. But he's also very quick to do something when he sees an opportunity. He sees it; he hits it. And when he hits it, he hits it big. He's got balls, the Baron. Big balls."

"So you all like him?" Jonah asked, recalling that yesterday's visit had not been without its tense moments.

"Well, *we* all love him," said Franky, "but then, we're on his team." The weasel-faced man, Dog, had appeared. Franky turned to him. "Isn't that right, Dog? We all love the Baron."

"Oh, yes, indeed. The Baron we do love. Totally loyal we are," said Dog, bowing as he spoke.

Franky cackled. "Don't mind Dog. He and the Baron have had their share of differences, but he's still a Bunker Boy through and through, aren't you, Dog?"

"That's me!" Dog sang out.

"He's big into loyalty, the Baron," Franky continued. "You'll hear him say, 'My word is my bond.' It's the motto of the City of London. It means honesty, loyalty, and trust, although really it's about the money. Lots of money. Work with the Baron and you can make more money in a week than some people make in their lifetime. Millions of pounds. Even tens of millions of pounds. That's *really* why we all love him."

Jonah was making calculations in his head. He knew a millionaire was a rich person, and these people were more than millionaires—they were very, very rich!

"It's all about the money, sonny," said Dog grinning. "Contrary to what the Beatles taught us, money *can* buy you love." He turned to Franky. "And I've got a feeling we're going to make loads of it today. The Baron's on to something, Franky. He's just rung. Better get the lad sorted out before he gets back."

Jonah saw them exchange a knowing glance before she turned back to him. "Did you hear that?" she asked, yesterday's air of superiority having completely disappeared now that the thrill of the chase was upon them. "This could be your lucky day. Let's run through a few inputting tests. Things are about to get hot!"

Jonah was running through the inputting test for the fourth time when the Baron returned. "Franky! Dog! Schnell! Schnell! Gather the foot soldiers and let us talk gold. It's killing time!"

Jonah couldn't help but feel exhilarated to see him again.

Dog shouted, "Cockpit!" and Jonah watched all the Bunker Boys leap out of their seats and head quickly toward him. Dog was there first, and Jonah could see a hungry look in his eyes as he licked his lips in expectation. He looked up at Franky, and she, too, had switched into hunter killer mode. A pale flush was spreading down from her cheekbones to the top of her chest. She took a deep breath in through her nose and breathed out a sigh of pleasure while fingering the necklace around her neck. "Mmm. Gold. My favorite," she purred.

Once all the Bunker Boys had gathered, the Baron started speaking, quietly and urgently. "Something is rumbling in deepest, darkest Africa. A takeover in the gold sector. I don't know who, and I don't know when. But I've spoken to the top brass, and we're clear to go within the hour. Stealth stuff, mind you; we don't want anybody to see us coming."

Jonah could sense the heart rates quickening around him and feel the bodies pressing in even closer.

The Baron continued. "Lads, this is a big one. So clear your positions, phone your loved ones, and most of all . . . think of what you're going to buy with the bonuses you'll make!" He paused to let his words sink in and turned to Jonah. "Here's your chance to shine, sonny."

Jonah swelled in anticipation. He was in on the action. He was part of the team.

"Yeah. We'll need breakfast before we get going," said the Baron, handing him a piece of paper and a pen.

"What?" said Jonah. This wasn't what they'd talked about him doing.

"Breakfast, mate. A very important job. Take the lads' orders and ring Amelia on extension 1736, and she'll bring it up. Can you manage that?" he mocked.

Jonah inhaled deeply. He didn't want the Baron thinking that he considered himself above the task, but he also hadn't convinced his dad to come back to his office to be some kind of lackey. "I won't need those," he said, indicating the pen and paper. "I have a very good memory."

The Baron's eyebrows went up. "Good memory, eh? Are you sure? These people can get quite nasty if they're not fed properly. You wouldn't want to get it wrong."

Jonah stood his ground. If yesterday had taught him anything, it was that backing down wasn't an option. "I'm sure."

"Well, all right then," said the Baron, his eyes flashing. Turning back to the traders, he added, "Did you hear that, lads? Our young guest is doing the breakfast order today . . . from memory! So don't make his life difficult, eh?"

The group pressed even closer around Jonah, all of them grinning wolfishly. Dog patronizingly called out, "We'd never do that!"

"Yeah, we had such a nice time together yesterday," Jeeves added for effect.

"I'm sure you did. Oh, and sonny," the Baron turned his attention back to Jonah, "don't forget to get yourself something. My treat. I can afford it."

The traders' grins turned to laughter, and Jonah heard Milkshake whisper to Dog, "A hundred quid says the kid fails." As the group broke up and headed back to their desks, Jonah wondered what he'd gotten himself into.

He started with Franky, since she'd been so surprisingly pleasant this morning (Jonah couldn't help but wonder if her mood had anything to do with that chap whom the Bunker Boys had said she was seeing). He then worked his way around to the others on the desk, none of whom made it particularly easy. Milkshake was the worst of the bunch, and Jonah suspected that he could sense that being difficult was the name of the game. Five minutes later, he finished with the Baron himself, scarcely managing to contain his surprise at the comparative healthiness of his order.

Back at the Cockpit he dialed up extension 1736 as instructed, and a woman's voice answered. "Breakfast time, Jammy?" The voice was posh and sexy, not at all what Jonah was expecting.

"Er—it's not him," he replied. "My name's Jonah. I'm working with the Baron today while Jammy is out. I'm learning about trading."

"Oh!" Jonah's obviously wasn't the voice she was expecting either, but she quickly recovered. "Well, welcome to Hellcat, Master Jonah."

"What do I do?" Jonah asked. The order was a large one, and he wanted to place it as quickly as possible for fear of forgetting something.

"You tell me what you want, and I'll get it all ready and bring it up to the floor. Give me the name of each person when you give the order, and we can package it all together so there are no complaints."

"Is that it?"

"That's it," she purred. "Hellcat knows its traders are too busy making money to leave their desks, so we here are happy to get you whatever your heart desires."

"So it's like room service at a hotel?"

"Yes. But better. Much, much better, darling boy. We can get you food, toothbrushes, clothes, books, newspapers, CDs, jewelry, Christmas presents, birthday presents, apology gifts for wives, girl-friends, children, you name it. We did an engagement ring once. Marriage didn't last, I seem to recall. But breakfast for the Bunker is a specialty. The Baron likes a show, and the breakfast trolley comes with a certain pizzazz."

"Sounds cool," said Jonah. "Well, here goes." He began to relay the traders' breakfast demands, using the skills he'd developed play-ing parlor games on rainy days when his parents were still married. When it came to his own order, he went for another cappuccino, looking for that buzz again, plus a doughnut. Then he had another, riskier thought. He had once done something similar when his school headmaster had sent him to buy sweets from a local shop, and it had worked so successfully that the other older boys had begun treating him as a kind of hero. That time he had used all the change to buy himself more sweets than he had bought his headmaster. This time he was thinking bigger.

"So the Baron said I can get something on him . . ." Jonah began.

"Oh, isn't that sweet?" Amelia singsonged. "What did you have in mind?"

"Can you really get anything?" he asked.

"Try me, darling."

He told her what he wanted.

"Oh, that will be easy," she said. "We always have a few of those in stock. Give me twenty minutes, Mr. Jonah, and I'll be up to make your dreams come true."

# CHAPTER 6

**Franky and Dog** were back in a huddle with the Baron when Jonah put the phone down. He watched as every now and then the Baron tapped some keys on his keyboard and the three of them looked at the screen, the acute hunger in their eyes growing as the seconds passed. They were talking very quietly, and Jonah could only hear snatches of their discussion: *stealth, option trades, Cayman Islands, SIVs, collars, out of sight, foreign exchange, Rand, minimum visibility,* and *gold.*

When they finished, Dog and Franky returned to their desks, and the Baron turned to Jonah. "Now sonny, I gather that Franky has provided you with a more thorough understanding of our technology than I had the opportunity to do before yesterday's interruption." He waved nonchalantly at the bank of screens in front of them.

Jonah nodded, his fingers itching with excitement. This was what he'd been waiting for. He was finally going to get to help the Baron for real.

"Based on our discussion yesterday, I assume you've already had substantial experience using a computer before. Am I right?"

"Yes," Jonah said, flattered that the Baron had picked up on his prodigious familiarity with the subject. "I even write my own programs."

He immediately regretted his enthusiasm when Dog looked up from his own computer screen and yelled to whomever would listen. "Did you hear that, everyone. He writes his own programs. La de bloody da!"

"Does that mean that some basic inputting is beneath you?" Jeeves sneered.

Jonah reined himself back, his eyes darting between the Baron, who seemed slightly aggravated by his underlings, and the Bunker Boys. "No, I didn't mean it like that. I just wanted the Baron to know that I know how to use computers. Inputting's fine. Sorry."

"I thought I told you to never apologize, mate," said the Baron more brightly than Jonah would have expected. "I like a bit of chutzpah. You need that to work here."

"Hah!" Dog snorted, and under his breath he added, "That kid's got more chutzpah than is legal for a twelve-year-old."

The Baron ignored the murmuring. His focus was now solely on Jonah. "Maybe one day you'll do a bit more than basic data inputting, eh? But today it is just inputting, so why don't you give me a demo of these skills of yours." He grabbed a handful of old trading tickets that were in a tray on the top of the partition and handed them to Jonah. He looked at his watch and said, "Three. Two. One. Hit it!"

Jonah whipped through the tickets, reading each one over and inputting the details as quickly as his fingers could type. He finished inside a minute. "Done," he called out and pushed the pile of tickets back toward the Baron.

The Baron nodded, still looking at his watch. "Swift, sir. *Très vite*. *Mucho speedio*. I like what I see."

Jonah was about to say thank you when a sudden bout of whistling erupted around the trading floor. He looked out across the floor to see what looked like an electric golf cart cruising toward them. It was driven by a woman dressed in a housemaid's black uniform with a white apron and hat. The skirt was short, the heels were high, and the legs were clad in black stockings. Bright red lipstick provided the final touches to a very different dinner lady than the ones at his school.

"Ah! The gorgeous, pouting Miss Amelia is here with our breakfast," the Baron called as she came to a halt next to his desk. "You are looking particularly gorgeous and particularly pouting this morning if I might say so." He adjusted his prominently displayed neck tie, and Jonah instinctively drew his hand up to his collar, wishing that he had one of his own.

"All to keep you boys happy," Amelia singsonged. "All to keep the wheels of finance suitably lubricated. I am here to please." Jonah recognized the voice that had been at the end of the phone earlier. She stepped out of the cart and stood, one hand on her hip, posing provocatively for her audience. She was probably in her late twenties. "But enough of this idle talk. It is breakfast you need to keep the money flowing, not chatter." With that, she sashayed around to the back of her cart and began to withdraw boxes from a heated compartment.

Jonah began to feel butterflies in his stomach. He hadn't thought about the order since he'd placed it. What if he hadn't gotten it right?

"So true, Amelia. So true," the Baron replied. "And we also need to find out whether our young friend here has been able to deliver on his confident statement that no pen and paper were necessary to ensure that my loyal foot soldiers receive their correct rations."

Heat rose to Jonah's cheeks. He watched anxiously as Amelia strutted around the desk and delivered the first box to Dog. "One double decaffeinated cappuccino, with just a dab of foam. One egg and bacon sandwich, lovingly made with brown bread, expertly toasted on one side only, and with a side order of tomato ketchup," she announced.

"Correct," responded Dog. He made a rude sign at Milkshake.

Jonah sighed inwardly, ignoring the sign which he knew wasn't for him. One down.

Amelia delivered the second box to Jeeves. "One chai latte, a subtle blend of Indian spices mixed with steamed milk. One bacon sandwich on white bread with the bacon grilled to perfect crispness and not a trace of tomato ketchup. And one freshly squeezed orange juice, no ice."

"Correct," Jeeves proclaimed.

*Two down,* thought Jonah.

Amelia worked her way around the Bunker, dropping off the boxes with a variety of pouts, hair tosses, and hip sways. Each time she arrived at a new trader's desk, she'd repeat their order aloud and receive a "correct" in response, until she was back at the Baron's side. "And finally, one herbal tea and fruit salad for the king of the

Hellcat trading floor, who wishes to keep his instincts sharper than a leopard's claw." As she handed the Baron his box, Jonah noticed she brushed against him like a cat does against its owner.

"Correct on all counts, Amelia. Extraordinary scenes indeed, as the sports commentators say!" the Baron pronounced. "Which means that young sonny here has delivered the goods." He stood up and faced Jonah. Clicking his heels together, he raised his hand in the flat-handed salute Jonah had seen all the traders give to him the day before. "I am impressed."

Jonah smiled nervously back as Amelia presented him with his own box, giving him a conspiratorial wink, her lips pursed, trying hard to conceal her own smile. She turned to the Baron and presented him with the bill.

Jonah's stomach plummeted as the reality of what he'd done sunk in.

"Your receipt Mr. Baron. One hundred and ninety three pounds and thirty-five pence, service not included," announced Amelia to the whole trading floor.

"How much?" cried the Baron, grabbing the leather folder she was proffering him. The Baron's face reddened as he opened the check case. "What is the meaning of this?"

*Here goes*, thought Jonah, his heart quickening. *Do or die time.* "Well," he piped up, "you said I was to get something for myself. And you said you could afford it. So . . ." He stood up and extracted a plastic container from his breakfast box. "I bought myself an iPod!"

The Baron was speechless. The rest of the Bunker, however, was in an uproar as guffaws of laughter exploded from the mouths of the traders.

"Hey, Milkshake!" shouted Dog. "That's a ton you owe me!"

Franky yelled out, "I reckon we've got his nickname now. He's IPOD!" There was even more laughter, and a chant of "iPod, iPod, iPod" started up.

"You cheeky little f—" the Baron started and then stopped, controlling himself and nodding. "But nice. Very nice. Chutzpah indeed. Chutzpah indeed." He peeled off four fifty-pound notes from a gold money clip and handed them to Amelia as the chanting of "iPod! iPod! iPod!" continued. "You'll be needing some music for it, though. I might be able to help you there," he added, turning back to Jonah.

Jonah glowed. It had worked. He felt the same as he had at school after the candy incident—accepted, appreciated, valued. He looked toward Drizzlers' Den wanting to tell his dad what had happened, but he was hunkered away on his phone, oblivious to the two Neanderthals throwing a ball of paper to each other back and forth over his head.

Jonah glanced down at his brand new iPod and back up at the Bunker Boys, who were even now dancing around him, shouting their approval. If Jonah had been ever so slightly confused before, now he was filled with absolute certainty—he was no Drizzler.

# CHAPTER 7

**At eight thirty** A.M. precisely, the Bunker went into overdrive. The comms screen in front of Jonah lit up like a cruise ship leaving port: lights flashing quickly; lights flashing slowly; lights on constantly. Everyone on the desk was attached to a phone: murmuring, cajoling, buying, selling. It was clandestine and secretive, and Jonah found himself at the center of the action.

He was sitting to the right of the Baron, as he had been the day before, but this time he was the keeper of the trades. Franky would bring him the trading tickets that the traders filled out, and it was his job to input them on the computer. First, he'd enter the stock's ticker code—every stock had a code—then the price and then the amount. If it was a buy order, he gave it a plus number; if it was a sell order, a minus number.

The biggest trades came from the Baron. He was a general who led from the front. He had two phones in his hands at all times, and somehow he could carry out two conversations at the same time, flicking the mute switches alternately with his thumb. Every now and then, he would add his cell phone into the mix, always holding it a few inches away from his ear. His concentration was intense, but his voice gave nothing away to the person at the other end of the phone. He might have been booking a holiday for all Jonah could tell, or at least it sounded that way when he closed his eyes. It was only when he really watched him that he could see the focus.

One thing that Franky and the others hadn't told Jonah was that the Baron didn't write tickets for his trades. He just looked at Jonah and told him the deals directly. He'd say things like "40k short Anglo at 1254," and Jonah would have to deduce the meaning. Fortunately, Franky helped him get started, explaining the traders' language to him as they went along. "40k short Anglo at 1254" meant that he had sold (short) forty thousand (K) shares of Anglo American (a massive mining company) at a price of 1,254 pence.

Pretty soon the Baron gave up even looking at Jonah, such was his confidence in his abilities. He just spoke the orders out loud, so Jonah had to have his ears open to conversation, his eyes on the tickets, and his fingers on the keyboard, all just to keep up. Still, Jonah found the whole thing exhilarating. It was like a race at school, but far more intoxicating. There was the same thrill of leaving everyone in his dust, but this set every nerve ending on fire in a way that Jonah had never previously experienced.

Without meaning to, Jonah slipped into a style of working in which he used his right hand to input the Baron's trades and his left to do the rest. That way he could keep his eyes on the tickets, and when he heard the Baron announce a trade, he could lift his left hand up and switch to his right so that there was a division in his information processing.

"How the hell do you do that?" Franky exclaimed. She was standing behind Jonah, double-checking his work when she caught sight of Jonah's incredible speed and dexterity. Jonah acknowledged the question with a shrug, so focused was he on the task at hand. But inside he felt an indescribable electricity, as if every fiber of his being was telling him that this was what he'd always been meant to do.

"My work here is done," Franky said more to herself than to Jonah, though she did give him a punch in the shoulder for maximum effect. Then she went off to collect more tickets, only returning to Jonah's side for any real length of time when he needed her help to read a trader's writing. Dog's scrawl, in particular, was horribly appalling, but a few of the others weren't much better. Jonah was a bit apprehensive the first time he called her over for additional assistance—he'd thought she'd been glad to leave him to his own devices. But if anything, it seemed like, contrary to her behavior yesterday, she was actually quite relieved when her help was required. Every so often she'd say things like, "Ah! You still need me?" and "Not an expert yet, huh?" And while Jonah couldn't be sure, it felt like as the morning wore on, her words took on a slight bite.

At ten fifteen A.M. David Lightbody appeared at the desk. "We're going to have to leave soon, Jonah," he said.

Jonah turned around. "No, Dad, not again."

His father looked around, his expression a mix of disgust and intense apprehension as he took in the frenzied activity. "I have another client meeting, Jonah. And I'm sorry, but I don't feel comfortable leaving you here by yourself."

"Who with?" Jonah asked.

"Huh?"

"Who's your meeting with? Is it that Russian guy again, Scrotycz?"

His dad shook his head. "It doesn't matter who it's with. I said it's time to go."

Jonah resumed typing. "Dad, I'm inputting trades."

David sighed. "Are they being nice to you?"

"Really nice."

"What are you trading?"

The Baron had told Jonah not to tell anyone what they in the Bunker were doing. He'd sat him down and said, "Loyalty, Jonah. That's what I expect. Even if it's your dad."

So Jonah shrugged. "No idea, Dad. It's just numbers to me."

"Hmm . . ." David replied.

Jonah smiled to himself, his attention still on the screens in front of him.

"Well, I can give you twenty minutes, but after that you'll have to stop entering these mysterious numbers of yours."

"Dad—"

His father cut him off. "I'll tell you what—I'll ask the Baron if you can come back again tomorrow."

"You will?" Jonah exclaimed. He turned back around to face his dad, a giant smile plastered across his face.

"I will," David announced, grinning awkwardly in return. "But," he said, his features taking on their usual stoic arrangement, "don't get used to this. Tomorrow will be the last time you come to work with me, and that's only if the Baron says it's okay. You'll be going back to school on Monday evening, and I don't want you thinking about this place when you do." With that, David nodded, walked around to the Baron, said a few words in a hush, and returned to Drizzlers' Den.

The only thing Jonah could make out from his father's conversation with the Baron was the Baron shouting, "Of course! We'll have iPod again. Getting to be a regular part of the gang, that son of yours! I'm not sure I'll ever want to give him back to you."

Those four sentences were enough to make Jonah positively burst with excitement as he continued entering the trades.

As Jonah typed in the information, it seemed to him as if he wasn't merely inputting; he was building up an elaborate tapestry from the strings of numbers in front of him. There was a pattern to the trades, and two companies were at the center: River Deep Gold and Mountain High Minerals. But there was also a smokescreen being laid around everything so that most people would just see a series of unlinked buys and sells, the connections hidden to them. Jonah didn't have time to wonder why the Baron was doing this, but he knew in his gut that his intuitions were correct.

The tally on Jonah's trading screen kept growing larger and larger as the minutes ticked by—one million, five million, ten million, fifty million, one hundred million, two hundred million, three hundred million, four hundred million, five hundred million—until the Baron called time at ten thirty-two A.M. precisely.

"All right, lads, start closing down," he yelled out, flicking the mute switches on both his phones. "What's our final tally, iPod?" he asked, turning to Jonah.

Jonah looked at the bottom of the screen, doing a double take when he saw the number. "Five hundred and twenty million," he said, forcing his voice to be loud and clear because he knew that's what the Baron would expect. Inside, though, he was in total shock—$520 *million! That was a huge amount of money.*

The Baron seemed satisfied. *"Très fort. Très fort,"* he said. "Half a billion quid and not a sniff of a market reaction. They have no idea what's going to hit them tomorrow." He moved his eyebrows up and down and stroked his mustache, a smug smile playing around his mouth.

There were nods all around.

Or nearly. Dog was the only one of the bunch to look confused. "Wait, tomorrow?" he echoed. "We're not waiting *that long* to really drive it home, are we?"

"That we are, Dog. That we are," the Baron answered, nodding. "Our resident inputter, iPod"—here he looked at Jonah—"has to leave us again for the great and terrible wonderland that is adolescence. But fear not! He will return tomorrow."

"What about Jammy?" Jeeves asked.

*"What about Jammy?"* the Baron repeated, his tone aggressive, taunting. "I'll ask Amelia to call him and tell him to take the day off."

"You're giving him an extra day of vacation?" Milkshake asked, jumping on board the bandwagon.

"I wouldn't exactly call it that," said the Baron, attempting to push his chair under his desk—it wouldn't go very far considering its sheer size.

"So you're firing him?" asked Dog, his hands stretched out on his desk in front of him as if he needed to grasp something wooden, solid, to believe what he was hearing.

The Baron stroked his mustache. "Not yet," he said calmly. Then as if issuing a proclamation, he added, "Let this be a lesson to all of you. If a twelve-year-old can do your job better than you"—Jonah tried to resist the smile that began to take shape at this point—"you probably aren't true Hellcat material."

At that, the Baron gave a flourish of his wrist, motioning for everyone to continue about their business, and turned back to Jonah. "But you, sonny, that was good work. You're quick. Well done. I'm looking forward to having you back with us tomorrow."

Jonah positively swelled with pride. He didn't get much praise at home or at school. "What should I do until then?" he inquired.

"Till then?"

"Yeah, is there anything I can do so that I can, you know, go even faster?"

The Baron started cracking up. "You want to go faster?"

"I want to be the fastest."

There was a glimmer in the Baron's eyes. "That's what I like to hear." He reached into his top desk drawer and pulled out a CD-ROM. "Sometimes we get a little bored, and so to keep sharp we have this training tool," he explained, handing the disk to Jonah.

Jonah looked down at the case. The label had the letter "A" scribbled on it.

"You install it on your computer at home, and it will link you into our trading system."

"And this will teach me to be faster?"

"This, Jonah," the Baron said, using Jonah's given name for the first time since he'd introduced him, "will teach you to fly."

# CHAPTER 8

**When Jonah arrived** home he felt more stimulated than he ever had coming back to his room in the dorms after a class at school. He was so jumpy that he couldn't be sure whether he wanted to run up to his room to begin trying out the disk the Baron had given him (which was now sitting awkwardly in his pants pocket) or sprint through the streets and shout out at the top of his lungs that he'd just had the best morning of his life. Even better than yesterday's.

However, this enthusiasm was tempered by the rapid departure of his father. He didn't even follow Jonah inside the house; he just muttered something about how his meeting "might take all day," spun around, and marched off back down the road, leaving Jonah to close the door and stand alone in the hallway. For a second he took in the silence of the house, hating it, and the euphoria drained out of him. The house felt hollow and desolate, the exact opposite of the trading floor. Jonah sighed and took off his shoes. He thought about taking them upstairs so that they would be easier to slip on the following morning for what he'd been told—repeatedly—would be his final trip to his dad's office. But he remembered how he'd been reprimanded only yesterday morning, and thought better of it. He couldn't risk it.

So leaving the shoes in the pile by the front door, he trudged up the stairs and began heading for his bedroom. It was the sight of his dad's closed door that lifted his spirits. He looked both ways and chuckled to himself. It had to be done!

He pushed the door open and walked straight into his dad's room, his steps deliberate and his mind as singularly focused as it had been at the bank. The room's walls and carpets were beige, and there were old newspapers strewn about, giving the space a disheveled effect that ran counter to the composed air David Lightbody attempted to project. But Jonah didn't reflect on what any of that meant. He went directly to his dad's wooden armoire and opened one of the smaller drawers at the top. In it, he found what he was looking for—his father's tie collection. He ran his fingers along the silk material and reached through to the bottom to grab what he hoped was his dad's least favorite tie, and thus the one he'd be least likely to notice was missing. The tie he extracted was green with little flags all over it, nothing like the striped navy tie that the Baron had worn that morning, but it would do.

He carefully closed the drawer and headed back out to the landing where the silence enveloped him once more. This time though it didn't worry him as he looked at the tie and felt the circular shape of the disk in his pants pocket. He was going to recreate the trading floor in his head using the Baron's training tool!

Energized once more, he bounded across the hall into his own room. There, he awoke his desktop computer from sleep mode and swept his whopping two track trophies out of the way as he sat down in his grey, fabric desk chair. He pulled the disk out of his pocket, placed it into the drive, and carefully tied the tie around his neck while he waited for the old computer to chug to life.

It took him two attempts to knot the tie to his satisfaction, and as he finished a red triplane appeared on the computer screen. The plane swept upward to reveal the German Iron Cross on the underside of its wings before disappearing to be replaced by the words "LEVEL ONE—Ours is the invisible hand. Do you have what it takes to join us?" Jonah screwed up his face in puzzlement as three options popped up: "New recruit," "English Dummkopf," and "Manfred Albrecht Freiherr von Richthofen."

He waved his fingers in a moment of indecision before hitting "New Recruit." Text scrolled up the screen, telling him about the pilots of World War I and that the greatest of them all, with more than eighty kills, was the German pilot Manfred Albrecht Freiherr von Richthofen, more commonly known as the Red Baron. Jonah snickered, thinking that it was probably a good thing that he hadn't selected what was obviously the Baron's preferred character.

As soon as the text finished scrolling, the red triplane reappeared along with a graphic of keyboard controls showing how to land and take off, to turn and climb, to navigate and shoot. At this point, Jonah's puzzlement transformed into laughter that grew louder and louder until finally he had to hit "pause." How had the Baron called this a training tool?

This—Jonah was pleasantly shocked to discover—*was a video game*.

# CHAPTER 9

## Wednesday, August 25

**"Scramble! Scramble!" shouted** the Baron the next morning. "Let's go! Let's go! iPod, you're going to need to be really sharp this time. There won't be any tickets. We'll all be hollering at you, not just me."

"Why? What's happening?" Jonah asked, pulling at the tie he'd "borrowed" the previous afternoon.

The Baron shifted back to his desk and settled into his seat triumphantly. "The news is out! River Deep Gold is going to buy Mountain High Minerals. Market's moving. Probably shouldn't have waited for you to come back to us, but hey, when I start something with someone, I like to finish it."

Jonah thought he could hear Dog whisper something nasty under his breath. A second later, he and Jeeves were cracking up.

"Ignore them," said the Baron, eyeing Jonah directly. "Nice tie by the way." Jonah was about to say thank you when the Baron once again undercut his attempt at pleasantries. "No time for that. Get yourself set. We're going to be clearing out any minute now."

Jonah couldn't help but be struck by the similarity between this Baron and the image of the Red Baron he'd played against yesterday. This one was pressing buttons on the keyboard like a fighter pilot going through his preflight checks; the other had appeared on Jonah's screen out of nowhere, shooting to victory before Jonah could even blink.

Meanwhile, Jonah's screen was going berserk. The numbers next to everything they had bought and sold yesterday morning were changing by the second. And in the profit column it was all blue and climbing. Jonah marveled at how much he'd missed the energy and excitement, even though he'd only been gone for half a day.

Suddenly, the bellowing started. Jonah could hardly tell where it was all coming from: "Gold, platinum, silver, all rising!" "River Deep diving!" "Mountain High roaring!"

"TAKE THE MONEY! Put it all up on the big screen, iPod. We need to see where we are," ordered the Baron.

"I'm on it," shouted Jonah, hyped up by the frenzy that had erupted around him. He pressed the function button on his keyboard so that his screen was duplicated on the fifty-two-inch LCD TV on the wall behind him.

"Now go, go, go!" the Baron roared to his traders. "Give iPod the volumes; we'll do the prices afterward. TAKE THE MONEY!"

Everyone was standing, screaming, waving. One phone, two phones, three phones. It was mayhem as the traders sold everything they had bought and bought back everything they had sold.

"iPod! 20k Anglo gone!" someone yelled.

"iPod! 50k Gold gone!"

"iPod! 500k Katanga gone!"

The calls kept coming.

If the coffee Jonah had consumed over the past two days had heightened his awareness, this was sharpening his reflexes beyond belief. He was a machine. All sound other than the voices of the traders was closed down to white noise in his head. All he could hear was their shouts of completed trades: "5 mill platinum gone!" "70k Lonmin gone!" "Half a bar dollar rand gone!"

His fingers were unerring, punching in the trades and transferring the data back to the traders in real time. They in turn seemed to absorb the constantly changing picture on the screen behind him and use some sixth sense to close it all out without duplication.

"200k Barrick gone!"

"10 mill rouble/dollar gone!"

Next to Jonah sat the Baron, icy calm, and Jonah once again thought about how yesterday his avatar had swept in right when Jonah had believed he'd been about to win the dogfight on the training tool. At first, Jonah had thought it was a computer-generated character that had beaten him. But now he knew for certain that this wasn't the case. It shouldn't have come as such a surprise that the Baron would have been able to emerge victorious, even remotely. After all, he *had* told him that the program was connected to the trading desk.

"40k Norilsk gone!"

"20k Implats gone!"

As each position was closed out, the computer automatically wiped it off the screen, and after about half an hour Jonah could sense that the incoming trades were beginning to slow down. They had carved through the bulk of the deals and were now picking off the stragglers.

"500 Harmony gone!"

"500 Rio gone!"

Jonah could see the Baron in his peripheral vision. He was leaning back in his chair, his fingers stroking his mustache, contented. Jonah watched him as he leaned forward and punched one of the buttons on the comms board, picking up the phone at the same time. "Amelia, I am obliged to ask for your presence for a second time today," he said, the look in his eyes as hungry as ever. "A champagne moment is upon us. . . . Shall we say twelve forty-five? . . . Cristal . . . Yes, indeed, a very productive morning. So much so that I suspect the afternoon will be spent elsewhere. In fact, please book somewhere French for lunch . . . very expensive. . . . Thank you, Amelia. We look forward to seeing you soon." He laid the phone down gently and leaned back again, stretching his arms and calling out, "Franky, collect the tickets, will you? It's almost time for a Sympathy Session." Turning his head, he refocused his gaze on Jonah, and Jonah could see the same glimmer in his eyes that he'd seen there yesterday . . . the moment before he'd handed him the training tool.

# CHAPTER 10

**As Jonah worked** through the tickets that Franky had handed him—a slightly complicated task as these needed to be matched to the trades he'd already inputted—he could hear the Bunker Boys in the background. They were now in a state of post-battle euphoria.

"I love it when a plan comes together," Dog announced, leaning back in his chair and licking his lips.

"I dunno. That one bloke called me an inside trader," Franky admitted in a whisper, shaking her head.

"He's just pissed that you had information and he didn't," Jeeves reasoned, nodding at Dog. He adjusted his bow tie.

"Said he was going to report us to the authorities," Franky added, her eyes wide.

"Nonsense. He says that every time," Milkshake contributed, his eyes darting to Dog and Jeeves for approval. "He's only trying to gain an edge on you for our next battle."

"Yeah, we stuffed him," Birdcage mimed. Jonah almost glanced up from his computer to chuckle at the way he said it. The comment seemed devoid of logic, as if he himself didn't fully understand the words that were coming out of his mouth.

"Him and many others," Dog corrected, grinning.

"There's a few here who won't be happy," Franky said, more to herself than to anyone else.

"Ahh . . . screw them!" Jeeves yelled. Then with a wave of his arms, he added, "Another killing for the Baron and the Bunker Boys!"

Everyone cheered.

Jonah listened as the traders prattled on, smiling to himself as he continued inputting the data, but it was not until their discussion shifted to all the things they were going to purchase with the bonuses they'd make that Jonah's ears really perked up. Milkshake mentioned that he was going to buy a black Maserati to go with the five he already owned. Franky said that she was going to buy some more gold jewelry because her doctor boyfriend didn't have the cash, a comment that only led to the others mocking her for her poor choice in men. For his part, Jonah didn't add anything to the conversation. He'd already acquired an iPod, and he could hardly wrap his mind around what it would mean to buy even more than that in so short a span, even though it sounded tempting.

The traders' moment of exultation was cut short when the Baron yelled out, "Oi! iPod. You got those numbers done yet?" (Though Dog did add, "Yeah we've got stuff to buy!" for good measure.)

Jonah did have the numbers ready. He handed them to the Baron.

The Baron stood up, hit a button on his desk, and stood arms apart like a game show host. "Ladies and gentlemen, it's show time!" he announced, and the Bunker Boys cheered even louder than they had a few minutes earlier.

Jonah looked around the trading floor. Everything had stopped. Everyone was staring their way, though Jonah couldn't make out where his father was among the confused masses.

A drumbeat started to thump out of speakers hidden somewhere in the desks. It was the sound of tom-toms: dark and mystical to Jonah's ears. Suddenly there was a scream: "Yeow!" And again, "Yeow!" Now maracas joined the tom-tom beat. More screams followed, conjuring up images of black magic and witch doctors in Jonah's mind.

This was a song like nothing Jonah had ever heard before. The drums were driving it with a dark satanic beat, and the traders tapped along with their hands on their desks. Suddenly, the Baron's voice rose above the rhythm. It was a surprisingly soft voice from such a big man, but clear. "Please allow me to introduce myself," he sang.

A number flashed up on the TV screen, and Jonah's jaw dropped at the size of it: 123,749,666. This was the amount of money the Baron and the Bunker Boys had made this morning. One hundred and twenty-three million, seven hundred and forty-nine thousand, six hundred and sixty-six dollars.

Even the traders seemed shocked at the sheer scale of their profit. For a moment their drumming ceased, their mouths fell open, and their eyes opened wide. The whole floor was silent in shock, the only sound being the Baron's voice, singing about the devil, Lucifer, the crucifixion of Jesus, the murder of the Russian

Czar, Adolf Hitler's blitzkrieg across Europe, stinking corpses, bad cops, and pain.

And all at once everyone on the trading floor was on their feet cheering, and the Bunker Boys were screaming and laughing. Jonah turned back to the screen and sat there transfixed by the number. It was pulsing in time to the music, changing color and rippling. In Jonah's mind it had a life of its own. He couldn't take his eyes off it.

He was vaguely aware of Amelia materializing next to him carrying a tray of champagne glasses high above her head. "Ooo Baron, that's a very big one," she cooed as she offered him the first glass, but it was only when Dog grabbed his arm and put a glass of champagne in his hand that Jonah tore his eyes away from the number before him.

"Come on, mate! I didn't like you before, always hanging around, but you're one of us today," Dog said, grinning feverishly. "Made me a hundred quid and a monster bonus. Grab my back, we're going to start a conga!" He turned around and started dancing in between the desks, shouting, "Conga! Conga!"

Jonah snorted at Dog's honesty, stood up, placed the champagne glass on the desk, and fell in behind. Before he knew it, he was grinning madly and shouting, "I'm going to be a trader when I grow up!"

Within seconds the rest of the team had joined them, and they congaed around the Bunker, glasses of champagne in their hands, singing along with the Baron. Around and around they danced, summoning the other traders as they moved out to the main part of the floor, the conga line growing longer and longer.

Suddenly Jonah felt a hand on his shoulder, sliding down to grab the top of his arm roughly and forcing him out of the conga line. It was David Lightbody, grim-faced and angry. "That's enough!" he screamed above the noise. "You're out of here, Jonah."

"But Dad, I'm having fun," Jonah shouted back. "And you're the one who said I could come back!"

"I don't care, Jonah. Your time here is *over*."

With that, Jonah's father began to propel his son away from the Bunker. As he passed the Baron, he yelled, "I said no funny business! He's a kid. Keep your circus to yourself and your bunch of clowns."

The Baron sneered, put his fists up in a mock fighting pose, and carried on singing, "Hope you guessed my name."

Jonah felt as if the Baron was looking directly at him alone, singing at him and no one else. He started squirming, trying to break free. "Let go of me, Dad! I don't want to go."

But David gripped tighter and pushed harder as the conga approached them around the other side of the desk and all the traders started pointing at them like football fans. Dog leaned into David Lightbody's face, his teeth bared, and screamed, "Aggggghhh" as they went by, but David didn't react. He just pushed Jonah on toward the exit, Jonah wriggling as the conga line snaked on without him.

"Why do I have to go? What have I done wrong? Tell me! Tell me!" he shouted until the doors closed behind them, killing the sound, killing the song.

## CHAPTER 11

**Once they were** outside, David changed his grip and grabbed Jonah's hand, pulling him down the corridor toward the escalators. He was walking so fast that Jonah had to run.

Jonah tried again to understand why his father was so angry. "What have I done wrong?" he pleaded.

"You? Uh, nothing," David said, his pace as fast as ever.

"So why did I have to leave?"

"I never should have allowed you near that lunatic," David snapped, and shaking his head, he added, "And then I let you back there. Twice!"

"But it was brilliant!" Jonah declared, unable to contain the excitement in his voice. They were now heading down to the lobby with its shark tank. "We made one hundred and twenty-three million dollars in one morning."

"You made! You made!" David exploded. "That type of money doesn't come without a price. He'll bring the whole bank down one day, if not even more than that."

"What do you mean?" Jonah asked. They were on the pavement now, Jonah's father hailing a black taxi.

"Forget it. You wouldn't understand." He had his mobile phone out. "Hi. Yes, I'm putting him in a cab now. . . . I'll give him cash to pay for it." David bundled Jonah into the back of the taxi, then bent down through the front window to give the driver the destination.

"I was hoping we were finally going to go to lunch today," Jonah implored.

"Well, we're not," came the harsh reply. "You're out of here. The au pair is expecting you, and here's some money to pay the driver." He handed Jonah a twenty-pound note. "That's the end of it. And stop stealing my ties." David gave the back of the cab two final pats, and the car sped away.

Jonah sat alone in the back of the taxi, glumly removing his father's tie from his button-down shirt as he watched the City of London pass by. From his seat, he could make out Cheapside, St. Paul's Cathedral, the London Stock Exchange, a glimpse of the old City wall, a sign to St. Bartholomew's Hospital, and finally Holborn Circus, where the City of London finished and the City of Westminster began. But none of the sights, as impressive as they were, did anything to cheer Jonah up. Like his father had said, "That was the end of it."

Except it wasn't. Jonah had left the iPod on the Baron's desk.

# CHAPTER 12

## Saturday, August 28

**Three days later** a package addressed to Jonah was delivered while David Lightbody was out running. Jonah weighed the parcel in his hands and pressed his thumbs into the brown padding, feeling a sense of glee that in his hands might sit a massive secret, some part of his life that his dad would hate if he knew about. It felt like a book, but there was something else there too. Jonah tried to gauge the size of the second item by searching for its edges with his thumbs, but the padding of the envelope was too thick.

Jonah had been trying to think of a way to return to the Bunker, or to at least get the iPod back, ever since he was forced to leave the trading floor on Wednesday. He couldn't ask his father, and he didn't have the courage to pick up the phone to call the Baron. He had tried to construct an e-mail to Franky, since she'd grown friendlier throughout his time at the desk, but again his courage had failed him. By Friday, he had accepted that the iPod was gone, one part of a dream that was fading as quickly as school was approaching.

Jonah calculated that David wouldn't be back for at least half an hour and took out a knife from the drawer by the sink. He cut the envelope open at the top and ran the knife down along the side so that he had created a flap. When he pulled the flap back, it revealed first the corner of a paperback book, then the corner of a folded piece of heavy white paper, and finally the rounded corner of an iPod—*his* iPod.

"Yes!" Jonah screamed as he pulled the iPod from its wrapping, the earphones wrapped around the device. He picked it up in all its white, tactile glory and pressed the center button to switch it on. The logo came up, followed by a menu with the word *music* highlighted in blue at the top. He pressed again and scrolled down to the songs section. As he did so the fingers on his other landed on an oddly shaped groove on the back of the device. Jonah turned the iPod over and saw that it was engraved with the Baron's motto—MY WORD IS MY BOND.

Jonah felt tears welling up in his eyes and bit his lip to hold them back. Nobody had ever done something this nice for him—not his classmates at school, not his deserter mother, and definitely not his father, as cold and removed as he was.

Jonah put the iPod down and turned his attention to the book, leaving the folded piece of paper until last. The book said that it was for "Anyone intrigued by the allure of million-dollar deals." *That would be me*, thought Jonah, a grin spreading across his face.

Next he focused on the folded piece of paper. He picked it up by the crease, and as he did so another piece of paper fell out, face up. It was a check. A check made out to Jonah Lightbody. A check for ten thousand pounds.

Jonah felt his pulse quicken. Bloody hell! What was he supposed to do with that? He didn't have a bank account. He couldn't possibly ask his dad to cash it for him. *The iPod and the book were enough, thanks, Mr. Baron.* Money was a different issue. And not only money, but serious money of an amount that twelve-year-olds did not have access to. To the Baron, ten thousand pounds might be loose change, but to a kid? From a stranger?

Perhaps the note would provide an explanation. Jonah opened it. The paper was thick and expensive, and at the top was an unusual embossed coat of arms, made up of a triplane, a trading screen, a bear, and the German Iron Cross. The handwriting was big, bold, and in black ink. It all seemed strangely reminiscent of the training game.

Dear iPod:

You left your new toy behind, so I've filled it up with proper music.

There's also a book and a check. I've sent you the book because I think you have a talent for this game. I admit that I got you on the desk to wind up your dad, but I was impressed. I have never seen anyone pick things up as quickly as you. In fact, it made me APPRECIATE how useless Sammy is. So he's gone. Guess I'll have to look for another trading assistant now, though I'd doubt if any of these fresh-from-university blokes live up to the feats you performed in three days on the desk.

You also brought us good luck, and I never underestimate the importance of luck. That was one of the most profitable days in Hellcat's history, and I reckon you deserve a slice of the cash that will be coming my way at the end of the quarter. Hence the check.

*Have a listen to the music and read the book. Also, be sure to keep up with that training tool I gave you. It's good stuff, and besides, then I can always shoot you down when you get too cocky! If you want more, please feel free to get in touch. My personal e-mail is probably best. If you think I'm a filthy pedophile, then don't (but at least keep the cash).*

*Yours sincerely,*

And it was signed with a flourish with a B, followed by:

*P.S. Listen to "Sympathy for the Devil" first. It's by the Rolling Stones. I think you'll recognize it!*

*P.P.S. I'm not a filthy pedophile by the way.*

*Bloody hell and blimey! The Baron thought he had talent! The Baron thought he had talent!* His father had never said he had talent in anything, but Jonah didn't let himself think about that for the time being. Instead, he slipped the note and the check into his back pocket and grabbed the iPod. This required a Sympathy Session!

He fixed the earphone buds in his ears and scrolled through the songs until he found "Sympathy for the Devil." The sound of satanic tom toms filled his head, transporting him back to the trading floor and its thrills. It was the same song the Baron had played at the end of Jonah's time at Hellcat. He turned the volume up to maximum, closed his eyes, raised his arms in the air, and started to dance. Singing out loud, he felt lost in the music and the memories and the sheer joy of the moment.

The first he knew of his father's presence in the room was when the iPod was torn from his hands.

# CHAPTER 13

"'**My word is** my bond'!" He gave you this, didn't he?" David shouted. "He gave you this, and he put that song on it."

"Dad, uh, it's not what you think," Jonah said, fear in his voice. He had seen his father cross before, but never angry like this.

"And what is this?" David had seen the book and snatched it up off the table. "Did he give you this too? What else did he give you? What else, Jonah?" he screamed and started coming toward Jonah, his eyes wild, his pupils dilated, the muscles on his neck protruding. "What else, Jonah?"

Jonah backed away until he was up against kitchen cupboards. "Nothing, Dad, nothing," he lied.

"Don't lie to me! What else, Jonah?" Now his father was right on top of him.

Jonah dropped to his knees, wanting to cry, but finding something in him that held his tears back. "Nothing," he lied again. "Nothing. I promise."

"I told you to forget it. Didn't I?" David shouted.

"Uh, uh . . . yes, Dad," Jonah mumbled.

David took a step backward. "The sooner you go back to school the better. That man is dangerous. You are to have nothing to do with him. Now stand up. I'm returning these to where they come from."

Jonah stood up, hearing the Baron's words in his head. *Drizzlers all the way through. Say boo to them and they run a mile.* He wondered if he'd proven that the description applied to him as well.

David pointed to the kitchen stools. "Sit down," he ordered.

Jonah moved over to a stool, keeping his back away from his father in case the note or the check was visible in his pockets. When he sat down, David put the book and the iPod on the table and continued firmly. "Jonah, this isn't about you and me. It's about that man. He's a bad influence. Do you understand?"

Jonah resisted the urge to cower. "No, Dad, I don't understand," he said, his memories of his time in the Bunker spurring him to fight back. "I had a great time at Hellcat until you decided to end it."

His father glared back at him, the anger rising once more. "Don't be taken in by it," he replied. "He really believes in all this Baron stuff, and it's gone to his head. That man is only interested in himself."

"Says who, Dad? He told me I was talented. He *praised* me. When was the last time you did that?"

"I, uh . . ."

"Don't worry, I remember. I think I was about five years old. It was your birthday. I wanted to make you happy. I made you breakfast in bed, but as I brought it into the bedroom I dropped the tray. You said 'well done' then. 'Well done for ruining the carpet.' " Jonah's voice had risen, and he could see from the expression on his father's face that his words were upsetting him. But now that he'd started, he couldn't stop. He decided to twist the knife. "You're jealous, aren't you? He's better than you, isn't he? That's why you hate him."

"Jealous! What is there to be jealous of?" David shouted back.

Jonah momentarily wondered whether he'd pushed things too far, but still, he kept going. "One hundred and thirty million dollars in one day?" he chirped.

"How dare you! Like I told you, nobody makes that type of money in that amount of time without being very lucky or cheating. Nobody has that much good fortune. He'll bring us all down one d—"

Jonah didn't wait for him to finish. "Is he the reason you're called Biff? Did he challenge you to a fight, and you were too scared to fight back?"

His father answered far more calmly than Jonah had expected. "Yes, Jonah. He's the one who gave me that awful nickname. And yes, it's because I refused to fight him. But no, I wasn't scared."

"So what was it? You knew you were going to lose?"

"No," said David, gaining control of his temper. "I didn't fight him because I don't fight."

"What's that supposed to mean?"

"I don't fight," repeated David, crossing his arms. "Simple as that."

"Why not?" Jonah pressed.

"It's too complicated to explain."

"Why is *everything* too complicated to explain?" Jonah implored, and without waiting for his dad to reply, he added, "Forget it. I get it—why you hate the Baron, why you and Mom divorced, why Mom never wants to speak to me." His eyes bored into his father's. "You're a Drizzler and a coward and a bully."

David looked on, helpless. "That's not it, Jonah. You've got it all wrong. There's a lot you don't understand about me, your mom, my time in Africa, the Baron. . . ." His voice trailed off.

"But you're not going to tell me about any of that, are you? Not really?" Jonah prodded. "Well, that's fine by me. Good thing I'm going back to school soon. It's not as if I like it here anyway." He ran out of the kitchen and upstairs to his bedroom, slamming the door shut behind him and collapsing on his bed.

# CHAPTER 14

**Jonah finished the** book the Baron had given him in twenty-four hours. He'd simply gone out on Saturday afternoon and bought a new copy after his dad threw away the original. He read late into Saturday night and through Sunday, keeping the book hidden from his father at all times. The only time he put it down was when he became lost in thought about the differences between the man who'd brought him into the world—a dour, absent man who was a drizzling, bullying coward—and the man who had given him this book, told him he had "talent," filled his iPod up with music, and sent him ten thousand pounds. As far as Jonah could tell, *this* was the man who had given him life.

Jonah wrote an e-mail to the Baron as soon as he turned the book's final page. He told him what his father had done. He told him he wanted to be a trader. He told him he wanted to work for him and asked him to set up an online trading account with the ten thousand pounds.

It was time to declare himself a Whistler once and for all.

The Baron responded almost immediately from his Blackberry. His message was one word in capitals: "DONE."

On Monday, Jonah received another e-mail from the Baron. It had the details of the trading account, the user name, and the password. The account would be in the Baron's name—that way, nobody would be able to tell it was a kid doing the trades—but it would only be activated once Jonah had been trained. The Baron asked for Jonah's address at school so that he could send more books and a new iPod. Jonah gave it to him. He trusted him. His word was his bond.

On Monday night, Jonah went back to school and away from the prying eyes of his father.

Four years later, Jonah Lightbody was back at Helsby Cattermole. He was four hundred thousand pounds richer and was—at age sixteen—about to become the youngest trader Helsby Cattermole had ever employed. He was also about to walk into a global financial firestorm.

## Part Two

# LONDON
# ZURICH
# NEW YORK
# JOHANNESBURG

# CHAPTER 15
## Monday, September 8

**Jonah walked through** the doors of the Helsby Cattermole building and into the "shark tank" at eight twenty-five A.M. He was dressed in a slim-cut, single-breasted black suit, white button-down shirt, black boots, and a silk Hermès tie as classy as any he'd seen the Baron wear. His clothes were all tailor-made and topped off with a pair of solid gold cufflinks, a dollar sign on one cuff and a pound sign on the other. A Breitling Navitimer watch adorned his wrist. He glanced beyond the building's revolving doors to check that the car valet was giving his antique 1960s Vespa scooter the careful attention it deserved, nodding when he saw the way that he was admiring the original details as he cautiously wheeled it down to the underground garage. Jonah normally only used the Vespa to get around on weekends, but he couldn't resist driving it to work on this, his first day back.

At the reception desk, he asked for the Baron and gave his own name. The receptionist, a pretty blonde girl called Sophie, according to her badge, smiled at him and asked whether he had been to Hellcat before.

Jonah smiled back. "I have," he said. "But it was a long time ago."

"Let's have a look," she replied, tapping his name into the database. She stared at the screen for a moment, raised her eyebrows, and looked back up at Jonah. The photo on the monitor showed a pale-skinned boy with fair, straight hair, cut short so that it was above his collar. His face had the chubbiness of childhood, and his brown eyes were soft and innocent. The person in front of her was touching six feet and broad across the shoulders. His hair had darkened from fair to light brown, and was well below his collar and flopping over his forehead. His skin was tanned, presumably from the summer holidays, and all of that puppy fat had disappeared to reveal sharp cheekbones. The darker hair seemed to have softened his eyes even further, but the innocence had definitely departed.

"I think we'll need a new photograph," she laughed, and Jonah had to stand self-consciously at the desk while she pointed the digital camera at him. "Take a seat, and I'll tell him you're here, Mr. Lightbody," she said, causing Jonah to look over his shoulder in a panic, thinking that she was referring to his father. He'd managed to evade traveling to work with him this morning by using the lame excuse that he had to polish his shoes before beginning his first day, and it wouldn't have surprised him if his father had been waiting there in the lobby, eager to tell him once again that he was making the wrong decision by joining the firm, even if it was only temporary. Fortunately, there was no one behind Jonah, and he acknowledged his error quickly enough to turn back around and say thank you without the receptionist noticing any odd behavior.

There was only one set of chairs in the reception area. They were made from black leather and chrome and arranged around a glass table. Jonah walked over to them, sat down, and threw his newspaper on the table. He'd read it already, and regardless, anyone in banking—and for that matter, the world at large—knew what it said. Another two banks deemed "too big to fail" had been rescued over the weekend, and there would probably be more.

The world had changed since Jonah was last here. It was now in the midst of a massive financial crisis, one that looked like it was to have global ramifications. Jonah looked upward to the towering ceiling, then downward at the modern art on the walls, and back across at the sharks, the solidity of the building around him warming his heart. Despite all the chaos out there beyond the firm's revolving doors, Hellcat itself hadn't changed. It was as invincible as ever.

Jonah smiled to himself. *Kind of like him,* he thought. He sat back in his chair, reached into his inside pocket, and pulled out a well-creased old letter, the one the Baron had made sure was waiting for him upon his arrival back at school four years previously.

When Jonah caught sight of a woman coming down the escalator that led to the trading floor, he promptly put the letter away and watched as she, a grim-faced man behind her, and a security guard—carrying a black garbage bag—descended and crossed the reception floor, never once exchanging a word between them. The receptionists, too, stopped talking as they passed. The only sound was footsteps on the marble floor. Jonah found himself frozen with fascination. The trio reached the revolving doors, and the woman stopped and turned to the melancholic-looking man. She held out her hand, and he took off the security pass from around his neck and handed it to her. The security guard gave the man the black garbage bag. Still there was silence. Finally the woman spoke. "I hope it all works out," she said.

"Yeah right," the man replied and walked out of the revolving doors, garbage bag in hand.

Jonah watched the security guard and the woman head back toward the escalator and saw Sophie the receptionist walking toward him. *She really was very pretty*, he thought, standing up. She stopped in front of him, handing him a security pass. "This is valid until the eighth of December, three months from today."

"Great, thanks." Jonah placed the pass in his pocket, nearly forgetting the spectacle he'd just observed as his heart began to race in anticipation.

If Sophie noticed Jonah's excitement, she kept it to herself. She simply said, "The Baron says you can go straight up."

"Excellent," Jonah replied. "I know the way."

# CHAPTER 16

**Jonah ran the** security pass across the sensor and watched as the double doors opened up. A shiver went through his body, and he shook his head as if trying to wake himself as his eyes swept across the cavernous space in front of him. It was smaller than he remembered and quieter too. Many of the desks were empty, their chairs devoid of jackets, casualties of the financial crisis. Jonah could sense immediately that, despite his impressions of the lobby, this was no longer an army on the charge. This was a force in retreat, hunkering down in the trenches, waiting for the next barrage of market-crippling news. These were individuals hoping to just get out alive, to return home each day with their jobs intact.

Or at least that was the case outside the Bunker. With a quick glance at his (still tie-less) father over in Drizzlers' Den—no Neanderthals there anymore, he noticed—Jonah strode over to the Bunker, where he could already hear a buzz of determined activity. *Here was the Resistance!* The Lego fort and airplanes were still there, as was the fishless tank above which now hung a row of plastic trash bags, lifeless and black, the antithesis of Christmas stockings.

"Achtung! Achtung! Heeeeere's iPod," the Baron shouted when he saw him. "And he needs a hair cut!"

Heads popped up around the desk like meerkats in the desert. There were smiles and thumbs-ups and high-five signals. Then, just as quickly, the heads went down, back to work. Jonah couldn't be certain, but it dawned on him that, despite how positive his last interaction had been with the Bunker Boys, maybe Dog and the rest of them weren't actually all too happy about having him there.

"Hello, mate. Glad you could make it." The Baron shook his hand. "Summer off looks as if it treated you well. What's with the hair?" he teased.

"What's with the trash bags?" responded Jonah, refusing to be drawn into a discussion of his barbering decisions.

There was no sign of Franky.

"Oh, them? A mark of disrespect for the departed. One for every job lost. Another one went this morning," the Baron answered loftily.

Jonah thought about the grim-faced man in reception and nodded. "Yeah, I saw him."

"Terrible business, it is," the Baron added somewhat unconvincingly. "But fortunately, we have little of that here at the Bunker." The Baron raised his voice. "Right, boys?" he called out.

"Hell no!" came a combined military-style chant.

"What goes in the trash bag?" Jonah asked, still trying to absorb the change in atmosphere since he'd been here last.

"Possessions." The Baron waved his hand airily. "When you're chopped, we don't want you hanging about. You might smash up a computer or put through some dodgy trades. So it's desk cleared and into the bag, and you're out of the door, security guard on your shoulder, check in the post, game over."

Jonah counted twenty-seven trash bags below the fish tank. "That's not what happened to Franky, is it?" he inquired.

"Naaaah," the Baron sneered. "I told you we don't have any of these corporate-mandated layoffs here in the Bunker." The Baron punched Jonah in the shoulder, laughing heartily. "No, she'd had enough. Made enough money, she said. Though who knew there was such a thing? Her doctor boyfriend proposed and that was that. Off to get married and have babies."

"Good for her," said Jonah, though his enthusiasm was cut short when he noticed a shadow pass across the Baron's face.

"Yeah well. Maybe. But it's been carnage without her. She'd been doing some assistant duties for me as well—as you know, I never could find an assistant who I felt could really follow in your footsteps." Here the Baron shook his head despairingly. "The whole lot was as bad as Jammy. Which is why you're back!" He paused for a moment before adding, "By the way, what did your dad say about you coming to fill in for the next few months?"

"Pretty pissed off but not a lot he could do," said Jonah. "I cleared it with the school first. They think it's a great idea. Kind of like the exchanges we do with other schools, only this one is giving career experience."

"Ah, I knew I liked you!" the Baron exclaimed. "Smart approach."

Jonah nodded casually in agreement. "Then I told the Drizzler that they'd said it was a good idea, and if he didn't let me do it I'd leave school."

The Baron cracked up. "Wish I could have seen the look on his face."

"Me too," Jonah replied, though that wasn't entirely true. "But I did it over the telephone!"

"Good man, good man," the Baron muttered, nodding his head. "No reason to drag it out."

"Guess not," Jonah agreed, and falling more completely into the rapport he and the Baron had developed over the last four years, he added, "Would have helped though if you'd told me I was only here until you found a full-time replacement for Franky!"

"Did I not mention that?" the Baron replied, a mock guilty expression on his face.

"You did not. You just said to 'come for a few months.'"

"Well, you know, we're looking really diligently." Here the Baron rolled his eyes.

"I can see that." Jonah gestured at the files on the Baron's desk, which he guessed were unopened job applications.

The Baron laughed heartily, his hands on his stomach. "So have you seen the old man at all this summer?"

"I'm not looking at him?" Jonah teased, causing the Bunker Boys to glance up from their work, their faces filled with shock that the kid would try something like that with their boss.

Dog whispered to Jeeves, "Fifty quid he doesn't let him get away with that."

"Haha, I had that one coming," the Baron said, patting Jonah on the back, causing Jeeves to cackle. "So tell me what you were doing this summer?"

Jonah tried to ignore Dog, who was now swearing. "I've been all across Europe touring music festivals like you suggested. Best time of my life!" he said to the Baron

"Hence the hair," noted the Baron, cocking his head.

"Hence the hair," Jonah repeated, standing his ground. There was a moment of silence when Jonah wondered whether the Baron was going to tell him to get it cut, but instead he sat back down and motioned to Jonah to do the same.

"Right. That's enough banter. Let's get to work. We don't want to make the rest of these punters jealous, now do we?" He shot a glance at Dog, who was shaking his head in apparent disbelief, and then returned his attention to Jonah, raising his voice a fraction. "You're being paid now, so I'd better get my money's worth! You'll remember what *this lot* is like: badly written tickets, mismatches, screw-ups. We are trading our socks off, and there's been nobody to clear up *their* mess. Clive in Settlements, you'll meet him later, has sorted some of it, but he's got the whole floor to deal with. So, you're stepping straight into Franky's shoes as well as those of my long departed trading assistant. All right?"

Jonah looked at the overflowing tray of tickets sitting on the desk. He'd thought he'd come here to trade, not input. "Yeah, I reckon that'll be all right. Though I'm not sure high heels suit me," he quipped.

"Ha bloody ha. Good. What's the time? You've got to see some people this morning." He glanced at his watch. "Eight fifty. Amelia's first, at nine. Remember her?"

"The breakfast lady? I'm not doing breakfast again, am I?" Now Jonah was really concerned.

"No," said the Baron. "Those days are gone, and she's gone up in the world since then anyway. You'll find out." He winked. "After Amelia you'll do Pistol—Harry Solomons—in Legal—Compliance we call it—at ten, boring but legally necessary. That'll be followed by a visit from the tech boys at eleven thirty and a twelve o'clock with Clive." He changed his voice to a sneering cockney accent and was rubbing his fingers and thumbs together and screwing up his face. "After that it's on the desk making money . . . loads of money."

Jonah smiled, the excitement reaching his eyes. So he would be trading.

The Baron reverted to his normal voice. "Now go, or you'll be late for Amelia, and that will upset her. You don't want to upset Amelia. If there's a Hellcat in this place it's most definitely her. Fifth floor, follow your nose."

Jonah stood back up again, removed his jacket, and placed it on the back of his chair.

# CHAPTER 17

**In Switzerland it** was nine fifty in the morning, one hour ahead of London time. Kloot stood at a window of his mansion in the Oberstrass, the wealthiest area of Zurich. He was smoking a cigar and contemplating the five hundred million dollars he had made from trades relating to the U.S. government's bailout actions over the weekend. *These governments were so predictable,* he mused. Two banks rescued so far but there would be more. He'd seen it happen twenty years ago with the savings and loan crisis. What had they pumped into that one? Over a hundred billion dollars, and he'd taken a good slug of that, thank you very much. This wasn't the end of this latest financial crisis, and if he got it right he could make a financial killing even bigger than the one he'd made twenty years ago or what he'd earned from the Russian Crisis in 1998 or even the attacks on the Twin Towers in 2001. This was a special time. Situations like this were precisely what the Apollyon Fund was designed for, a situation in which fear reigned. He would drive the fear and Apollyon could feed its greed.

His plan was simple: force the U.S. government into another rescue situation. Stage one would be to harness the power of the financial markets to create a complete crisis of confidence in New York's banks. There was so much panic around, it wouldn't take much to cause another stampede of investors to the exit doors. Once the market had flushed out the next target, his operative inside the Federal Reserve would be in the position to feed him the information he required to execute the trade. And stage three would be the trade itself: a massive bet that would reap massive profits.

He took a long draw on his cigar, blowing a series of smoke rings into the air, and turned toward his desk with its encrypted telephone. He didn't want anyone listening in to what he had to say. Once he had marshaled the Apollyon network, he would return to Africa, his original home, and admire the carnage from somewhere warm. Switzerland was too cold, even in the summer.

## CHAPTER 18

**Jonah was outside** Amelia's "Boudoir," as the sign on her office advertised itself, when he heard her unmistakable high-class purr. Up here the smell was a long way away from the blood, sweat, and tears that pervaded the trading floor. "Mr. Lightbody! iPod!" she exclaimed. "My, haven't you grown into a fine-looking man!"

Her mouth was now on his cheek, her hands holding his shoulders. Her lips were soft, lingering, as she kissed him first on the left and then on the right. He was uncomfortable: uncomfortable with her attention and flattery, uncomfortable with her proximity, and uncomfortable with the feeling of butterflies at the base of his stomach.

She stepped away, her eyes finding his, her hands still on his shoulders. Four years ago he'd hardly thought of her at all—she was a minor character he had to deal with in order to impress the Baron. Things had changed since then. He noticed the fullness of her lips, her high cheekbones, her clear and taut skin, the way her blonde hair was pulled back from her face to reveal her blazing eyes. He stood, rigid, his own hands firmly by his sides, unable to hold her gaze lest she read his mind. A slight smile flitted across her mouth as he looked away. "Come, let us go somewhere more private," she said, leading him into her office.

He looked around. There was no desk in the Boudoir. Instead there was a glass dining table with six chairs, along with a matching glass coffee table surrounded by a rainbow of armchairs, poufs, and a sofa. There was also a bookshelf-cum-display cabinet along one wall, containing a variety of objects that Jonah couldn't identify. Hanging on the opposite wall was a single painting, an explosion of color within which Jonah could make out the discrete form of a naked woman. Otherwise the walls were covered in grey, textured wallpaper. The floor was carpeted, also in grey, and as the door closed, the soft furnishings deadened all sound, and Jonah felt cocooned and cut off from the world outside. He settled himself into a plump, cerise velvet armchair, wary of the consequences of choosing the sofa. He hadn't fallen in love during the summer, but he had had a good time with a couple of girls. But they had been girls. This was a woman.

Amelia walked toward the dining table and picked up a telephone that was lying on it. Turning, she asked Jonah, "Cappuccino?" Jonah nodded, wary of speaking lest his voice do something weird. She punched a button and spoke into the phone, staring at Jonah the entire time.

"Creedence darling, would you please make my guest a cappuccino? And do join us when you're finished. Thank you, darling." She released the button and walked over to where Jonah was sitting. She placed the phone on the coffee table and perched herself on the arm of Jonah's chair, her arm along its back, her bare thighs highly visible to Jonah's rabbit-like stare.

"So here you are, all grown up," she almost whispered. "Do tell me what you have been up to."

Jonah started from his erotic reverie. *Come on, Jonah, pull it together*, he silently castigated himself. *You're with the big boys now. Don't give her the pleasure of teasing you. Play the game.* He gave the most obvious answer he could think of: "Making money."

Amelia jumped up from the chair, smiling widely. "My darling," she said with a gasp, "if it's money that you've been making, you have come to the right place." She pirouetted so as to sweep her arms around the whole room and on completion flicked her right hand as if casting a spell. "It's all here, darling. Anything you could ever desire. No need to leave the building."

Jonah now had the chance to scrutinize what was on the shelves of the display cases. Luxury goods would be the correct collective term—jewelry, handbags, shoes, gadgets, model cars, boats, planes, signed photos of some of the world's best clothing designers, auction catalogues, books on art, books on homes, books on travel; the possibilities seemed infinite.

"Only thing missing is breakfast," Amelia said, her face now close to his, her expression stern. "We don't do that anymore. Traders are up in arms, of course, but in these times of trouble we all have to accept certain reductions in privileges."

There was a gentle knock on the door, and Amelia straightened up. "Come in," she called out. The door opened and into the room stepped a girl, not much older than Jonah. She held a tray of coffee and biscuits that she placed on the table. Then she curtseyed.

Jonah was taken aback. "Did she just curtsey?" he asked Amelia.

"She most certainly did. I like to maintain standards." She held out a hand toward the girl. "iPod, meet Creedence Clearwater."

Jonah stood up and stretched out his hand, about to apologize for being so rude, though he knew the Baron would have thought it beneath him. But before he could speak, Amelia jumped in again, "Creedence, this is iPod. He will be working as the Baron's right hand."

Creedence raised her eyebrows a fraction at this statement.

"He has been sent here to get everything he'll need for his new job. Would you be so kind as to do the honors?"

"It would be a pleasure, Miss Amelia," she said. "But I'm sorry, sir," she added as she turned to Jonah. "You were going to say something?" Her brown eyes sparkled with amusement, and her voice was much deeper and stronger than Jonah had expected. There was a hint of an American accent in there somewhere. She was elfin, dark, and her hair was cut boyishly short with long bangs. She had three earrings in her right ear and one in her left, and Jonah suspected that she was not quite as demure as her introductory curtsey suggested.

"I was. I was," he stuttered. "Jonah is my real name. Jonah Lightbody. And I would like to apologize for being so rude." He extended his hand further toward her, and she placed hers inside his in a formal handshake.

"Apology accepted. And I'm pleased to meet you." She paused. "Jonah."

That voice again. Almost rasping. It made the hairs on his arms stand on end. "Is it Creedence Clearwater as in the band?" he asked.

She jumped back, surprised. "One and the same. Not many people our age have ever heard of them. My parents were hippies. When they had me, the temptation to combine Creedence with Clearwater was all too great."

"It's cool," responded Jonah.

"Thanks." Creedence smiled. "I like it too."

"I knew you two would hit it off," interjected Amelia in a suddenly maternal tone. "But we must get to work. The Baron doesn't like to be kept waiting."

Jonah realized he was still clasping Creedence's hand and sheepishly pulled away. Creedence grinned again, more broadly this time. She didn't seem to mind the extended shake. They continued staring at each other, only starting when Amelia placed a dark brown leather attaché briefcase on the table between them.

Once they all taken their seats, Creedence pulled the case toward her, snapping the locks and lifting the top open as she did so. She was now very businesslike. "First, your phone," she announced. Like a magician she withdrew a smartphone from inside the case. "This is a next-generation prototype: faster, longer battery life, and no dropped calls. It's been preprogrammed with all the necessary numbers and e-mail addresses from the Baron's address book, plus a selection of useful and relevant websites and apps. There's a real-time market prices feed, no twenty-minute delay, a fully operational trading platform, and a stealth function so that you can use it on airplanes without the crew knowing. In these markets we can't afford for our traders to be out of touch for any time at all."

Jonah gazed longingly at the device in Creedence's hand, though he remained far more impressed by the woman holding it. "Very useful," he said in what he hoped was also a businesslike manner.

"It is. The bank picks up all your telephone costs, and if you do use a second phone you must register it with Hellcat. It's a requirement. The easiest thing to do is cancel any other contracts you have and transfer the number to this phone. If you leave your phone with me, I'll sort it out."

Jonah extracted his old phone from his pocket, placed it on the table, and took the new one from Creedence. No contest.

"Laptop." This time an ultra-slim slab of anodized aluminum came out of the magic case. "Again a next-generation prototype and the thinnest laptop in the world. Externally it's no different from the one you'll find in the store. Inside it's a souped-up beast with an HD screen and more processing power than Mission Control in Houston. It's set up for remote access and a personal Hellcat trading account with fifty thousand pounds worth of credit on it. For compliance reasons you must use this account for any personal trading. If you have any other accounts, close them down." Creedence hesitated. "Do you have any others?"

Jonah was going to say yes, but remembered that his trading account was actually in the Baron's name. Probably best not to mention that. He shook his head. This was better than Christmas.

"Credit card. The American Express Centurion, or Black AmEx as it's more commonly known." The black card took its place on the table. "It has an exceptionally high spending limit. The most expensive purchase known to date on a black card is that of a thirty million dollar private jet, although you might have to wait a while to hit those heights."

Jonah tried to look cool and unconcerned. He failed. "Thirty million bucks on a credit card!"

"Apparently so," Creedence replied with a smile twitching around the edges of her mouth.

The next card was purple, with no other markings on it except Jonah's name.

"This gets you into the VIP section of any club you might want to go to, here in London or in any other major financial center. It will also—"

Amelia interrupted. "Yes, I'm particularly proud of this one, darling. I call it the Purple Nicey." Her tone had changed from charm to firm. "This is what I really do, Jonah. Erase any images you may have of me dressed up like some tart for the traders to ogle at. This card makes money for us. It doesn't only do clubs. You'll find that if need be it might even get you into an embassy or two. All our clients will recognize it and do whatever they can for you. A Black AmEx is just money. This card is power and contacts. And that's what makes this business function, the ability to reach what others cannot." She made a point of looking Jonah in the eye and ensuring that he had understood. "Treat it with care."

"Wow!" said Jonah, all attempts at grown-up behavior falling away.

"Wow is right, darling. Wow is right."

Meanwhile, Creedence was returning the booty to the briefcase. "You get the case too," she said. "It has a secret document compartment to protect confidential information, a thumbprint locking system, which you'll need to activate, and a built-in solar powered phone and laptop charger." She pushed the case across the table toward him. "Happy?" she asked.

"Happy?" Jonah exclaimed. "It's like being James Bond. Does everyone get all this stuff?"

"Oh no. Only the biggest swinging dicks get this stuff, the masters of the universe," Amelia admonished, causing Jonah to shift his attention away from the case. "You are working for the biggest swinging dick of them all, darling, so you get everything. But keep it quiet." She put a finger to her lips. "We don't want to incite too much angst among those less fortunate. You are only a temporary employee after all."

A thought flashed across Jonah's mind. "Does my dad get this stuff?" he asked.

Amelia put on an expression of theatrical dismay, brought her hand to her forehead, and pretended to faint.

Jonah laughed. "I guess not then."

"Correct," said Amelia, now fully recovered. "Which reminds me, your iPod. The source of your music collection also resides in this room." Amelia raised herself from her chair and crossed the room to a steel cabinet Jonah hadn't previously noticed. She ran her security pass across a sensor on the right, and the front of the cabinet slid back to reveal a stack of eight briefcase-size black boxes behind a glass door. She stroked the door lovingly. "The Baron's hard drive," she sighed. "He likes me to look after it for him."

"Pardon?" said Jonah.

Amelia simply smiled and carried on. "On here is the Baron's complete music collection, among other things. You will find a database on your new laptop. When you need your iPod updated, mark the songs you want, bring the laptop and the iPod to me, and I'll get it done. It has to be me. Nobody else has access."

"Oh. I see," said Jonah. "Right. Yes. Thanks. Out of interest, how many songs are there?"

"Oh, thousands. Tens of thousands. I have no idea. They download automatically. I can't believe he listens to them all, but there you go. It's his passion, and money buys you the ability to fulfill those passions, no matter the cost." She ran the card over the sensor again, and as the front slid back she looked at her watch. "Nine fifty-two. Time to move on."

Jonah and Creedence stood up, Creedence handing him the case with one hand and a business card with another. "If there is anything else you might need, day or night—travel, tickets to the theater, sports, music, limousine service, restaurants, you name it—ring this number," she said, her suggestive glance hinting that Jonah could find more than the aforementioned items at the other end of the line.

"Thanks. Thanks for your help," he said, wondering if perhaps he'd read too much into what was, at the end of the day, a simple gesture.

"I hope we meet again," came the warm reply, and Jonah felt himself flush.

He had to find some reason to call her.

Having left the Boudoir, his heart still racing over the encounter with Creedence, Jonah took the elevator up another five floors to see Harry Solomons in the Legal Department, or Pistol as the Baron had called him. He was made to wait ten minutes until a secretary ushered him into a large office with a large desk, behind which sat a small man in a dark suit and waistcoat. He was writing, his head down, revealing a bald patch on top. The secretary gave Jonah a weak smile and left, but Mr. Solomons carried on writing, leaving Jonah standing and feeling increasingly uncomfortable in the silence. Finally, after well over a minute, the man put down his pen and looked up at Jonah with disgust.

"I am Legal Counsel to Helsby, Cattermole, & Partners," he said in smooth, well-educated tones. He then proceeded to lecture Jonah about how he alone was the guardian of the firm's reputation and how he—Jonah—had a choice: he could either follow in the Baron's "dangerous" and "egomaniacal" footsteps or adhere more closely to his father's example by sticking to the straight and narrow. Jonah wasn't sure whether he was supposed to respond to any this and felt that it was all coming a little late in the game—he'd already chosen sides. So he nodded in the appropriate places, hoping that would be enough to appease the man in front of him and get him back to the Bunker unscathed. It worked for a while until Pistol made him sign a bunch of forms, handed him a giant-looking file with the word "Compliance" printed on it, and sent him on his way, muttering, "Reprobates, all of them," as he did so.

Jonah was twenty yards away from the Bunker when the Baron's voice hit him like a sledgehammer. "iPod! Where the hell have you been? Get your arse over here now!"

Jonah quickened his stride, holding the file Solomons had given him as far from his body as possible. It was like being summoned by the headmaster. For a second he felt small, a child among men once more. "I've been seeing Amelia and Mr. Solomons like you told me to," he explained.

"Did I?" The Baron seemed genuinely surprised. "Oh yeah." He looked at the file in Jonah's hand. "Is that Pistol's file of death?"

"That it is." Jonah grinned, pretending to struggle with its weight. "Why do you call him Pistol anyway? Is it because he shoots the traders down or something?"

"That's what he thinks." The Baron laughed, a glint in his eyes. "The reality is we call him that because he's a small bore."

Jonah cracked up. "Genius."

"Yeah. I thought so when I made it up. Anyway, if he's said you can't do anything until you've read his file of death, forget it." He paused and grabbed the file from Jonah's fingers. "Here, let me help you." He chucked the file into the trash can, a wild expression on his face. "Now, get all the tickets and start inputting."

Jonah could feel his fingertips tingle with excitement, but he still had his wits about him enough to make sure he'd dealt with all the preliminary nonsense. "What about the meetings you wanted me to have with Clive and the tech boys?" he asked.

"Screw them! Do them tomorrow," the Baron replied gleefully. "We're bank bashing, and we're about to go supersonic!"

"Bank bashing?" Jonah echoed.

"Shorting the crap out of them. Selling their shares," the Baron explained. "The market thinks that the weekend's rescues mean the end of the financial crisis. It's not."

"No?"

"No!" The Baron smiled. "The banks are going down, and we're going to help them on their way. He crunched the knuckles on his left hand, then the knuckles on his right. Finally, he kissed the skull-head ring on his finger. "Come now, iPod, cry havoc and let slip the dogs of war!"

"Yeah!" shouted Dog. Jonah looked across the desk to see he was holding a hammer in one hand and his phone in the other.

Jonah put his new briefcase down, took a deep breath—inhaling the scent of the hunt—and began rushing around the Bunker, collecting the trading tickets from each of the traders. Back at the Cockpit he quickly refamiliarized himself with the computers, making a mental note to be in first tomorrow morning so that he could press the button that made the screens appear. Nothing much had changed in the four years he'd been gone except for a fingerprint security device to activate the computers. Now that was cool.

The Baron was on the phone but signaled to him to put his finger on the pad and mouthed, "It'll reset with your fingerprint." Jonah did so, and the screens lit up. After some security wording, it all came to life: there were the numbers, red and blue; the newsfeed in a window on the right; the e-mail chat from the market; the profits and the losses. Jonah scanned the information—absorbing it, understanding it. They were selling bank shares, betting that the share prices would fall and that they could buy them back cheaper in the next couple of days. And they were doing it on a massive scale.

Jonah turned to the Baron. "Jesus. You're not joking about shorting the crap out of them!"

The Baron raised his arms in the air like a boxing champion and started singing, obviously enjoying himself. "I'm going supersonic, bring me a gin and tonic."

Jonah's fingers started rattling across the keyboard. The Bunker was hunting the banks down one by one. Royal Bank. *Bang*. Hudson Building Society. *Bang*. Banque de Triomphe. *Bang*. Saxo Kash Finanz. *Bang*. Nordic Insurance. *Bang*. The biggest names in European finance were coming under heavy fire from the Baron and the Bunker Boys.

And still the Baron continued to sing, "Going supersonic, their management's moronic."

At one o'clock the New York markets opened and they turned their sights to the United States. Allegro Home Finance. *Bang*. National Mutual. *Bang*. OPM Insurance. *Bang*. DebtGroup. *Bang*. Lads Bellowing & Brothers. *Bang*.

"Going supersonic, they've all got plague bubonic."

Jonah struggled to keep up with the volume of trades—they were coming so fast. All afternoon he pounded away at the keyboard, loving the buzz around the desk. His only frustration was that he wasn't trading himself. After having spent the last four years huddled in his dorm room working with the Baron on his portfolio, it struck him as odd that he'd keep him at arm's length now when the heat was really on.

"Going supersonic, let's give them some colonics."

Jonah tried to calm the itch inside him. In the choice between sitting in a classroom at school learning about glacial erosion or being here on the trading floor with the Baron and the Bunker Boys, the answer was obvious.

"Going supersonic, the market's catatonic."

Five o'clock passed, then six, and then seven. Jonah was beginning to wonder whether they were going to push on through the night until finally, at eight o'clock, the Baron stopped singing, leaped up, and shouted, "Got to run. Going to Switzerland. Nearly forgot. Doesn't time fly when you're having fun?" To Jonah, he said, "Good work, fella. I won't be in until lunchtime tomorrow. Go and see Clive and the IT trainspotters in the morning and start on the backlog, will you?" He squeezed Jonah's shoulder, practically threw his laptop into his case, and headed rapidly for the door, still singing, "Going supersonic, the Baron is iconic."

Jonah watched him leave, a sense of pride filling his very core. This was the man who had chosen *him*, who had picked him from among the endless number of college graduates who were trolling for jobs in the city. His methods may have been crazy—all the singing and the adornment of the desk with souvenirs of successful trades—but the Bunker's continued success, in spite of horrible market conditions, didn't lie.

The other traders, including Dog and the rest of them, trickled out shortly after the Baron, barely nodding to Jonah as they went.

As Jonah input the final trades, he did not let himself be concerned by the dismissive attitudes of the boys in the Bunker—they'd get over his being there just like they did the last time. Neither did he let his mind linger on the bank share prices that had risen on the back of the rescues and the fact that they were sitting on a loss of twenty-four million pounds. Instead, he remembered the complicated tapestry the Baron and his Boys had woven the last time he was here, the patterns that weren't visible to anyone but those most in the know, and he felt certain that tomorrow all would be made clear. He stood up and headed for the door, feeling for Creedence's number in his pocket, convinced that he'd just lived through the first day of the rest of his life.

So long as he didn't run into his dad at home, the day would be perfect.

# CHAPTER 19

## Tuesday, September 9

**Jonah was woken** the next morning by the radio on his alarm clock. He tried to focus on the red numbers that the clock beamed up onto the ceiling. "Four fifty-five A.M.," it read. *Why so early?* his unconscious mind asked. *Work,* his now semiconscious mind replied. *Hellcat! Bank bashing! The Cockpit!*

*Hit it!* he thought, leaping out of bed and heading to the shower. He lived in the old au pair's flat at the top of the house, now complete with a 56" LCD TV screen, a very substantial sound system, an Xbox, a PlayStation, and two electric guitars, all purchased since he began trading back at school. On the wall were two framed posters from early Rolling Stones concerts in Richmond, bought at auction, and from one of the frames hung his gold medal from the National Under 16 Cross Country championships. He'd cleared the rest of his track cups and medals from the room in preparation for his soon-to-be acquired trading trophies.

In the shower he turned the heat up a fraction more than normal to really feel the sting and then switched it to cold, gasping as the water crashed onto his head. He brushed his teeth and got dressed so quickly that it was only five fifteen A.M. when he quietly opened the front door and slipped out of the house undetected, relieved that he had avoided his father. Logically, Jonah understood that eventually the two of them would be stuck in a room together for more than ten seconds, but still the prospect filled him with horror given the acrimony of their recent encounters.

It was dark and damp outside with a light drizzle filling the air. Sunrise was not for another hour, but Jonah felt invigorated. At Hammersmith Bridge he stopped before crossing the river. He could see a taxi approaching, its yellow light illuminated. He held his arm out to hail it, reasoning that he shouldn't suffer the crush of the Underground when he could afford the comfort of a cab.

When Jonah arrived at the office, it was still not yet six o'clock. He pushed through the glass doors of the entrance, which were never locked, nodded to the nighttime security guard at reception, went through the turnstiles, up the escalator, onto the trading floor, and over to the Bunker. He was first in. The Cockpit was his. He reached under the desk and pressed the button, mouthing, "We have ignition," as he sat back triumphant, taking in the grandeur of the double desk coming to life around him.

Suddenly it struck him that this was the first time he'd ever been on the trading floor while it was as deathly silent as his father's house. The thought repulsed him, and he quickly sought to remedy it.

Item number one: Clive. Clive was in charge of Settlements and saw every trade that was made. Rumor had it that he never actually left the office, so Jonah assumed he'd be in despite the early hour. He was right. Clive came over to Jonah's desk and told him about how he was the one who made the corrections when the traders input the wrong amounts or client account numbers. He was the safety net, the one who made sure that all the money and the trades went to the right places. Jonah soaked up everything that Clive had to say, mostly because he was a big fan of the Baron's, and—after Jonah had worked so hard that morning to avoid interacting with someone who felt the opposite—he was happy to talk to an individual with whom he had at least that in common.

Item number two: the tech guys, or IT as they were properly known. There was a large crew of people in IT, and many of them worked late nights and early mornings. Two of them walked over to the Bunker—one fat, Lardy, and one thin, Jez—fixed up Jonah's new laptop and showed him everything about the state-of-the-art technology on his desk. Neither looked too thrilled to be doing it.

Item number three: the backlog. Jonah punched the keys on his computer and pulled up the mismatched trade folder. He looked at it, memorized it, and closed it down. Next he picked up the pile of unresolved trading tickets and deciphered the scrawls and scribbles against the photograph in his mind.

His concentration was only broken by the incessant ringing of an unanswered cell phone. He looked around to see where it was coming from—other traders had begun arriving at this point—until finally his ears settled on his own briefcase. It was his new cell phone. He hadn't recognized the ringtone. He put his thumbs on the lock sensors so that they could read his thumbprints and flicked the lock to open the case. He picked up the phone and looked at the screen. It said, "The Baron."

"iPod," said Jonah, briefly wondering why the Baron hadn't called his work line.

"Bloody hell, that took a while," came the reply.

"Yes, sorry. You're the first call on the new phone," Jonah replied, oddly nervous. He suspected it had something to do with the sudden tumult amid the silence.

"That so?" The Baron didn't wait for a response. "What's news?"

*This has to be a test*, thought Jonah. *As if the Baron didn't know what was going on!* He scanned the screens quickly. "More of the same from last night really. Overnight markets up. London and Europe opening up as well. Financials ahead. Only bank that got hurt yesterday was Allegro Home Finance, off fourteen percent. Rumors that the deal with the International Development Bank is going to fall through. Wisemen Thryce have put some research out this morning saying that the financial crisis for the banks isn't as bad it seems. It's pushed the sector up further."

"Nah," the Baron drawled, "Wisemen's trying to push their own book. They're long and they're wrong"—he meant that Wisemen and others were *buying* stocks because they believed the prices were going to go up, that the banks' stocks were going to improve. "I want *you* to do some trading this morning—*more selling.*"

For a moment Jonah felt fear rising in his throat, taking him back to his first ever trade three years previously. He had worked hard the previous year and all through the summer holidays to learn the financial and legal stuff the Baron had thought was most important. But still the closest he'd come to betting real money were the few times the Baron had let him make some virtual trades on the video-game training tool. When it came to actual investing, his mentor would still only allow him to run a shadow portfolio of stocks and shares. And it was a good thing too—the first five trades Jonah did were disastrous. If he'd had real cash invested, it would have been gone in a few weeks.

However, a full year after Jonah had begun his training with the Baron, Jonah woke up at seven o'clock on the first day of the new term and went straight to his computer to check his e-mails. There was a new message from the Baron: *Playtime over. Account is activated.*

Jonah's heart rate accelerated, his mind raced—he could finally trade for real! His hand hovered over his mouse, about to pull the trigger on his first trade when another message came from the Baron: *Show me that I was right to believe in you.* Jonah pulled his hand back, hesitating. From there, he came up with one reason after another for why he should wait—he needed to unpack everything for the new term; he had to buy groceries; there were classes to attend; the timing wasn't right. The reality was he couldn't bring himself to put actual money on the table. If he did, and he was wrong, would the Baron abandon him, leave him to his own devices, to school, to running, to his father? It was as if a wall of anxiety and indecision had been erected around him.

On Wednesday night there was another message from the Baron, short and sharp as ever: *Whistler or Drizzler?* Jonah cringed. He was no Drizzler. He had to break through the wall.

He decided to invest in a company called Games Boutique, a major retailer of video-game software and hardware. He had three reasons for thinking that Games Boutique would be a good trade.

First, they had recently made an announcement that—in the absence of any new devices—their quarterly earnings had been poor, bringing their stock price to unusually low levels. Second, consoles and handhelds kept getting better and better, and there was another new one due out in one month. And third, he felt that the market had not adequately factored in the extent to which kids loved video games. Sure, investors knew that there were various waiting lists for the next-generation consoles. But what they, as adults, couldn't understand was that video games were *the* thing. Forget books, forget movies, forget TV—if you wanted to capitalize on every young boy's wish list, you went for video games.

Jonah bought five thousand pounds' worth of shares at sixty-five pence per share. Three weeks later, the stock skyrocketed up to ninety pence, and Jonah sold all his shares. He'd made a profit of 3,600 pounds.

From that day on he forgot about fear.

Back in the present, Jonah quashed the tinglings of apprehension that had begun to take hold. "Sure," he said calmly. "How much do you want me to do?"

The answer came quickly. "Another hundred million. Pile on the pain! Focus on Allegro and OPM Insurance, but choose a couple of others and hit them hard."

*One hundred million!* Jonah's biggest previous trading outlay had been fifty thousand. He knew enough, though, to keep that information to himself. "I'm on it," he said.

"Good," the Baron replied and hung up.

For the rest of the morning, Jonah set about placing his trades, quietly singing as he did so. "Going supersonic, I'm feeling so bionic!"

Jonah jumped when the Baron's briefcase landed on the desk beside him a few minutes before one o'clock. He was absorbed in the screens and eating a sandwich he'd had delivered. He'd had to pay for it himself, a fact that was annoying but that plagued everyone on the trading floor equally.

"Are we in?" the Baron demanded.

Jonah finished his mouthful, swallowing frantically as the Baron ripped off his jacket and logged on to his screens. "We're in," he eventually replied. "I've also cleared your backlog. There's only one trade I can't work out." He picked the offending trading ticket out of the tray and held it up.

The Baron turned, raising his eyebrows, impressed. "One trade only? Good lad. But that can wait." He dismissed the ticket with a quick flip of his right hand and turned back to the screens. "How much have we got on the table?"

"Five hundred and fourteen million pounds," Jonah answered automatically, calling up the information that was stored in his head. "Market's still up this morning, and we're down, uh, thirty-five million on the price rises."

The Baron swung his chair around to face Jonah directly. "You sound twitchy, iPod. Are you worrying that I'm steering you wrong?" Jonah was about to lie that of course he wasn't, but the Baron didn't give him a chance. "I've been speaking to a few boys over the water in New York. There is going to be a lot of selling pressure on these markets in the coming hours. A *lot* of selling pressure."

Jonah glanced at the time. It was twelve fifty-six, four minutes until the New York Stock Exchange opened.

"This is a dead cat bounce, iPod. Mark my words."

"A dead cat bounce?" repeated Jonah, relieved that he hadn't had the chance to fumble his way through an answer about whether he questioned the Baron's judgment.

"An old market term—refers to a market rally in a bear market. Even a dead cat bounces when it's dropped!"

Jonah grinned. He'd been told about bull markets going up and bear markets going down, but now he had to add dead cats to the list? The financial markets were a zoo!

"So let us sit back and let the games begin," the Baron continued. "These babies are about to go down in flames!"

It was now two minutes to the New York open, and while the Baron fiddled with his computers, Jonah wolfed down the rest of his sandwich, counting down the seconds, his eyes glued to the screens.

At one P.M. precisely, his screen went red as the markets opened massively down.

"Blood on the screen!" screamed Milkshake.

Jonah turned to the Baron, who gave a wry smile and said, "I thank you," before standing up and shouting across the trading floor as if he were a flight attendant giving the safety briefing on a plane. "Ladies and gentlemen, if you would kindly take your seats and fasten your seatbelts, we are about to hit some severe turbulence. Anybody who is long, the emergency exits are over there"—he pointed toward the windows. "Those of you who are short"—he turned back to the Bunker Boys and raised his voice another notch—"TUCK IN, LADS! FIRE AT WILL!"

Jonah joined the Bunker Boys in roaring back, "YES SIR!" as the adrenaline rose in him as fast as the number at the bottom of his trading screen was climbing. A tsunami of selling swept around the world. Fear and panic abounded, and the Bunker fed on it as a hyena feeds on rancid meat. They tore at it, savaged it, and devoured it in a state of frenzy, helping to drive the prices down further as their losses of the previous thirty-six hours reversed and Jonah's trading screen turned from red to blue. They were now in profit: *Ten million. Twenty million. Thirty million.*

"Allegro Home Finance rating to be downgraded. International Development Bank deal unlikely to materialize," shouted Dog as the headline flashed across the news screen, sending Allegro's share price into freefall.

"Allegro, Capital Mutual, and OPM Insurance most likely next to go bankrupt, say analysts," yelled Jeeves.

"Treasuries rallying as investors fly to safety," Jonah chipped in.

"The market has given up resistance," said the man on the television.

"Shares driven down by heavy shorting," flashed a headline on Bloomberg.

*Forty million. Fifty million.* With the profits escalating, the Baron telephoned upstairs for clearance to increase the bets. It came without issue, and they sold another one hundred million—piling on more pain, feeding the panic that the world's banking system was rotten to the core, that it would fail, possibly taking the world's economy down with it—and all the time reaping more profits for themselves.

"Analysts say massive shorting renews fears about the US financial system!" shouted Birdcage.

"Crisis at New York's banks," announced Jeeves, reading the first edition of the evening newspaper.

"Who cares!" laughed Dog. "The Bunker's bonuses are going to be huge!"

*Sixty million. Seventy million.*

Jonah was in awe. The Baron's bet had become a self-fulfilling prophecy. Where yesterday there had been inertia, today there was momentum, an unseen force pulling prices down, and an equal and opposite force driving their profits upward. They and the other shorts around the world had the market on the run.

Eighty million. Ninety million.

"It was a day of complete capitulation," said the man on the television at around seven P.M. that evening.

By that point, everything was winding down at the Bunker. Jonah was clearing out the last of the trading tickets, the Baron had disappeared upstairs to discuss further increases in their trading limit, and the Bunker Boys had begun heading out to the pub to celebrate, Jonah motioning that he'd join them as soon as he was done.

As Jonah entered the final piece of information, he felt spent with the excitement and the concentration, but was also happier than he had ever been before. It was as if he had just finished his most ambitious race.

The number at the bottom of his screen was more than one hundred million pounds.

# CHAPTER 20

**The opposite was** the case for David Lightbody. He'd left the Helsby Cattermole building long before Jonah. He'd had to get out. Scrotycz had been on his case all day, and the crash in the markets brought back dark memories. The Russian market, his main focus, had been one of the worst hit, even worse than in 1998.

He walked to Cannon Street and caught a District Line train home. There were no seats free, so he was forced to stand, hanging on to the overhead rail and gazing vacantly into space.

It had been ten years since the Russian financial crisis. Ten years since the model of the red Fokker triplane had arrived on his desk. And ten years since he had lost thirty million pounds on a single trade and with it his job. He'd been unemployable until Helsby Cattermole had knocked on the door. The salary was well below his previous one, but he didn't have a choice: He had a young child and large bills to pay.

At first he thought that maybe the Baron had felt some sense of responsibility for his firing and had arranged for the job offer. After all, he was the one on the other side of the original trade. But that thought was soon dispelled. From the day David arrived he was the butt of the Baron's bullying. He was assigned—at the Baron's insistence, he later discovered—to the Drizzlers' Den, greeted with a second model red Fokker, and subjected to a floor-wide welcome e-mail that read: *How do you make a small fortune in Russia? Start with a big one and give it to Lightbody.*

David complained. The bank did nothing.

The train stopped, and David looked to see where they were. It was Sloane Square, still another five stops until Hammersmith. He returned to his thoughts.

From then on, the Baron sought out every opportunity to make David's life hell. And it was at the office Christmas party that David finally cracked. The Baron had been overtly flirting with David's wife, Miranda, asking her why she was married to a Drizzler. David objected, and the Baron had mockingly suggested they fight for her hand in good medieval knight style. David immediately refused. He'd given up fighting a long time ago. By then, though, it was too late—the whole of the trading floor was baying for blood. It had been a set-up, a practical joke aimed at humiliating him once more. And it had worked. He became Biff, a Drizzler and a coward.

But that wasn't the worst part of that night's events. The Christmas party also seemed to trigger the beginning of the end of his marriage. It had been shaky ever since Jonah's birth and David's descent into depression, the "darkness" as Miranda called it. He had put it down to the stress of his job and the travel, but he knew that wasn't the complete truth. They lasted another three years, but divorce was inevitable. When Miranda was subsequently offered the job in America, she took it without ever looking back.

The train reached Hammersmith, and David began the forced march home, his thoughts turning to the son his wife had effectively disowned at the same time she'd ended things with him: Jonah. *What to do about Jonah?* It was bad enough watching the Baron and the other "shorts" driving the financial system toward oblivion, but to see Jonah at his side, laughing and grinning, was too much to bear. David hadn't seen it coming. He knew that Jonah had enjoyed the three days he'd spent on the trading floor a few years back and that his relationship with his son was nonexistent, but he had put it down to Jonah's adolescence. He'd had no idea that once again the Baron was working behind the scenes, acting as a mentor and guide while David had been too blinded by his own issues.

He had to come clean. He had to tell Jonah the whole story. Only then would he have any chance of getting Jonah away from Hellcat and the Baron.

The wind picked up as he stepped onto Hammersmith Bridge, whistling down the river from the west. He hunched himself up against it and increased his pace to get to the other side as quickly as possible.

He would do it tonight.

It was past ten o'clock when Jonah put his key in the front door. He wasn't expecting his father to be up and started when David Lightbody appeared at the door and greeted him with a polite, "Evening, Jonah."

"Uh, hi Dad," said Jonah, fumbling to put his keys back in his pocket. "I wasn't expecting you."

"We have to talk," David said, grimfaced.

"What about?" Jonah retorted, a belligerent edge to his voice. Whether his father was looking for him to rethink going to work with the Baron or to chastise him for arriving home so late, he knew the conversation wouldn't be a pleasant one.

"Jonah," David said as he opened the door wider, "you're still my son, and you're living in my house. And I say that it's time for a chat."

"Fine," Jonah grunted. Putting his briefcase on the floor, he followed his father into the sitting room. The room—with all its open space, white walls, straight lines, and contemporary furniture—was as cold as ever, and that didn't even account for the lack of radiators (his mother had thought these were unsightly and so had instead opted for inferior underfloor heating). Like the rest of the house, this particular space had never been set up with a child in mind.

"Why don't you sit down?" David asked, motioning to the chaise beside him, which Jonah knew to be uncomfortable.

"No thanks," he replied, leaning against the wall. He wanted to make it clear he wasn't interested in this "chat" taking any longer than necessary. Plus, he needed to use the bathroom after having spent three hours at the pub.

"Jonah," David began, his tone firm, "what do I have to do to persuade you to go back to school?"

"Dad," Jonah sighed, mimicking his father, "we've had this conversation. Forget it."

"No, I won't forget it," David replied less calmly. "It's a disgrace what is happening at the moment, and to think that you are a part of it is unconscionable. I've been here before. You, the Baron, and the rest of the shorts are driving us to oblivion. You might make a lot of money, but the long-term cost is going to be enormous."

"Uh huh." Jonah shrugged. "And your point is?"

"My point is, Jonah, you are too young to be doing this."

"The Baron doesn't think so."

"The *Baron*"—David said his name with even more disdain than usual—"is leading you down a dangerous path."

"Is he?" Jonah answered sarcastically. "Well, can you explain to me why our desk made more money today than you've probably earned in your entire life?"

David snorted, "I guess we have different perceptions of what it means to *earn* money. And I as your father—"

Jonah cut him off. "The father card? Really, Dad? That's what you're going for? You've had sixteen years to be that person, and, as I recall, instead you decided to ship me off to boarding school."

"Jonah, I—"

Jonah continued as if there'd been no interruption. "And honestly, Dad, that would have been fine if you hadn't totally ignored me, if you'd shown up for a few track meets or sent me a card sometime, but instead you basically only remembered my existence when it meant telling me *not* to do something. And that's okay—that's a fatherly thing to do—but you don't get to have it both ways."

Regret seeped into David's voice. "This is not what I wanted for us. It's just that ever since Africa"—David's voice broke—"and losing my job and your mother . . ."

"Oh, don't go blaming it on her. The two of you deserved each other. You both like to pretend that you never had a son."

"That's not true, Jonah. I—"

Jonah waved his hand dismissively. "If you'll excuse me, I'll be going to bed. Early start tomorrow." He headed for the door and began slowly trudging up the stairs. "And don't follow me," he added.

David didn't.

# CHAPTER 21

## Wednesday, September 10, morphing into Thursday the 11th, and roaring through Friday the 12th

*"Allegro's going down!"* Dog shouted, popping out of his chair.

"Blitzkrieg! Blitzkrieg! SELL AGAIN!" screamed the Baron.

*Fantastic*, Jonah thought as he read the headline on his Bloomberg screen: "Allegro Home Finance fails to secure new capital. Takeover or bailout now only chance of survival." He felt a hunger in the pit of his stomach: He wanted to see more collapses, more precipitous declines, to see this crisis play out to its worst possible conclusion. The feeling scared him, but he wouldn't allow himself to admit as much, especially after last night's lecture from his father. (That and the fact that the profit on his own trades was now through fifteen million.)

They had been working flat out all morning—selling, selling, selling—and they continued all afternoon, all through Thursday and on into Friday. The continuous bombardment of the banks became a blur in Jonah's mind as the profits climbed ever higher.

*One hundred and sixty million. One hundred and seventy million.*

The only pause was at one forty-six P.M. on Thursday, September 11, in observance of the anniversary of the attack on the Twin Towers in New York. Jonah remembered the day even though he was eight years old at the time. The pictures were all over the television: the collapsing towers, the flames, the smoke, the people jumping. But that wasn't the only reason these images were burned indelibly in his memory. Two weeks prior to the terrorist attack, his parents had told him they were getting a divorce. One week later, he'd been sent away to boarding school.

For two minutes the trading floor was silent, the traders' heads bowed, the lights on the comms board extinguished, and Jonah relived those first days and months away from home—the feeling of desertion and loneliness, of waking up each morning expecting his mother to come and collect him, of finally understanding that it was never going to happen. He looked across the trading floor at his father and felt only disappointment.

Suddenly there was a nudge in his ribs. "One of the great trading weeks, iPod," the Baron whispered. "I had a man who stood his ground there as the planes came in, picked up the phone, and talked me through it. The market dived, I hit it hard and made a lot of money."

Jonah's stomach dropped. "Did he get out?"

The Baron shook his head, locking his eyes onto Jonah's. "No, he knew he was going to die. But he delivered. True loyalty."

Jonah shivered, and the hairs on his forearms stood on end. Loyalty and trust, that's what the Baron had given him, and what he now expected from him in return. He was the one who had guided him, who had molded his passion for finance, who had mentored him when the other boys had looked at him oddly for being too busy trading to leave his room, who had motivated him in his running, and who had taken him out for lunch to celebrate his excellent exam results. And now he was the one whose expectations of loyalty and trust deserved to be met, not Jonah's father's.

Jonah nodded at the Baron, about to say that if given the choice, he'd die for him as well, but then the alarm rang, signaling the end of the two minutes of silence, and before he knew it they were scrambling back to their screens and phones.

The earlier cacophony only grew more intense with their arrival back. "Confidence and perception issues are overwhelming Allegro Home Finance's franchise value as its shares fall forty percent," reported the man on the television.

"Financials drag Europe stocks lower," flashed the headline on the screen.

*One hundred and eighty million. One hundred and ninety million. Two hundred million.*

The words "Bank shares battered" scrolled across the bottom of the television.

A research analyst messaged them on the chat screen: "Restructure doubts over Allegro Home Finance hammer markets."

*Two hundred and fifteen, two hundred and twenty.*

"We've got another ton cleared, iPod. You take fifty and I'll take fifty," whispered the Baron.

"I'm on it," said Jonah.

And then it was as if there were an echo in the room.

"I'll sell you ten million of OPM," said the Baron.

"I'll sell you five million Allegro," said Jonah.

"I'll sell you five million National Mutual," said the Baron.

"I'll sell you fifteen million Debtbank," said Jonah.

*Two hundred and forty, two hundred and forty-five.*

For three solid days they sold the life out of the world's banking system, until finally at three o'clock on Friday Jonah saw the Baron lay his phones down on the desk and close his eyes.

"What's happening?" Jonah asked, worried. Up until now the work had been so unrelenting that the events that normally punctuated the day—waking up, going to the office, eating lunch, going home—had begun to give way to a steady hum of work, work, work, and nothing else. Jonah even suspected that Milkshake had reworn one of his shirts from one day to the next—that's how bad things had gotten.

"Our work is done, iPod." The Baron smiled at him, his eyes giving off their usual twinkle. "It's time to take the money." He stroked his mustache, stood up, and coolly announced to the desk, "Silence please."

The Bunker Boys turned to look at him.

"Gentlemen, it is time to buy. Cover our positions if you will. I am going for a short walk . . . to the pub! Join me when you are finished. I am calling a Sympathy Session in honor of the obscene bonuses we will be receiving." The Bunker Boys cheered, and the Baron gave them the flat-handed salute before packing his laptop into his briefcase. He snapped the briefcase shut and turned to Jonah. "One final thing, iPod. Buy an extra twenty-five million dollars of Allegro Home Finance stock. There's a chance the U.S. government will find a way to save it—it's too big to fail—and after they do, the price could easily skyrocket in a couple of days. It's worth a small punt."

"On it!" Jonah shouted, pressing the function key that transferred their trading positions from his screen onto the TV behind him.

Now everyone in the Bunker was on their feet screaming and shouting, reversing their short positions in a frenzy of buying at lower prices than they had sold.

"Buy twenty Allegro!"

"Buy fifty National Mutual!"

"Buy ten OPM!"

"Buy thirty Banque de Triomphe!"

Jonah was inputting and trading at the same time, his left hand working the keyboard, his right hand punching the comms board. His phone was tucked into his neck, and his eyes jumped from screen to screen, his ears alert to the trades going on around him.

"Financial sector gets boost from expectations that Allegro Home Finance could be taken over!" shouted Birdcage, reading a headline. "This is too easy!"

Jonah shook his head—if it was too easy for Birdcage, he didn't know what to think. "Market recovering strongly!" he screamed, the headline invigorating him further.

"I'm going to the pub," cried Dog. "Enough of this nonsense. We've made our money."

"I'm coming too. iPod's got it covered," answered Milkshake. "Though I think I'm going to run home to pick up a new shirt before I go."

"Is that right?" said Birdcage.

"About the shirt or iPod?" Jeeves taunted.

"Both," replied Birdcage.

"Failure is not an option," shouted Jonah.

"Well, there's your answer," Jeeves said, adjusting his bow tie and standing up.

"Ale, ale, we want more ale," sang Dog.

Suddenly Jonah was alone on the desk. It was past six o'clock by the time he processed the final trade. Despite the enormous profits Jonah had become used to lately, he still couldn't get over the number he saw in front of him: more than a quarter of a billion pounds!

They had made a killing.

Six thousand miles south, Kloot was looking to make an even larger killing. He was at his hunting lodge, a short helicopter ride from Johannesburg, South Africa, the gold mining capital of the world and the source of many inside trading tips over the years, including his highly successful River Deep Mountain High coup four years previously. He was accompanied only by his bodyguard, Klaasens, so that there was no chance of any witnesses to what he was about to do.

It was time. Allegro Home Finance was on the brink, driven to the precipice by its own stupidity and the power of the Apollyon network. The next stage was to confirm what the U.S. government was going to do about it.

Kloot's operative at the New York Federal Reserve, the organization that was at the epicenter of the U.S. government's frantic efforts to prevent the complete collapse of its financial system, would let him know the second the Americans decided whether or not Allegro Home Finance was worth saving.

At that very moment the operative was making the first in a series of calls to the CEOs of Wall Street's biggest banks. The message was simple: the U.S. government needed them to rescue Allegro Home Finance before the markets opened on Monday morning. It was in their own interests. After all, if Allegro Home Finance were to fail, any one of them could be the next to go. . . .

Kloot would have his answer within the next couple of hours.

# CHAPTER 22

**The pub was** heaving when Jonah arrived, packed shoulder to shoulder with Hellcat traders celebrating and commiserating the end of a long week all around. Jonah had hoped that Creedence would be there, but he couldn't see her anywhere through the thick and chaotic crowd. Fat wedges of bank notes were being handed over the bar, champagne was being drunk straight from bottles, and it was so noisy that all conversation had to be done by shouting and hand signals. Jonah forced his way through the melee to where he could see Birdcage, a head taller than the rest of the crowd. When he reached them, a bottle of champagne was thrust at him, but Jonah shook his head.

"Come on mate, you've got to celebrate being a millionaire," said Dog, waving the bottle in front of him.

"What do you mean?" Jonah shouted back.

"Bonus mate. Bonus," Jeeves explained, waving a huge wad of cash in the air.

"Yeah!" Milkshake added. "On the numbers we pulled today you'll make it straight into the million club after only one week."

Dog squeezed Jonah's shoulder. "HOW DOES THAT FEEL?!"

Jonah stared at their expectant faces, totally baffled. *Was it that quick? Was it that easy? One week and he was a millionaire?* If he were stuck at school, he'd be busy doing homework, hoping that the Baron would call to save him from his misery. "IT FEELS GOOD!" he shouted and grabbed the bottle of champagne. As he was about to take a swig, the noise in the pub suddenly died, and everybody turned toward the bar. Jonah turned too: The Baron was standing there, his eyes closed and his arms raised. The power of his presence had silenced the room.

He brought his arms down and opened his eyes. As he did so, Jonah guiltily hid the bottle of champagne behind his back before any alcohol had touched his lips; the Baron didn't drink and had advised Jonah to do the same. "I thank you, ladies and gentlemen," said the Baron when all was quiet. "And I agree with young iPod. IT FEELS GOOD!" he roared, and the traders roared with him. He raised his arms again, and the noise died. "Ladies and gentlemen, good things seem to happen when iPod is on the trading floor."

There was another cheer, and Jonah felt slightly uncomfortable at the attention, particularly with the champagne bottle in his hand.

"The last time we had a Sympathy Session he had to leave. This time he's here to stay!" Another cheer went up, and the sound system began to pump out the tune that Jonah now knew so well. Some of the traders began to join in with the drumming, but they were silenced by the Baron. He wanted the stage to himself. He breathed in deeply and began to sing his own parody of "Sympathy for the Devil":

*Please allow me to introduce myself*
*iPod is my name*
*I've been around for only a week*
*But I'm well pleased that I came*

A random hand slapped Jonah on the back, and Jonah could see other traders straining to see his reaction.

*I was there when Homeloan Corp*
*Crashed and burned, went down in flames*
*Saw the U.S. government*
*Pump in twenty bill to ease the pain*
*Ain't it awesome?*
*The market's gone insane*
*Makes it easy for us to play our games*

The pub was now rocking, everyone was singing, jumping up and down, champagne bottles raised in the air. All Jonah could do was shake his head and laugh along.

*I took a chair in the Baron's lair*
*When he saw it was the time to go short*

Now he could feel hands grabbing him and beginning to lift him. Someone grabbed the champagne bottle out of his hands. "What's happening?" he shouted.

*Blasted shares all around the world*
*Saw their values fall close to naught*
*We stuffed the banks*
*'Cause let me be quite frank*
*Their management reeked*

*And their loan books stank*

Jonah was up in the air, on his back, helpless, and could hear a chant of "Crowd surf! Crowd surf!" around him.

*Ain't it awesome?*

*The market's gone insane*

*Makes it easy for us to play our games*

The hands were moving him around above them, and he could do nothing except trust them not to drop him.

*I laughed with glee*

*As their gluttony*

*Paid the price in spades*

*For its grand charade*

He was being maneuvered toward the bar.

*I shouted out*

*Who's next for bankruptcy?*

*I'll tell you what*

*It won't be me*

*Let me please introduce myself*

*iPod is my name*

"Yeah!" he shouted as he was deposited safely on the bar next to the Baron.

*I short stocks for the fun of it*

*And the bonus that's on its way*

Finally, the music stopped, but if anything, that only made the din of the tightly packed space seem louder. "Big hand for iPod?" the Baron called out over the noise.

There was a tumultuous roar of approval from the crowd.

Jonah gave an embarrassed smile, grateful to the Baron for

the attention but unsure what to do with it now that he had it. He decided that now was a moment for loyalty. He waved his arms as he'd seen the Baron do, attempting to capture the same level of poise. It worked—for the most part. The crowd grew silent and Jonah pointed at the Baron. "That was nice and everything, but we all know it's not me who's the lucky one. It's this man!"

The masses erupted in applause. "Baron! Baron! Baron!" everyone screamed.

Jonah took that opportunity to tiptoe off the bar.

That's when he collided into Dog. "Hey, Dog," he said.

Dog grimaced. "You."

"Yeah . . ." Jonah raised his eyebrows.

"He certainly likes *you* enough."

"Huh?" Jonah noted that he hadn't actually seen Dog actively participate in the latter half of the Sympathy Session.

"I said he likes you"—he burped—"the Baron, I mean." Now that Dog continued speaking, Jonah could tell that he'd become a lot more intoxicated since he'd seen him last.

Jonah shrugged. "Same as he likes everyone, I suppose."

"Nah." Dog flicked his hand. "Probably sees a lot of himself in you."

"I don't know if that's—"

Dog cut him off. "Him being an orphan. Your practically being one. Plus, you're both nasty buggers, aren't you?"

Jonah froze. This wasn't the turn he'd expected the conversation to take.

"Ahhhh, I'm kidding," Dog slurred, playfully punching Jonah. "Come and join the rest of us. We is cookin'!" He dragged Jonah over to where Birdcage, Milkshake, and Jeeves were standing.

"Heeere's iPod!" shouted Birdcage. "Who do you think is the better dancer?" He bopped his head and shook his hips in a way that made him look even more like a giraffe than usual. "Me or Milkshake?"

"You call that dancing?" Milkshake said, breaking out a move of his own.

Jonah cracked up laughing. He was one of them. This was his tribe. This was where he belonged—not at school where the boys his own age couldn't understand his interests, but here, with people like himself. The bar was going wild, singing and dancing along as the Baron's voice rang out with song after song, Jonah and the Bunker Boys at the center of the action.

From there the evening descended into chaos. The Baron even had Jonah sing the chorus of Muddy Waters's "Mannish Boy" into the microphone. And at one point all the Bunker Boys stood up on the bar and created a manmade pyramid. To Jonah, it felt like he was floating on an ocean of euphoria.

This lasted for a couple more hours until Jonah's tiredness kicked in. He looked at his watch—it was nine twenty-five. He had a race the following day, and the lack of sleep of the past week was taking its toll.

He gestured goodbye to the Bunker Boys, but most people were so drunk they didn't even notice him sneak out. Even the Baron didn't acknowledge his departure, though that was because he was outside, engrossed in his phone. *Back in the money-making zone*, thought Jonah. *What a god!*

● ● ●

Kloot's operative left the meeting room inside the Federal Reserve at four twenty-five P.M. New York time and headed downstairs for a cigarette. He slipped out of the entrance onto Maiden Lane, parallel to Wall Street, and turned away from the posse of media photographers and TV camera crews camped outside the building waiting for news of the Allegro rescue. Once clear, he pulled out a box of cigarettes from his pocket and put one in his mouth. Across the road a man watched him carefully flick the flint on his lighter and light it.

That was the signal. He had indicated that yes, Allegro would be rescued.

The man across the street flipped open his cell phone and sent a blank text to Kloot, who in turn sent texts to five traders positioned in major financial centers around the world: one in London, one in New York, one in Hong Kong, one in Chicago, and one in Zurich.

These texts weren't blank.

What appeared instead—or what would have appeared to someone who wasn't in the know—was a telephone number consisting of seven digits. In reality, each number had an important meaning. The first number was a one or a two: one for buy, two for sell. The next three numbers were the size of the trade in millions of dollars. The final three numbers were the price. All communication was done through untraceable prepaid cell phones. Even if the authorities had ever worked out what had happened, they would have never been able to follow the trades back to their original source.

Kloot removed the SIM card from his phone and stepped out onto the terrace of the hunting lodge, a cigar in hand, his bodyguard, Klaasens, standing off to the side. He blew a smoke ring with his second draw on the cigar and admired its purity as it rose into the air before disintegrating in the light breeze that was blowing from the southwest. He'd made a five-hundred-million-dollar bet using derivatives that the Allegro Home Finance share price would go up over the next month. He expected to make at least three billion dollars, probably five. He blew another smoke ring. All so easy. He tossed the SIM card into the dying embers of the fire that had cooked his steaks earlier in the evening and watched it disintegrate. "Another day, another billion dollars," he murmured.

In London, Jonah went to the office to collect his briefcase—the pub was only two doors over—and back outside to wait for a taxi. It was five minutes before one pulled up to drop someone off, and Jonah readied himself to claim it once the current occupant had departed. The door opened and out stepped Creedence Clearwater, looking cool in a black skirt and a very un-businesslike leather jacket.

Jonah's heart skipped a beat. She was the one person who could make this night even better.

"Blimey, you're late for a Friday," she said, shaking her head. Then taking a better look at him—the loose neck tie, the messy hair—she added, "And you look like you haven't been to bed all week."

Jonah gave a tired smile and said in a theatrically distressed voice, "I can't take it anymore. I've had enough. I'm leaving." Creedence's face dropped, and he quickly added, "Not really. But I am going home to get some sleep. It's been a mad, mad week."

She brightened up. "Oh! Are you going to Barnes? If so, you can share this cab and drop me off in Fulham on the way. I've just got to dump these packages at reception." She held up two Louis Vuitton bags. "Some girlfriend's birthday present. No thought, all money."

"Works for me, if you don't mind," said Jonah, his fatigue falling away.

"Great. I'll be one minute."

Jonah got into the cab and told the driver of the change of plan, while Creedence dashed inside the building, dropped the bags off, sprinted back out, and climbed in next to him.

"So how's it been?" she asked. "What you expected?"

Jonah launched into a summary of his week at work. He was pleasantly surprised by how easy it was to talk to Creedence—she was incredibly attentive and continually fired questions at him.

"I can't work out that man," she said after Jonah had begun telling her what it was like to work for the Baron. "Sometimes he's charming. Sometimes I'm invisible."

"Yeah, I know what you mean. I think it's because he's so focused on what he does."

Shifting gears, Creedence asked Jonah about his running, which took him aback. "How do you know about my running?"

"Oh, I read your file. It has press cuttings in it."

"Jesus. No secrets, eh?" He tried to sound upset, but in reality he was pleased. "I'm not sure there will be many more of those after this week. I've got a race tomorrow. Boy is that going to hurt."

"Really? Whereabouts?" she asked.

"Richmond Park."

She seemed so genuinely interested in his life that they were in Chelsea before he managed to turn the conversation onto her. He discovered she was taking a year off before going to university, but she had jumped a year at school, which made her only a year older than him. Her passion was singing. She sang mainly jazz and blues, and Jonah told her all about the singing he and the other Bunker Boys had done that night, which made her laugh. He learned about her relatives, an exotic bunch of French aristocrats, burlesque artists, restaurateurs, and hippies. Her parents lived in California, where they owned vineyards and made wine, but her grandmother still lived in England and was, by the sounds of it, a wild old girl even at the age of seventy. Creedence was going to stay with her this weekend.

It was all a far cry from Jonah's own broken family. He had never met any of his grandparents. They had all died before he was born, and he realized that he didn't even know their names.

The taxi pulled up to the curb outside a line of terraced houses in a street off Fulham Road, and Jonah found himself disappointed that the journey had ended.

"Well, this is me," said Creedence, and Jonah felt a sudden sense of awkwardness where previously everything had been so relaxed. He was wondering what to say when she added, "You'll have to ask me out if you want to hear about the rest of my fabulous family tree." She was looking at him, challenging him almost.

He felt the butterflies in his stomach again but managed to stay cool, revealing nothing. He pretended to be thinking hard. "Mmmm. Let me see." He scrunched up his face. "Oh, stuff it. I'll live on the edge. Are you free for dinner and a movie next Saturday?" he asked.

Creedence laughed. "Mr. Lightbody, it would be my pleasure."

She leaned over and kissed him on the cheek before getting out. "Good luck tomorrow, and maybe I'll see you around sometime next week." She slammed the door shut, waved, and turned toward the building entrance.

Jonah watched her go, wondering what excitement lay beyond those closed doors. He would never tell the Baron this, but he expected it might even be better than the million dollars that was soon to burn a hole in his pocket.

# CHAPTER 23
## Saturday, September 13

**Jonah looked around** at the runners warming up beside him in Richmond Park. He had slept well and felt refreshed, ready for the challenge of the seven-and-a-half-mile race that was about to start. The weather was overcast and cool, not ideal given that the opposition was mainly made up of fully grown men. Jonah was at his best in bad conditions or difficult courses, when a strong mind could make up for any relative physical frailties. A win today would require his "brain and pain" strategy. His plan was to go out fast and try to break his nearest challengers well before the finishing line. He knew he wouldn't be able to compete in a sprint finish with these older men.

Jonah had first taken up running because he wanted to find something he and his father could do together. It quickly became clear that running was something Jonah was good at, but not something his dad wanted to do with him. David Lightbody preferred to exercise alone, and if it had not been for the Baron's urging him to keep going—along with a healthy diet and alcohol abstinence, physical fitness was on the list of things the Baron felt most traders overlooked—Jonah probably would have given up. And it was a good thing he hadn't—running had since become an essential part of his life. It had really helped in year three of his training in particular, when he'd become so obsessed with trading that his father had refused to speak with him for a month. Of all the ways Jonah knew to release stress, running was by far one of the best, just as the Baron had told him it would be.

The announcer was now calling the runners, and Jonah made his way to the start. This was his first race since the end of the term and the summer holidays. It was a new set of competitors, and he had no coach with him and no teammates. He was on his own.

The starter called out, "On your marks," and Jonah stuck his elbows out to create space for himself. "Get set!" He bent his legs further. "Go!" He rocketed away, almost sprinting to get to the front, his pace at one hundred strides a minute, wanting to nose in front before the curve in the track four hundred yards after the start. "Got it, through it, now pump it," he said to himself. It was one of the motivation techniques he used: a constant commentary rolling through his mind.

The track was brown gravel, and Jonah wore spiked shoes to give himself an added advantage over this opening stretch. His feet would hurt later on, but he'd cope with that. The first two miles of the race were flat, but after that, there was a short, steep hill. This was where he'd bargain on opening up a gap. They'd expect him to ease off at this point, not hit it harder. He accelerated up the hill, his heart rate rising, and felt the cool air streaming past his face, barely noticing the rabbits scurrying for their burrows as he pounded past them, determined to show the other racers that Richmond Park was his to win.

Four miles later and with a little more than a mile to go, his body was beginning to rebel against his earlier aggression. His breathing was becoming ragged, and pain suffused his whole body. He had set a furious pace that had opened up a substantial gap at halfway and held it for the next few miles. Now it was a case of trying to hang on until the end.

He was passing Richmond Gate when a female voice shouted. "Go Jonah! Go! Go!" He allowed himself a moment to glance over. It was Creedence! She was riding on a bicycle alongside the track, hair flowing behind her.

Jonah couldn't believe she'd actually come to watch him. He couldn't lose now, not in front of her. He'd have to dig even deeper.

Half a mile to go.

Jonah was feeling real pain now. His face was screwed up, his head thrown back, his mouth open gulping oxygen to feed his rapidly tiring legs. He used Creedence as a pacemaker as she rode alongside him, standing on the pedals, shouting encouragement, her center of gravity slightly behind the seat to counter the effects of the slope they were now cutting across. But it wasn't enough. He knew they were catching him.

Five hundred and fifty yards to go.

"He's closing!" Creedence yelled.

Jonah glanced behind to see a tall, dark-haired runner closing the gap fast. The man was twenty yards away; now fifteen.

"Go Jonah! Go!" screamed Creedence again.

Jonah could feel his heart rate speed up past his usual 175

beats per minute. There were two hundred yards to the finish, and Jonah was only five yards in front. *Come on Jonah!* he screamed at himself.

Fifty yards ahead was a small bridge, at each end of which were double fenced gates to slow cyclists pedaling along the track. Jonah knew that these would also bring the runners to a near standstill. There would only be room for one at a time through the gates, and whoever was through first would be almost guaranteed victory. Jonah had to get to the bridge before anyone else managed to reach it.

He saw Creedence veer off to the right to find another way across the ditch, and he could feel the other runner on his shoulder. The runner pulled out to the side and moved ahead of Jonah a fraction. Jonah tried to up his own speed, but there was no kick left. He wouldn't make it.

But as he raced toward the first double fence ahead another option entered his head. A risky option. A Whistler option. There would be no margin for error.

The bigger runner was a yard ahead now and began to slam his feet into the ground, reaching out his right arm to use the fence post to help slow him down and maneuver himself through the gate.

Jonah, however, did the opposite. He didn't slam his feet into the ground. He didn't slow down. He ran hard straight at the fence, pushing up and over it with every ounce of energy he had left.

And somehow it worked. He was over the fence and back in front. He would be through the second gate in the lead, and from there he knew he could hold on. The crowd roared with excitement, and Creedence appeared again to his right, screaming, "Yeahhhh-hhh!" and punching her arm in the air. "Yeahhhhhh!"

Jonah crossed the line, breaking the tape, gasping for breath. His knees buckled and he fell to the ground, shaking, and close to retching. A pair of feet materialized in front of him, dancing up and down manically, and he felt two hands reach under his armpits, helping him to his feet.

"You're amazing! Amazing! Amazing! Amazing!" screamed Creedence, holding him upright with her tight embrace.

Jonah rested his chin on the top of her head, relishing the warmth of the hug and the smell of her hair.

They rode back to the house together on Creedence's bike. Jonah was on the seat, hands on Creedence's waist as she stood and pedaled them along Roehampton Lane from the park toward Jonah's house.

"Sit still, you fool! You'll kill us both," she mocked.

"You should sit where I'm sitting and tell me if you could stay still," Jonah replied.

"Shut up and enjoy the view."

They cut across Barnes Common, rode down the bus lane on Castelnau, and turned left into Lonsdale Road before ending up at Jonah's house. "Do you want to come in for a coffee?" he asked. "My dad's away. Meeting with one of his Russian clients again, I presume."

Creedence pursed her lips. "Sadly not."

"Oh, can you not stand my musky male scent?" Jonah flexed for effect. He really was quite sweaty from the race.

"Actually, that's a reason to stay. I love *eau de* need a shower." She pretended to take a whiff of him, giggling. "Unfortunately, the issue is that I'm supposed to be on a train to East Anglia to see my grand-mother. Instead I'm on my bike in West London talking to you."

"Oh, that's not an issue," Jonah replied, leaning against the doorpost. "Phone her and tell her you've come down with a horrible case of must-hang-out-with-Jonah-itis."

Creedence laughed. "She won't believe that. I'll have to tell her the truth: that I was watching a potential Olympic superstar."

Jonah shrugged. "Guess as long as you tell her the superstar part."

"Oh, I will."

He leaned forward to kiss her on the cheek, but she turned her face so that their lips met. The kiss was magical, their first real one. It was soft and tender, and Creedence tasted of cappuccino and cherry, the latter most likely from her lip gloss. It was a kiss that Jonah never wanted to end.

Eventually, though, like all things it did. "Thanks for coming," he whispered as she pulled away.

"Of course," she whispered back, her eyelashes self-consciously fluttering.

"I'll come and find you at work. Okay?"

She nodded. "Definitely okay!" she answered with uninhibited enthusiasm, playfully shoving him toward the house. "Now go and have a hot bath. I bet you won't be able to move tomorrow!" She turned the bike back down the road and cycled away, waving at him as she went.

Jonah let himself into the deserted house, taking a deep breath as he did so. The effort of the race was now hitting him. At least sleep would make Monday arrive quicker.

# CHAPTER 24
## Monday, September 15

**Monday didn't turn** out the way that Jonah had been hoping for, however. He woke up to discover that Allegro Home Finance was going down. Overnight in America, the U.S. government had made a public statement that there would be no bailout or rescue. It was all over the radio. Bankruptcy was the only option. For the first time since Jonah knew him, the Baron had got it wrong.

In Africa, Kloot was catatonic. He had been given incorrect information and was now sitting on a two-billion-dollar loss. As soon as Allegro Home Finance formally declared its bankruptcy, he would be asked for the money to cover those losses, money he didn't intend to part with. Time was of the essence. Operatives placed inside trading teams would offload the trades onto someone else; hit teams would ensure no further collateral damage from this disaster. There was one thing Kloot knew for certain: If Allegro was going down, they weren't taking him with them.

• • •

Jonah arrived in the office by six o'clock on Monday morning and was thankful that he had. When the Baron arrived an hour later he was in a foul mood and merely grunted at Jonah as he passed. He was unshaven, wearing clothes that looked as if he had slept in them, and mentally he seemed to be somewhere that no one else could enter. He was a man possessed: punching buttons on his keyboard, punching buttons on the comms board, punching buttons on his phone.

Jonah didn't know what to do, so he kept his head down and out of the Baron's way. He was tempted to tell him that it really wasn't *that* much of a big deal—they had made two hundred and fifty million last week and had only lost twenty-five million with the Allegro bankruptcy. But he reasoned that there was no way the Baron would look on this comment favorably. He really hated to lose.

Jonah thought that the Baron's ill temper would be the worst of it, and perhaps a slight scaling down of bonuses, but at eleven o'clock the news began to spread that Clive from Settlements had been found dead at his home.

It was Birdcage who was first on the case. He shot upward out of his desk like some amphetamined jack-in-the-box and shouted, "Oi! Apparently, Clive has killed himself."

The other heads in the Bunker all popped up. They, too, had been keeping a low profile until then. "What?" they chimed in unison.

"Topped himself," Birdcage repeated. "Dead. Kaput."

"What happened?" Jonah asked. He'd only met Clive once a week ago, and the only thing they'd had in common was their mutual admiration for the Baron. He'd struck him as a harried, overworked man who didn't seem to grasp the excitement of trading, only the logistics. He couldn't imagine what it must have come to for him to take his own life.

"Killed his wife and then shot himself." Birdcage shook his head. "I've just spoken to his secretary." Turning to Jonah, he said, "Been banging her." Then he refocused back on the group, leaving Jonah to wonder exactly what kind of girl would go for Birdcage's particular brand of cluelessness. "They've had a call from the Essex police asking them if they could confirm he worked at Hellcat. She took the call. Cops told her the cleaner found him."

"Was there a lot of blood?" ogled Dog.

"For God's sake, Dog," Milkshake admonished. "It's someone we know, not some scene from a Tarantino film."

Jonah was surprised to see that for once Milkshake had pulled himself from the fray enough to make a reasonable point.

"It was just a question," Dog insisted, his expression completely devoid of any semblance of guilt. "Anyway, I bet he did it because he found out his wife was shagging someone else."

"How much?" challenged Jeeves. "Let's take bets." He walked over to the empty fish tank and grabbed a felt-tip pen.

"Good idea!" Dog exclaimed. "Crime of passion: evens."

"Stock market losses?" suggested Birdcage.

"Could be, could be," said Dog. "Give you twos on that. Fives it was because he was gay and she found out."

Jeeves scribbled the odds on the glass.

Jonah couldn't believe what he was hearing. *Were the Bunker Boys really taking bets on why Clive had committed suicide?* He knew they dealt with stress in unusual ways—he never forgot how they all piled on Birdcage his first day on the desk—but this was a whole other level.

"Maybe she shot him and then herself?" Milkshake offered, joining in on the action.

Jonah sighed. He guessed his original impression of him was right.

The sound caught Dog's attention. "Oh, Jonah, we almost forgot about you! What'll it be?"

Jonah struggled for a response. "No thanks, I—"

Suddenly the Baron's voice roared violently out above the grim chatter. "Will you shut the hell up! This is not the pub or the bookies or your poker school. Get on with your work. Make some money."

The heads went down. This was a day to keep your mouth shut.

# CHAPTER 25
## Tuesday, September 16

**"Your cappuccino. Not** too much milk this time." Jonah looked up from the newspaper he was reading at the coffee shop the next day to see a smiling woman, probably in her mid-forties. She'd somehow remembered him from the previous week. It was the first time since last Monday that he'd been late enough for the coffee bar to be open, and this time it was mostly because he could barely bring himself to face another day like the one he'd had yesterday.

"Thanks," he said, folding his newspaper as he took the coffee. Still, though, his eyes kept trailing back to the front-page headline: "City Trader Tops Himself." The article went on to ask whether this was the first suicide of the market crash and recalled stockbrokers jumping from the window ledges of their offices in 1929 after the markets went similarly bust. *Dog would be happy*, thought Jonah as he walked the last few hundred yards to Helsby Cattermole—there had been plenty of blood. "Blew his head off with a shotgun after blasting his wife," according to the article.

He pushed through the glass revolving doors into the "shark tank." It seemed very quiet. Clive's death hung heavily in the air. The receptionists always wore black suits, but today they looked more like funeral suits than ever. Jonah ascended the escalator and walked down the corridor toward the trading floor. The sense of foreboding grew greater. *What was it? Was it Clive's suicide? Or was there something else?* The doors opened, and Jonah was hit with almost complete silence. There was no trading activity. *What was happening?*

He walked down the avenue of desks to the Bunker, feeling that everybody was staring at him. "What's the story? What's going on?" he asked as he placed his briefcase and coffee cup on his desk. The Baron was nowhere to be seen.

The reply took seconds to come back. Jonah could feel his heart beating faster and louder, could feel his face flushing. He understood now that those stares had been malevolent.

It was Dog who spoke first. "Dunno mate. You tell us." His voice was loaded with sarcasm.

Jonah's legs began to shake.

"We're toast." It was Birdcage.

"I, uh, I don't know what you're talking about," Jonah stammered.

"Your dad's shafted us. Shafted us all." This time it was Jeeves speaking. He adjusted his bow tie but only managed to make it even more askew.

*His dad! What had his dad done?* He'd been away all weekend and yesterday. He'd only come back late last night. "My dad?"

"Yes, your dad. Your bloody dad." Dog's voice was rising. "We're blacklisted! We're going down!" He was shouting now.

"My dad?" Jonah repeated, aware that the whole trading floor was looking at him, hating him. He mind raced back to four years ago and those first minutes in Drizzlers' Den. That time the Bunker had come to his rescue. Now they were his accusers. Once again he wondered if he could hide under the desk. He could feel his mouth quivering as if he was about to cry.

"Yeah. What's he dropped this time?" Jeeves taunted. "Three hundred? Four hundred? Five hundred? More?"

Milkshake spoke up. "Nobody will trade with us. Nobody will touch us."

"They say we're going down," Birdcage exclaimed, shaking his towering head. "WE ARE TOAST!"

Jonah collapsed into his chair.

Suddenly everybody turned toward the doors. Jonah turned too. It was his dad, a security guard in front of him. Pistol, who Jonah had never expected to see again after that one day in Compliance, was waiting for them at the door. The silence was deadly, his father's face expressionless. He looked straight ahead, avoiding any eye contact with anyone as the security guard followed him to Drizzlers' Den to collect his belongings. When they reached it, the security guard handed David Lightbody a black trash bag. David opened his three drawers one by one and emptied the contents— a few pens, a stapler, a notebook. There was nothing on top of the desk, and they turned and walked slowly back to the door, Jonah's father carrying the garbage bag in his right hand. The doors swished open and someone shouted, "Get lost, Lightbody! Don't come back!"

Jonah watched his father leave, anger welling inside him. The

Drizzler had messed up, and he, Jonah, was being associated with it by virtue of their shared genetics.

Jonah's line on the comms board began to flash. He saw it but didn't move. The flashing stopped. He heard Milkshake's voice. "Yeah he's here." There was a pause and then, "Pick it up, kid. Baron for you."

Jonah leaned forward, stabbing the now slow-flashing button as he picked up his phone. He took a deep breath. The Baron would sort this out, just like he had when the Neanderthals were being horrible. The Baron would protect him. "Hello," he said eagerly.

"I suggest you go home." The Baron's voice was ice cold.

Jonah's heart fell. "What! Why?"

"Don't argue with me," the Baron snapped. "Go home. We'll need to talk to you once we've gotten to the bottom of this mess. Until then you're suspended."

*Suspended! What!?* "But I haven't done anything wrong," Jonah argued.

This time the Baron's reply was harsher. "Get out, boy! I'll be the judge of that." With that, the line went dead.

Jonah stared at the phone for a moment before replacing it. The Baron thought Jonah was associated with whatever his father had done. He didn't trust him. Jonah sniffled and his mouth again began to quiver. He refused to believe that the Baron had turned against him too. There *had* to be a reason for his behavior. Jonah couldn't be sure, but he thought he sounded almost pained when he spoke to him, as if the choice was out of his hands.

Jonah stood up and picked up his briefcase. Out of the corner of his eye he saw Dog make his fingers into a gun and point it maliciously at him with a "Click, click. Bang!" There were tears in Jonah's eyes as he walked shamefully toward the exit, praying that nobody would shout, "Get lost and don't come back" to him. As if the last sixteen years of neglect hadn't been enough, his father had now ruined his future.

# CHAPTER 26

**Once he was** out of the Helsby Cattermole building, Jonah walked toward Cannon Street station intending to go home. That was before he realized that he couldn't. To go to his house would mean seeing his father. He turned right at the end of New Change Street and left to cross the Millennium Bridge. From there he walked along the River Thames, past the Tate Modern and the Globe Theatre and onto London Bridge and Tower Bridge, great landmarks of the City of London. He shuddered—the city where he was now a pariah.

His phone rang incessantly as he walked, so he switched it off, recrossing the river at Tower Bridge and turning right toward Canary Wharf. The towering skyscrapers of London's other financial district looked down and mocked him. "You can't work here either," they seemed to say. He was hungry, but he didn't eat. Instead he turned and retraced his steps to Waterloo and Vauxhall, passing the MI6 building. At Westminster he crossed the river again, noticing that his feet were leading him home despite his mind's protestations. He'd run this route a few times before he'd started working to see if he could use his commuting time as training time. It had become so familiar to him that he was now operating on autopilot.

He walked along the river through Chelsea and Fulham, thinking of Creedence as he did so. Well, that was blown too now. She wasn't going to want to be associated with a loser. At Putney he crossed the river one final time, picking up the tow path that would take him to Barnes and his lockup garage. He would collect the Vespa and find a hotel for the night. The only one he could think of was the one at the top of Richmond Hill, by the gates to the Park.

He switched on his phone to get the number of the hotel. There were nine new messages, three of them voicemail. The first two were from his father. He deleted them. The third was from Pistol, requesting a meeting on Friday. It could wait. The fourth was a text from Creedence. He nearly deleted it, not wanting to see her cancel their date, but in the end read it anyway: She had heard what had happened; could he please call her? *Maybe*, he thought. The fifth was his father again. He deleted it. More messages from his father and Pistol followed. The last was a voicemail from Creedence, asking him to please, please call him. She was worried.

Jonah hesitated for a moment and then dialed Creedence's number.

She picked up on the first ring. "You're alive then?"

He felt guilty. "Yeah. Alive if not kicking."

"Where are you?" she asked, her voice mixed with relief to be hearing from him and annoyance that he hadn't called sooner.

"On my way to Richmond."

"What's in Richmond?"

"A hotel. I can't go home. I can't face my dad." Jonah wondered if Creedence could tell that he was shaking his head from across the phone waves.

"Why don't you want to see your dad? Surely he needs your support."

Jonah snorted with derision. "Creedence, we don't get on. We hardly speak. If he wants my support, he's not going to get it."

"Is that so?" she asked, a slightly disapproving note in her voice.

Jonah charged on. "Yes it is. Thanks to him I've been kicked out of Hellcat. Kicked out by the Baron. I hate him. Hate him more than I ever have, and that's saying something."

"I see." She paused. "Where's your mother?"

"In the States. I haven't seen her since they got divorced. She doesn't even send me a Christmas card. I can only guess what he did to her."

"Blimey, Jonah," she replied, her tone shifting. "I never knew. I'm sorry."

Jonah's tone became more subdued as well. "No need to be. It's not your problem."

"Well, don't go to the hotel. Come to my flat. Being alone will be hideous."

Jonah was taken aback at her offer, but he worried that it would be wrong to impose this early on. "That's very kind of you, but I'm not going to be much fun. It's probably best if I reserve a room at that hotel in Richmond."

"What!" Creedence exclaimed. "Nonsense. Stay with me."

"I thought that you wouldn't want to have anything to do with me after today," Jonah answered softly.

"Why would you think that?" Creedence asked. "And anyway, I'm not inviting you round to be fun. I'm inviting you round precisely because you're *not* going to be fun. Maybe I can help. I'm leaving the office now, so get in a taxi and I'll see you there."

Still Jonah hesitated. "Honestly Creedence, it's re . . ."

"Oh, stop being so English. I'll send you the address, and if you're not there in half an hour I'm going to send the police to find you. Bye!"

Ten seconds later the information popped up on his phone.

Jonah looked at the address and realized that he did want someone to talk to, and not just anyone either: Creedence. He walked to the lockup garage, collected the Vespa, and headed to Creedence's flat, stopping off only to buy some flowers and clothes.

It was six o'clock when he rang the bell of Creedence's flat. Hers was on the ground floor of an old house that had been converted into two separate living arrangements. He was holding his helmet, the bag of clothes, and a bunch of flowers. The flowers seemed like the right thing to do, though Jonah didn't know for sure what type they were, except that they weren't roses. He thought that roses would have been wrong somehow. Either way, he was nervous. It felt like a date even if it wasn't one.

Creedence opened the door.

"Err, these are for you," he said, holding out the flowers.

She smiled. "Oh, Jonah. I wouldn't have thought you'd have time for thinking about anyone else at the moment. That's really sweet." Then she saw the helmet. "Did you come here by motor-bike?" she asked, peering over his shoulder.

"Scooter." He stepped back so that she could see the Vespa.

"That's really cool!" Creedence exclaimed, making Jonah pleased that she shared his view of the Vespa. "But don't you need to be seventeen to ride one of those?" She cocked her head to the side.

Jonah grinned mischievously. "I have my ways."

"Tut, tut, tut," she said in fake admonishment. "Well, you don't want to leave that on the street. Wheel it through to the back. That's where I keep my bike. Here, let me take your stuff, and I'll get the key to the gate." She grabbed his bags and disappeared back inside, returning a second later with the key.

Jonah wheeled the Vespa down a narrow alley alongside the house that led straight into a small, overgrown courtyard garden at the back. The flat's kitchen opened directly into the courtyard via a set of French doors, so Jonah found Creedence waiting for him there. "Come on in," she beckoned. "And apologies for the mess."

Jonah followed her inside.

The flat was light and airy with a modern, open-plan kitchen and dining area leading to a sitting room. The walls were off-white, the kitchen Shaker style, and the furniture a mishmash of colors and fabrics: a huge dark blue sofa, a cream armchair, a small yellow leather mini sofa, and a wrought iron and glass coffee table. One wall of the sitting room was filled with books, and scattered around were a variety of shopping bags, magazines, and CDs. Jonah didn't think it was necessarily messy, more lived in and comfortable—nothing like his own house, or rather his father's, with its stark white modernism and hard edges.

"Is it yours?" Jonah asked, running his fingers along the cotton fabric of the sofa, fully appreciating what a warm and welcoming place it was.

"Kind of." Creedence gave a half nod. "My granny owns it, but I live in it, and my parents use it when they're over from the States, which isn't very often."

"It's awesome," Jonah said wistfully. The day he had his own flat couldn't come quickly enough.

"Thanks." Creedence blushed. "They gutted it a couple of years ago and updated it. I do my best not to trash it." Creedence walked over to the refrigerator. "Sit down at the table, and we can talk while I make some dinner." She opened the fridge and took out a bottle of champagne. Then she removed two glasses from a cupboard. "But first a drink!" she announced, turning back to face him. "Granny says that champagne cures all ills, and I reckon you're in the bracket of 'ills' at the moment. Wouldn't you agree?"

Jonah was about to give his automatic response—he didn't drink alcohol—but instead he simply nodded and said, "Champagne would be great, thanks." He'd seen more champagne in the last week than he had in the rest of his life combined.

She opened the bottle expertly and poured two glasses.

"You look as if you've done that before?" he joked.

"Haha!" she laughed. "With wine as the family business, I was brought up opening bottles. With champagne, you must hold the cork and turn the bottle. None of this Formula One stuff. We don't want to waste it." She handed him a glass and raised hers. "To adulthood and all its crap!"

"To adulthood—" Jonah repeated, hesitating before finishing

the toast; it was his turn to teach her something. "We'll have to do that again. You didn't look me in the eye. My dad says you have to look someone in the eye when you toast. Some African tradition."

"You're African?" Creedence raised her eyebrows.

"I'm not, but my dad's from Zimbabwe," Jonah replied.

"Why'd he leave?"

"Don't know. Don't care." He shrugged. "Let's get back to the toast."

"Let's!" Creedence exclaimed. She raised her glass again. "To adulthood and all its crap!" This time she held his gaze as their glasses clinked.

Jonah felt pleased that he could tell her something she didn't know. "To adulthood and all its crap," he replied, taking his first swig of champagne. It was cold and light, and the bubbles fizzed in his mouth, but the taste was cloying. He swallowed, and the cold swiftly turned to warmth as it entered his stomach, infusing his whole body.

"Speaking of which, don't you think it's about time you told me what happened today? From your perspective, I mean."

"There's not much to tell," Jonah sighed. "Sounds like my dad made some kind of bad trade, and I guess people think I was involved."

"Why would they think that?" Creedence asked, taking a delicate sip of champagne.

"No idea. I haven't talked to the man in days. And I certainly never traded with him."

Creedence nodded sagely. "It's been carnage in our office. Miss Amelia disappeared for most of the day and was in the foulest mood. I hate to say this to you of all people, but apparently Hellcat can't do any business because of what your dad's done."

"That would figure," said Jonah, taking another sip of champagne, this one larger than the last. His palate had become accustomed to the syrupy taste now, and he savored the feeling of cold turning to warmth as it slid down his throat. While coffee had enhanced his awareness, this champagne made him feel relaxed and uninhibited even as he recounted his humiliation on the trading floor.

As the champagne did its work, he started to really vent—to tell Creedence about his anger over his parents' divorce and his subsequent neglect at the hands of his father. He explained how everything changed when he met the Baron and that this was why his being kicked off the floor cut so deeply—the Baron had been his mentor and guide for the last four years, and without him he felt directionless.

Creedence busied herself by preparing dinner and refilling empty glasses while he spoke, asking questions only when absolutely necessary so as not to interrupt the flow of his thoughts. When he had finished talking, just in time for dinner, she was silent for a moment. "You really hate your dad, don't you?"

"Well, I—" Jonah sighed. "I've always thought I did, but I don't think I ever really and truly hated him until this whole debacle. Before this I guess I was just disappointed and"—he looked to gauge her reaction—"sad."

"Sad?" Creedence echoed. She took a forkful of pasta and motioned for Jonah to do the same.

"Yeah," Jonah began, slowly wrapping his spaghetti around his fork. "All I wanted was for him to be a regular, loving dad, and he couldn't be that person." Jonah paused. "Or maybe he didn't want to be."

"Doesn't sound that hard to me . . ." Creedence mused.

"You'd think that, but I can't remember the last time we sat down and ate a meal like this." Jonah swallowed a mouthful of spaghetti, the pasta catching in his throat.

"*You had to eat* . . ." Creedence said, pointing her fork at him.

"I guess . . ." Jonah replied, shrugging. "But we rarely did it together, especially after I went to boarding school. And when we did, every meal was a ready-made one, and we hardly ever talked about what I was up to."

"So what *did* you talk about?"

"Imagine a job interview," Jonah replied automatically.

Creedence's eyes glimmered. "And here I thought you were going to say the Spanish Inquisition."

Jonah smiled. "Close."

"He sounds massively depressed to me."

"Well, he should have done something about it," Jonah snapped, then immediately apologized. "Sorry, Creedence, I told you I wouldn't be much fun."

Creedence waved it off.

"You know," Jonah added, "you're the first person I've ever told all that stuff to."

"The beauty of champagne," she replied. "Loosens the tongue. But don't worry, your secrets are safe with me." She motioned zipping her lips shut. "It's heavy stuff, Jonah, what you've been through, but you'll cope. The Baron wouldn't have had you work for him if he didn't think you were going places."

Jonah paled at that, and she squeezed his hand, immediately sensing she'd said one thing too much. She paused, and Jonah could tell that she was weighing her next words carefully. "But you know you have to see your dad, don't you? He's very upset for you. He's outraged that you've been sucked into this."

Jonah froze with a forkful of pasta hanging in midair. "How do you know he's upset?" he asked, his eyes narrowing.

"He rang me."

Jonah dropped the fork into his plate. "He rang you! What the hell was he doing ringing you? How does he even know about you?"

"He saw us at the end of your race on Saturday."

"How could he? He was supposed to be out of town."

"Apparently, he *was*, but he drove up in the morning to watch you run. That was how he saw us together and decided to ring me at the office to see if I knew where you were. He told me to tell you he thought you ran an incredible race."

"Oh! Did he? How nice of him. Shame he couldn't be bothered to tell me himself." Jonah wasn't sure whether he was more or less angry at this praise from his father.

"He needs to speak to you, Jonah. He says he needs your help." She was pleading with him now.

Jonah leaned toward her. "Is that why you asked me here? Are you my father's ambassador?"

Creedence didn't rise to his taunt. "No, Jonah. He rang me while you were on your way here. I was pretty pissed off that he'd brought me into it at all, so I didn't promise him anything. I didn't even tell him you were coming here. But he did sound desperate, and given what has happened to him you should at least hear what he has to say. Hell, just think if you were in his position and needed help. Can you honestly say he wouldn't help you?"

Jonah gave a snort of contempt and slumped back into his chair. He wouldn't want his father's help even if he offered it.

"And you know what happens if you don't see him?" Creedence asked, her eyebrows raised.

"What?" Jonah deadpanned.

"I'll cancel our date on Saturday."

"But that's blackmail!" Jonah exclaimed, his face aghast, though the expression was admittedly somewhat forced.

"All I'm saying is think about it. You have nothing to lose by hearing what he has to say." She handed him a piece of paper with a telephone number on it. "This is his number. He doesn't want to use his usual one." She let her words sink in while she cleared the plates away and poured the rest of the champagne into their glasses.

Jonah sat back in his chair, his eyes darting down to the piece of paper and then back up at Creedence as if afraid of being caught. After a while, he put the number in his pocket.

Creedence saw him do it and smiled to herself. She grabbed his hand and flirtatiously pulled him along to the sitting room. "Come on, let's put on some music."

"What are we listening to?" he asked once Creedence started furiously rummaging through her CD collection, most of which were out of their cases and in a pile on the coffee table.

"Well, given tonight's theme of ills and angst I reckon it's got to be the blues." Creedence found the CD she was looking for and put it in the machine. "Muddy Waters," she said as the music started playing.

"The Baron made me sing a Muddy Waters song on Friday at the pub," Jonah said, seriousness once again taking over.

"I know." Creedence chuckled.

"You know?"

"You told me!" she explained, twirling around him. "But this being the blues, we need the right lighting."

Creedence skipped off back to the kitchen, giving Jonah a second to glance at his watch. His mouth dropped when he saw the time: It was past ten. They'd talked for more than four hours. Creedence reappeared a minute later with four candles, two of which she placed on the coffee table and two on the mantelpiece above the fire. She lit them each with a match, then bent down to carefully ignite the gas fireplace.

Jonah took another sip of the champagne, wondering why he had been so strict with himself in the past. It seemed to him that Creedence's family had the right idea on the champagne front. He snickered to himself. If he were still at school, he'd be being told "lights out" right now, not drinking champagne with a gorgeous girl in her flat.

Creedence walked over to the light switch and turned the kitchen lights off, leaving only candlelight and firelight and Muddy Waters. She stood in front of him and began to sing, "The spark in your eyes sets my soul on fire . . ."

Jonah felt his heart race as she sauntered over to him, shimmying as she went. Her voice was extraordinary. It wasn't the power or the pitch; it was the passion that she brought to the music. The spoken voice that had made his hair stand on end now ripped into his soul. There was no way he could interrupt. This was something else.

She sat down on the couch next to him, and when she reached

the second refrain of "Baby, I want to be loved," he couldn't resist: He grasped her and raised her face to his, his lips meeting hers as they kissed long and lovingly in the candlelight.

Elsewhere in the world, Kloot continued to silence the operatives involved in the Allegro trade. In New York, his Federal Reserve operative lay on a slab in the mortuary of a Brooklyn police station, the apparent victim of a vicious mugging. In Hong Kong, a trader had been caught in the crossfire of a Triad drive-by shooting in the red-light district. And in Chicago, another trader had evidently committed suicide with an overdose of pills and alcohol.

Meanwhile, in Richmond Park, David Lightbody lay awake in his sleeping bag, hidden in the woods.

# CHAPTER 27
## Wednesday, September 17

**Jonah woke at** seven A.M., his head slightly heavy from the champagne. They had fallen asleep together on the sofa, but at some point Creedence had left for the comforts of her own bed, leaving him alone on the couch. He felt awkward. Here he was, fully dressed on the sofa in Creedence's flat, memories of the previous night floating back into his mind. He thought about doing a runner and saving them both the embarrassment of accepting that last night was a mistake. Not that that's what he thought it was—the night's emotions still burned bright in his mind—but if there was a chance that she thought as much, he didn't think he could bear the rejection, not after everything else that had happened.

It turned out he needn't have worried. "Ahhh. It wakes!" said Creedence, plopping down on the sofa next to him, a mischievous grin playing around her mouth and eyes. In her hands she held a coffee cup. "Boy you sleep deeply."

"This feels weird," said Jonah, shifting to face her.

"What? Waking up in some girl's flat? I should hope so. But you look very sweet when you're sleeping. Even cuter than when you're awake."

Jonah wasn't sure that he liked being called "sweet" or "cute," but she did seem to be using those words in an affectionate way.

"Anyway," she continued. "I've called out sick today, so I can spend time with a certain house guest!"

"You needn't have—"

"Oh, pshhh," she cut him off. "The sun is shining, the day is young, so get up and let's go out for breakfast."

He was about to ask about where he might find a towel and a shower when she swooped in with the details. "If you want a shower, you can use the one under the stairs. There's a clean towel in there too," she rattled on. "Now get moving. I want to ride on your Vespa! Do you think it's all right if I wear a bike helmet?"

Jonah sat up. "Are you always this hyper in the morning?"

"Yes. So get used to it," she said with mock firmness before grabbing him by the hand and pulling him up off the couch. "Like I said, shower's that way. You've got five minutes." Then she propelled him toward the door.

"I'll be there in four," he replied over his shoulder, feeling the warmth of the previous night all over again.

Jonah had never ridden the Vespa with somebody else on it before, and the experience wasn't made any easier by having an excitable Creedence pointing and screeching gleefully on the back. It did, however, make it a lot of fun. She made him go past the café and around the block three times before they eventually pulled in for breakfast. Finally, Jonah went to order coffees and croissants, and Creedence found them a table. He was trying to work out how he'd gone from the depths of despair and anxiety yesterday afternoon to his current state of euphoria when he saw the headline on the pile of newspapers next to the counter: "Rogue Trader Brings City Bank to Its Knees." He snatched the paper up and started reading:

London bank Helsby Cattermole is believed to be the victim of a rogue trader running up losses in excess of half a billion dollars following the crash in the stock markets. The bank, known as Hellcat in financial circles, declined to comment on the rumors, but sources on its trading floor confirmed that a trader had been suspended until further notice. Traders at other banks and brokers also confirmed that they had been advised not to do any business with Hellcat until its financial position had been clarified. "The market is very nervous after Allegro Home Finance. Nobody's going to touch Hellcat for the time being. They might as well all go on holiday," said one rival trader.

Jonah paused to place his order before reading on.

Hellcat is renowned as being an aggressive trading house, and if it is proved that the losses are due to insufficient risk controls, the bank is likely to be closed down by Financial Regulators. City lawyers suggest that Hellcat will be seeking to prove fraud in this case, and the trader concerned could go to prison for as long as ten years. It is the second time in two days that the highly secretive Hellcat has been in the news following the suspected suicide of one of its senior employees on Monday.

*Prison*, thought Jonah. It hadn't occurred to him that his father might go to prison. He paid for the breakfast and the paper and carried them over to where Creedence was sitting.

"We're in the paper again. Says Dad might go to prison," he said flatly as he put the tray down.

"Prison!" she exclaimed. "What for?"

Jonah sat down and handed her the paper. "Fraud. Here, have a read."

While he waited for her to finish, he tried to analyze how he felt. His anger had been softened by the events of the last twelve hours, but now it was returning with abundance.

"Jesus, Jonah. This is heavy stuff. Prison! That's for thieves and murderers. And if it's a choice between proving your dad guilty of fraud and closing down Hellcat, I don't think he stands a chance. From what I've seen of that place, they'll be doing everything to make sure he's convicted, regardless of what is or isn't true."

Jonah sipped his coffee. "What do you mean *they'll* do everything? He's either guilty or he's not, and I'm guessing it's the former."

"Well, you know. There's a lot of money at stake. And jobs. And reputation. It's in the interest of the bank for your dad to take all the blame. I hope he's got a good lawyer."

Jonah remained unsympathetic. "Do you want to know what I think happened?"

"What?" asked Creedence, sitting upright and laying her palms flat on the table.

"I think he was trying to be a hero like the Baron and got it wrong, so he hid the losses. When the markets dived and Allegro Home Finance went down, he couldn't hide them anymore." He took a big bite of his croissant as if that settled it. "In which case he deserves what's coming to him."

"Really?" asked Creedence with steel in her voice. "Is that really your view? Because if it is, I had better be going." Her mouth had turned down, and she was challenging him with her eyes.

Jonah was taken aback by her response. It was the first time she had said anything that wasn't positive. "Well, he could have done it, right?" he said, his voice wavering. "Who's to say he didn't?"

"Where I come from people are innocent until proven guilty, not the other way around." Creedence leaned over the table toward him. "Look at you—you've been kicked out without anyone telling you why, judged guilty without any proof. You're doing to your dad precisely what they're doing to you."

"No, of course I'm not. I've done nothing. I'm not part of it."

"Precisely!" She slammed her coffee against the table, shaking the croissants. "What are *you* going to do about it?"

Jonah rocked back on his chair. He didn't know what he was going to do about it. He hadn't thought it was his problem to solve. Even though it was the Baron who had kicked him out of the office yesterday morning, part of Jonah had still believed that he'd be the one to fix everything. But maybe that wasn't true. . . .

Creedence seemed satisfied that she had succeeded in making her point. She leaned back and in a much softer voice said, "You have to talk to him. You have to listen to what he has to say; find out if you believe him. It affects you."

Jonah knew she was right, but he wasn't going to back down completely. "Fine. I'll hear what he has to say, but I don't have to agree to help him."

Creedence rolled her eyes. "Why don't you make that decision *after* you hear him out?" She reached into her pocket and pulled out her phone, holding it out to him. Jonah shook his head, took out his own phone, and dialed the number without needing to look at the scrap of paper he'd been given the previous evening. It had gone straight into his memory.

The phone rang several times before Jonah heard his father answer. "Hello?"

"It's Jonah," he grumbled.

Creedence raised one finger in the air, motioning that she was going to move to an empty table in order to give him some privacy. Sitting down, she nibbled on her croissant.

"Oh, hi," said David, breathing an audible sigh of relief. "Are you all right? I heard they'd kicked you out too. I'm sorry about that."

Jonah was taken aback by this apology. His father sounded sympathetic. "Yeah, I'm fine. You want to see me?"

"Yes, please," his dad replied. If Jonah didn't know better, he'd have thought his dad was nodding vigorously on the other side of the phone. "Where are you?" he asked.

"Dad, just tell me where you want to meet. I'm not coming to the house."

"I don't want you coming to the house," David retorted. "Can you get to Richmond Park at around twelve thirty?"

"Probably." Jonah shrugged.

"Okay. Meet me at Pen Ponds then."

"Fine," he answered, playing with the last of his croissant.

"See you," said his father, pausing. "And Jonah?"

"Yeah?"

"Take care of yourself." With that, his dad hung up.

Jonah put the phone back in his pocket, somewhat bewildered by the proposed meeting place as Creedence moseyed back over.

"Well done," she said. "Where are you meeting him?"

"He wants to meet at Pen Ponds in Richmond Park. Twelve thirty."

If Creedence thought that this was an unusual spot for a rendezvous, she didn't mention it. Her focus was instead on what they would be doing together until then. "Three hours. Excellent," she replied. "Let's get back on that Vespa and cruise the King's Road. Drink up!"

# CHAPTER 28

**Cruising the King's** Road, Jonah discovered, meant shopping, which he wasn't particularly keen about given his current employment prospects. Afterward, Creedence went back to her flat in a taxi, leaving Jonah to ride to Richmond Park alone. He reached the park at twelve fifteen P.M. and rode up to the Pen Ponds parking lot, walking down to the ponds on a path he'd taken many times before.

He thought it odd that his dad had selected this location of all places—it used to be their regular family Sunday afternoon "breath of fresh air." He would feed the ducks, always making sure he stayed clear of the old swan called Charlie that terrified him. He automatically scanned the ponds for Charlie this time and saw his father at the far end of the causeway that split the two small lakes. His hands were in the pockets of his old green Barbour jacket, and he was hunched up against the cold south-westerly wind that had replaced the morning sunshine. When he saw Jonah, he started to walk toward him. Close up, Jonah could see that his father hadn't slept much in the last twenty-four hours. He felt a pang of guilt that he'd been having such a good time with Creedence while his father was in this state. *Where had that come from?* he wondered.

"Thanks, Jonah. I appreciate you coming, and I'm sorry for any embarrassment I've caused you," David greeted him.

His apology again disarmed Jonah. "Yeah, well, okay," he said.

"I didn't do it, you know? I didn't make those trades."

Jonah shrugged his shoulders in a "if you say so" sort of way.

"Creedence seems like a nice girl," his dad continued.

This time Jonah cracked. "Dad, I didn't think we were here to talk about Creedence."

David looked sheepish. "No, you're right. Sorry." He took a deep breath and looked directly at his son. "I've been set up, Jonah. And the bank is going to hang me out to dry. Hellcat needs a quick fix to clear its name and get back in business, and they're not going to root out the truth if all it means is proving my innocence."

Jonah mused to himself that that was pretty much what Creedence had said to him as well.

David pushed his hands deeper into his pockets. "I don't deserve it, but I need your help."

Jonah staggered back. "You need *my* help? You've never wanted it before. . . ."

His father inhaled deeply. Then he looked beyond Jonah toward the parking lot and frowned before saying, "Point taken."

Jonah glanced to see what his dad was looking at. A black 4x4 was heading down the track toward them, probably some mother whose spoiled children couldn't be bothered to walk the four hundred yards from the parking lot to feed the ducks.

He turned back. "So?"

"So I need to get hold of the Baron's trading records."

Jonah shook his head in disbelief. "Oh, come on, Dad. You know I can't do that. And what's the Baron got to do with it?"

"I've told you before that he's dangerous. You know he hates me." David was strident now, and again he was looking over Jonah's shoulder. "Jesus, what are these idiots doing?" He moved toward Jonah as if to push him out of the way. Jonah looked back. The 4x4 was accelerating straight at them. They both jumped to the side as the car, an Audi Q7 with blacked-out windows, skidded to a halt on the gravel. The two right-hand doors were thrown open, and out leapt two huge men in black leather jackets.

"What the hell do you think . . ." His father was cut off as one of the men shoulder-charged him to the ground. The other one grabbed Jonah's throat and shoulder and spun him around to lock him in a half-nelson. Jonah yelped in shock and pain. *Who were these people? Were they being mugged?*

A third man appeared around the front of the car as the first man punched Jonah's father twice in the face before hauling him up by gripping him by the chest and spinning him around so that he, too, was in a half-nelson.

This man was wearing a dark, well-cut suit and black wrap-around sunglasses. He was holding a piece of paper. "Mr. Lightbody," he said. His English was heavily accented—Russian.

Jonah looked toward his father, who was shaking his head, trying to recover from the two vicious punches.

He regained his visual focus. "Yes," David said after a short pause.

"You remember me?" asked the man. It was more a statement than a question.

Recognition began to spread across David Lightbody's face now that he'd had a few seconds to recover from the assault. "Yes, yes. Mr. Scrotycz. Of course I remember you."

*Scrotycz!* Jonah gasped. *This was the "client" who'd kept his father so busy over the years?*

"Mr. Lightbody, I have received this letter from your employer. It says that 'unfortunately, unfortunately' "—the pitch of his voice rose a fraction—" 'we regret to inform you that your funds have been reduced by one hundred million dollars due to an unauthorized trade by Mr. David Lightbody. Mr. Lightbody has left Helsby Cattermole, and we are investigating the matter. But we regret that we cannot accept any responsibility for this loss. We remind you that investments can go down as well as up.' "

He stopped talking and looked at David, his gaze shifting as he caught sight of the boy standing next to him. "Is this your son, Mr. Lightbody?"

"No," came the reply.

"You lie," the Russian said, sounding bored. "I know it is your son. His name is Jonah. He also works at Helsby Cattermole. I know everything about you—where you live, when you get up, what car you drive." He raised his sunglasses to reveal a pair of heavily hooded eyes and stepped forward, leaning toward David Lightbody, his voice lowered to a menacing stage whisper. "I want my hundred million back. You have thirty days or you and your son will die."

The man holding Jonah wrenched his arm up until it felt as if his shoulder would dislocate. Jonah screamed in pain this time, and from the look on David's face the same was happening to him, although he didn't make a sound.

Scrotycz stood back. "We go," he ordered his men, who pushed their two charges to the ground and returned to the car, leaving Jonah and his father sprawling in the dirt. The Audi roared off, straight ahead up the hill to join the road that ran to the Sheen Gate exit.

Jonah was the first to get up, massaging his shoulder to ease the pain, still scared. "What the hell was that?!"

David Lightbody staggered to his feet, and his watch fell off his wrist, the strap broken. His face was already swelling up around the eyes where he had been punched. But beneath the swelling his eyes were blazing with cold fury. "Jonah, I told you—I've been set up. It's the Baron who's screwed up your future. He's the one you need to direct your anger toward. Not me."

"Oh, please, Dad. Not the Baron thing again."

"It's him, I tell you. He's the one who has done this. And I think he's had it planned for years."

"*Years?*" repeated Jonah.

"Yes!" said David. "Ten years ago I lost thirty million dollars in a trade, and he was the one on the other side. I was fired, and Hellcat was the only firm willing to employ me. You know what kind of influence he has there."

Jonah furrowed his brow. "So you're mad at him for doing you a favor?"

"I don't think it was a favor!" David practically screamed. He quickly reined in his temper. "Now look. He wants a fall guy, and I've got history."

Jonah shook his head. "You're obsessed, Dad. And anyway, the Baron doesn't trade clients' money. He's a proprietary trader. Besides which, I see every trade we do. Do you think that with my memory a one-hundred-million-dollar trade would have passed me by? Give me some credit."

"*You* don't trade clients' money. But he does. Big money."

"Dad, I really don't think—"

David didn't let him finish. "That's why I need his trading records. The only other person who might know what's going on is Clive in Settlements, and he's dead. Didn't that sound any warning bells to you? Clive? Dead? He's the only person who has access to every trade."

"Oh, come on, Dad. You've lost it. I'm going to the police now before another of your clients pays us a friendly visit." Jonah spun around and started running back up toward the parking lot. "The cops will sort it out."

"If you go to the police, we'll have no chance," his father shouted after him. "They're not going to help. Nobody's going to help. Only we can do this. You must help me Jonah. You must help me," he pleaded, desperation in his voice.

Jonah ran on, wanting to get away from the park as quickly as possible, away from the threat of violence. When he reached the parking lot, he turned around and looked back toward the Ponds. He could see his father walking up the hill on the other side, presumably back toward Barnes. He was a despondent figure with his hands thrust deep into his pockets and his shoulders hunched forward. For a moment, Jonah thought he might be crying, the way his shoulders were moving. But that was a ridiculous idea: David Lightbody didn't cry.

Still, though, Jonah felt a pang of guilt. He climbed onto the Vespa and phoned Creedence, his hand shaking as he held the phone, his eyes scanning the lot for any human movement.

Creedence's voice sounded brightly in his ear. "Hello! How was it?" she said.

"Well, we got attacked by some Russian heavies," Jonah blurted out, the shaking now moving to his legs.

"You what!" she exclaimed. "What do you mean? Are you hurt? Is your dad with you?"

"Look, Creedence, I need to get to a police station. I don't want to hang around here in case those thugs come back. But I'm not hurt. Not badly anyway. And no, Dad's not with me. He's mad. I'm going to Barnes police station to see what they can do. I'll come back to the flat afterward and give you the full story."

There was silence for a moment. Then Creedence spoke again, this time sounding as if she was close to tears. "I think I'm responsible for these Russians finding you," she confessed, sobbing.

"What do you mean?" said Jonah. "He said he knew where we lived. He probably tailed Dad. Look, I've got to get out of here and get to the police station. I'll see you at the flat."

"No, I'll meet you at the station." She hung up without waiting for an answer.

Jonah fired up the Vespa and rode it quickly out of the park, checking all the time in his mirrors for an Audi Q7. He was at the police station before Creedence, but not by much, and had only been waiting two minutes when she sped up on her mountain bike.

She looked scared. "I told Amelia where you were going," she babbled without even saying hello. "I told her yesterday I was going to see you, and she rang again this morning, asking how you were and whether you'd seen or talked to your dad. I was on such a high after last night that I told her we'd got on really well, that you'd told me all about how much you hated your dad so I doubted you were involved, and that you were seeing him at twelve thirty today. She asked where, and I told her that too."

Jonah pictured the Q7 coming down the hill from the parking lot and his dad walking away in the opposite direction. Surely if they had tailed his father, they would have appeared from the same direction as him, and not from behind Jonah.

"I'm sorry, Jonah. I'm so sorry. I thought I was being helpful. Please don't hate me," Creedence added, a tear dropping onto her cheek and catching the sunlight.

Jonah watched the tear make its way downward, unable to form a complete thought. Everything was once again spinning wildly out of control.

"She's a bitch, Jonah. I'm so sorry. I won't say anything else to her, I promise. This changes everything," Creedence pleaded.

Jonah stumbled over Creedence's initial statement. "What do you mean she's a bitch? I thought she was really nice." He thought back to how the Baron had called her a Hellcat. The description ran counter to how helpful and enthused she had been while setting him up with the Purple Nicey card and everything.

"Oh, she is nice to you and the Baron or any other rich trader. But if you're not likely to be useful to her, she'll chew you up and spit you out. You should see her in restaurants or with shop assistants—she's so rude. And once you're out of her good books, forget it. I've seen her reduce people to tears."

"So you wouldn't put it past her to tip off a client as to where to find me and my dad and have us beaten up?"

"No, I wouldn't. Amelia looks after herself, and as she says, 'It's *the clients* who pay our bonuses.' "

Jonah's eyes narrowed. "And how close is she to the Baron?"

"They're thick as thieves. Apparently he got her the job in the first place. Why? What are you getting at?" It was Creedence's turn to be quizzical.

"I'm not getting at anything yet," Jonah replied. "I'm trying to work out the facts. Apparently Dad's made a big loss before, and he reckons the Baron is using that to set him up. You think that Amelia sent Scrotycz to Richmond Park, and you're telling me that Amelia and the Baron are as close as can be. And I can't believe my dad would be so stupid as to make the same mistake twice or lose half a billion . . ." *Bingo!* Jonah realized that there was a single, simple question he had to ask his father.

"What is it, Jonah?" asked Creedence. "What have you worked out?"

"I need to find out how he managed to lose the money." He reached into his pocket for his phone and dialed his dad again.

# CHAPTER 29

**"Hello, Jonah,"** said David in a voice that sounded even more tired than he had looked half an hour ago.

Jonah went straight to the point. "What did you trade to make these losses?" he asked.

"What am I *supposed* to have traded, you mean?"

"Okay. Whatever. What are you supposed to have traded?"

David sighed. "I am supposed to have bought one hundred million dollars worth of a high-risk derivative in Allegro Home Finance. The bet was that the Allegro share price would go up. With Allegro Home Finance's share price now worth nothing, the loss is five hundred million."

A memory from four years back floated into Jonah's head: his dad telling him about finance by putting money on his desk and throwing it into the trash to demonstrate a loss. He'd thrown his whole wallet in the bin when he'd talked about derivatives.

His father didn't trade derivatives. He was a Drizzler. He was paid to make sure his clients didn't *lose* their money. He traded boring, low-risk investments. This trade was a huge gamble. It was a Whistler trade.

"So it's not loads of little losses hidden away. It's one big hit," Jonah said, practically whispering into the phone.

"That's right. One big hit."

"Using derivatives?"

"Yes, derivatives," David repeated.

"And what about the other loss? The one from years ago. Was that derivatives?"

"Yes," replied David sheepishly. "I didn't really understand them, and I paid the price."

"Is that why you don't trade them?"

"Correct," said David. "Do you believe me now?" Jonah could hear the hope in his voice.

He replied with another question. "Are you at home, Dad?"

"No. I haven't been home since Tuesday morning," said David.

The wheels of Jonah's mind were really spinning now. "Where have you been then?"

"Camping in Richmond Park," David explained. "I've been keeping my head down. People get killed for this amount of money. You saw what happened to Clive! And Scrotycz said it himself: He knows where we live."

David's sleeping in the woods struck Jonah as a bit weird, but he carried on his questioning regardless. "How did Scrotycz find us?"

"I assumed he must have followed you."

Jonah was silent.

"Jonah? Jonah! Are you still there?"

"I'll ring you back, Dad," Jonah exclaimed, ending the call. He turned to face Creedence, who was looking at him anxiously.

"What did he say, Jonah? What did he say?"

Jonah stood dead still, trancelike, nearly letting the phone slip out of his hand.

"What did he say?" Creedence repeated.

Jonah came back into the present. "He said . . . he said that the loss was all off one big trade, a big derivatives trade."

"Okay . . ." Creedence's voice trailed. "And?"

"And that doesn't make sense. He wouldn't do anything like that. That's not his style."

"And what about how those Russians found you? Did he have a different explanation?"

Jonah shook his head. "Actually, he said that he hadn't been home at all, so Scrotycz couldn't possibly have followed him."

Creedence's face fell again. "So it had to be Amelia who told him?"

"Looks like it." Jonah felt the fear grip him again.

"Do you think your dad is telling the truth?" she asked.

"I don't know yet. But there's still nothing to suggest that the Baron is involved. It's one thing for me to believe Dad didn't do it, but it's another for me to go against the Baron. I owe everything to him."

"What's your gut feeling, though? Isn't that what you traders go by?"

"I, uh . . ." The short sharp pangs of guilt he'd felt when he'd seen his father in the park began to develop into something more definitive, something that came from deep, deep inside him. *But it couldn't be right, could it?*

"Are you all right, Jonah?" Creedence asked, concerned, seeing the expression on his face.

He turned back. "My gut says Dad."

"That he did it or that he didn't do it?"

"It says I should side with him. Because he's"—Jonah couldn't believe he was saying this—"my dad."

"'An indissoluble bond which he cannot break if he could, for nature has welded him into it before he was born,'" said Creedence quietly.

"What?" said Jonah.

"It's something Pearl S. Buck wrote. It means blood is thicker than water," she supplied, looking embarrassed for a moment and swiftly returning to whether Jonah believed his dad. "Is that what you're going to do? Side with him?"

"Yeah, I, umm . . ." Jonah stammered. "I don't know."

"You don't? I thought you said . . ."

"The Baron's been there for me. Really. Truly," Jonah answered, the words tumbling out of his mouth. "I've yet to be convinced that he's behind it." He paused. "He and my dad could both be innocent, couldn't they?" Effectively answering his own question, he added, "I need more facts."

"Maybe your dad *has* evidence? Ring him again?" Creedence pushed. But then she held up her hands as if changing her mind. "No, don't do it while I'm here."

"What do you mean?" said Jonah, looking straight at her.

"I should go," she said. "I mustn't know anything more about what you and your father discuss or do in case Amelia quizzes me. This way I can't tell her anything."

Jonah thought hard. He didn't want to let her go, not even for a moment. But on the other hand he didn't want to encourage another run in with Scrotycz. He eyed her up and down, memorizing her every feature. If she stayed, she could end up getting dragged into everything. Or worse. As his father had pointed out, people got killed for this amount of money.

He decided she was right. "What will you say to Amelia if she rings?" he asked.

"I'll tell her what happened in the park and that you are shit scared and don't intend to have any other meetings with your father."

Jonah nodded. "And if she asks you what Dad and I talked about?"

Creedence thought for a moment. "I'll say that you didn't get a chance to talk because Scrotycz turned up and afterward you got out as quickly as you could."

Jonah nodded again. "Sounds good."

"And I'm not going to go back to the flat," she continued. "I'll head out to dinner tonight with a girlfriend. I'll stay the night there or longer if necessary. That way you will have somewhere to live until it's all sorted out." She reached into her pocket and handed him a key. "Leave it under the flowerpot by the door if you go out."

He took the key in silence as Creedence stood up. "You really want to do this for me?"

Creedence's eyes sparkled. "Ring me if you think the coast is clear," she said.

Jonah smiled weakly. "You betcha," he said, trying to sound strong.

She hugged him hard and gave him a long, lasting farewell kiss.

As she pulled away, her lips formed one of those closed-mouth sad smiles. She took a step backward to put her bike helmet on, and Jonah felt waves of loneliness flood over him again. He was losing his only ally. "Can I call you if I need to?" he asked.

"Of course," she replied without hesitation. "And will you still buy me that dinner when this is over?"

"I'd like to see someone try to stop me."

Creedence raised her eyebrows. That was far too close to what was happening to joke about.

Jonah struggled to recapture the moment. "I'll take you to Jake's Kitchen in Covent Garden." It was the latest trendy restaurant. He'd read about it in the paper before all the hoopla had started.

"I'll hold you to that," she said, wagging her finger. "I haven't been there."

"Well, in that case it would be my pleasure to accompany you." Jonah cupped her cheek in his hand and gave her a quick peck on the lips.

He gazed into her eyes. "You should go. I've got to make this call."

"Yup," she said and mounted her bike. "Good luck."

Jonah watched her cycle away along the river until she disappeared into the trees. Then he reached into his pocket and phoned his father for the third time that day.

"Jonah?"

"Yes. Dad, I believe you didn't do the trade, I think."

"Thank you, Jonah," said David softly. "That means a lot to me."

Jonah was again disarmed by the gratitude. "But I'm not ready to believe that the Baron is behind it. I need to understand what makes you so convinced." He paused. "Beyond the fact that you hate him."

"Where are you now?" came the curt reply.

"I'm at Barnes police station."

There was a pause. "I should have some evidence tonight. Will you meet me? I can't share it over the phone."

"All right," said Jonah, feeling the pain in his shoulder again. "Where this time?"

"I'll call you later, but it will probably be in the City."

"Okay," said Jonah and hung up. All at once the solitude hit him. He looked at his watch. It was now one thirty P.M. He had a whole afternoon by himself ahead of him. He went into the police station to file an assault complaint against Scrotycz, then crossed the road to the river. For a long time he leaned on the river wall, watching the boats, noting that the leaves on the trees that flanked it were beginning to change color as autumn approached. And all the time his mind was trying to find some sense as to what was going on: *Who could I believe? Who should I trust? What should I do?*

The questions only brought more riddles. And more anxiety.

"This line is secure. Yours?" asked Kloot from inside his stationary helicopter. He'd left a very important business meeting in Central Africa to check in with his chief operative in London. His bodyguard, Klaasens, stood outside the chopper, having been directed to use force if necessary to ensure that Kloot's conversation wouldn't be interrupted.

"Secure," said the man on the other end of the phone.

"You have an update for me?"

"I do. The loss is offloaded, and Lightbody's out. The bank won't make a fuss. They need a quick solution, and he has history."

"The Russian?" Kloot asked.

"Highly agitated. I have no doubt that his masters in Moscow are very unhappy. I understand he and a couple of gorillas have already paid Lightbody a visit. I'm sure Lightbody will be running for the hills."

"And what about the boy? Has he remained loyal? If he turns, it will be your responsibility to ensure that he is removed. We cannot afford any more mistakes. He is your recruit."

"Yes, I am sure," the man replied. "And I am fully aware of my responsibilities," he added with a hint of irritation in his voice. "One of Amelia's bimbos is close to the boy. She told us that he was meeting Lightbody, and we passed on the information to the Russian. The feedback is that he is terrified following the Russian's intervention and won't be going near his father again. As for his loyalty to me, training a child is like training an animal. Yesterday I took away everything he aspired to—the money, the independence, the status. Tomorrow I will give it back. He will know that it is better for him to denounce his father than lose his future, and I will be able to keep an eye on him."

Kloot chuckled, a rare sound for one of the world's most inscrutable criminal masterminds. "Ha ha. I taught you well."

"You did."

"Well, I hope you are right. He reminded me of you at around the same age. If he turns out to be half as good as you, our money will be in good hands for another generation. I will report back to my colleagues in the League that they have nothing to be concerned about."

"You might also add that I will now be looking after the Russian's money. Another lesson of yours I recall—keep your friends close and your enemies closer."

"Excellent! Excellent!" said Kloot. "Once more unto the breach!"

"Once more indeed."

# CHAPTER 30

**It was six** forty-five when Jonah's phone rang. He had spent the afternoon on the move, watching all the time for the Q7 or anything else suspicious. He was now in a café in Soho, drinking his sixth coffee of the day. He picked up his phone from the table and looked at the screen. It was an unfamiliar number. He let it ring three times before answering, and when he did, he stayed silent, waiting for the person on the other end to identify him or herself.

For a moment there was silence at both ends before the caller spoke. "It's me, Jonah—your father." Jonah breathed a sigh of relief. "I've switched SIM cards."

"Hi," said Jonah speaking quietly, one elbow on the table and his head down.

"When can you meet me at Helsby Cattermole?"

"Hellcat! You can't be serious?" he hissed.

"It has to be there, I'm afraid," said David. "The information I'm getting can't leave the building. That's the agreement with my inside contact. And don't worry about being caught. Everyone's gone home."

Jonah put his hand on his forehead and the other elbow on the table, gently shaking his head. "Well, how are we going to get in with all the security?"

"We'll meet in the underground garage. There's a fire escape on Foster Lane. It will be open."

Jonah was silent, weighing his options.

"Please, Jonah. You wanted evidence. I have evidence," David pleaded.

Jonah remembered Creedence's comment: *Where I come from, you're innocent until proven guilty*. He held the phone closer. "Okay," he said. "I can be there in ten minutes."

"Thanks. I'll see you there."

Jonah put his phone in his pocket and downed the rest of his coffee. He went outside to Frith Street, finding it packed with early evening drinkers spilling out of the bars and cafés. The Vespa was parked across the street, and Jonah weaved his way through the crowds to reach it, before heading east to the City.

Although sunset was not for another half an hour, Foster Lane was dark when Jonah arrived, the tall buildings around the narrow street shortening the day. He parked the Vespa and walked warily down the deserted lane, keeping his helmet on to ensure his face was covered. The fire escape was on the left and had been wedged open a fraction as promised with a small piece of wood. Jonah looked around to check that there was nobody following him and slipped through the door, noticing the descending staircase ahead.

When he closed the door behind him, he was in complete darkness and silence.

He took the helmet off and stood still, partly to let his eyes adjust to the lack of light and partly out of fear. What was the saying? Once bitten, twice shy. He'd already been beaten up once today. Why was he coming back for more? He didn't have an answer. As his eyes adjusted, he could make out the staircase once again, and, holding on to the handrail, he made his way carefully downward, acutely aware of the cold of the metal on his hand and the soft sound of his sneakers on the stairs. When he reached the bottom, he could discern the shadowy shapes of pillars and cars in the low light, but where was his dad? What was he supposed to do now? Should he call out?

A shaft of light speared down the stairs behind him and swiftly disappeared. Someone *was* following him! Jonah stepped quickly around to the left and pressed himself up behind a pillar, trying to control his shallow breathing. The person at the top wasn't moving. He was standing there listening. Listening for what? For him? Jonah held his breath. A thin beam of light from a flashlight flicked around and started coming down the stairs. Jonah could feel sweat breaking on his forehead.

"Jonah?" a voice whispered, and Jonah let the air out of his lungs. "Jonah? Where are you?"

"I'm here, Dad." Jonah stepped out from behind the pillar. The thin light moved toward him. "Thanks a lot for that, by the way," he said, crossing his arms. "I was scared witless."

"Sorry," said David. "I wanted to check nobody was tailing you." Then motioning to Jonah, he added, "Come with me," and began walking toward the far side of the garage. As he did, he flashed the light across the license plate of each vehicle, allowing Jonah a glimpse of the kinds of cars that were parked there. Jonah's jaw dropped as he took in the car manufacturers. He hadn't seen anything like this display since visiting the National Motor Museum. There were Ferraris, Aston Martins, Bentleys, Porsches, and what looked like a McLaren F1 and a Lamborghini. A row of Harley-Davidson and Ducati bikes also caught his attention.

As Jonah took in the cars and bikes one after another, his initial excitement began to waver. These were things he could never have unless he somehow managed to prove his father's innocence. And even then it wasn't likely, at least not without maintaining his relationship with the Baron, a relationship that still hung in the balance.

David stopped in front of a Bentley.

"Nice one, Dad," Jonah began, commenting on his taste in sedans. It was not until he followed the precise direction of his father's gaze that he saw that David was concentrating on the license plate, not on the car itself.

David walked around to the rear door, pulled it open, shone the light inside, and turned back to Jonah. "Here we go. Come on, let's get inside. We can talk in here without risk of being heard if someone comes down."

Jonah opened his eyes wide, and he followed his father into the Bentley's expansive backseat, smelling the leather, marveling at the space, and touching the wooden inserts. "Wow. Whose car is this?" he asked as David ripped open the top of a brown envelope and flicked through its contents.

"The same person who left this envelope here. He's someone in the Helsby Cattermole investigation team who's willing to help me, but only in a limited way, and he must remain nameless. Now close the door." David's tone was terse.

Jonah pulled the door shut. It was much heavier than he expected and closed with a solid thunk.

His father pulled down the cream leather arm rest between them to use as a table and placed the envelope on top. The lights in the car faded gently, putting them back into darkness save for the thin light from David's pencil flashlight. "Right, I'll give you the facts, and then I'll tell you what I'm thinking," he said, taking a sheet of paper out of the envelope and laying it face up on the armrest.

Jonah nodded along, eager to know once and for all what exactly was going on here.

"These are the official trading records from my computer for Friday, September twelfth."

Jonah looked down at the familiar layout of account numbers, dates, times, stock codes, volumes, and prices.

"At nine fifty-four P.M. UK time, I allegedly bought one hundred million dollars of Allegro Home Finance derivatives. For every dollar below five, there would be a loss of a hundred million. With Allegro Home Finance shares worth nothing, the loss is five hundred million. Make sense?" he said in a history teacher monotone.

Jonah nodded again. Of course he understood. They'd been trading derivatives all last week at the Bunker.

"I happened to have been online at nine fifty-four P.M. seeing what the U.S. markets were doing at the close, even though I was out of town. My online access can be traced, and so theoretically I could have been trading." David paused. "I wasn't." He searched

Jonah's eyes, desperate for him to understand. "Which means the records have been manipulated so that it looks as if the trades came from my computer. Agreed?"

"Okay . . ." Jonah replied cautiously. This was a lot to take in.

David continued, "At nine fifty-four P.M. the Baron was in the building. The access card records show that he entered the trading floor at nine thirty-five P.M. and left at ten twenty-five P.M."

Jonah remembered seeing the Baron outside the pub, engrossed in his phone call. It must have been just before nine thirty P.M. because he'd looked at his watch before waving goodbye to the Bunker Boys, and it had been exactly nine twenty-five.

David picked up the envelope and pulled out three additional sheets of paper. He laid two of them on the seat and shone the flashlight at them. "The telephone records of his cell phone and landline indicate that he neither made nor received any calls or texts during this time, or for the forty-five minutes preceding his entry into the building. However"—he paused and turned over the third piece of paper, a photograph—"this picture taken by the CCTV cameras in reception suggests otherwise."

Jonah leaned forward and peered at the picture. It showed the Baron with a phone in his hand as if just completing a call. It was a flip-style phone, not his usual smartphone.

"The phone you see here is not registered with Helsby Cattermole as is required," David explained, "and that makes his using it all that much more suspicious." Jonah tried to revisualize the Baron outside the pub. *Yes. He had been using the flip phone.* So, whatever conversation he had been having, it had taken him back to the office.

"Finally, the access records show that Clive from Settlements was in the building on Sunday evening," David continued. "After the announcement by the U.S. government that it would not bail out Allegro Home Finance." He took a second photo out of the envelope and laid it on top of all the other documents. "As you know, Clive is now dead."

Jonah gagged when the flashlight revealed what was in the photograph: a dead body with the top of its head missing and blood everywhere. David turned the photo face down and extinguished the light. Jonah shivered. The fear that had, for a short while, withdrawn to the background of his consciousness jumped to the foreground once more. "You think he was murdered, don't you?" he asked his father.

"I do," David answered bluntly. "I think that the Baron took a massive punt on Allegro Home Finance being rescued, based on some information he had received. When the trade went wrong, he couldn't accept the loss and persuaded Clive to switch the trade into one of my accounts on Sunday evening. And then he killed him. Or got someone else to do it."

Jonah swore loudly inside his head. *The Baron wouldn't kill someone, would he?!*

"I think he must have had inside information that turned out to be wrong. You'd have to be absolutely sure of your facts to put that much money down. And don't forget, he couldn't have done it through Helsby Cattermole. He would have had to have gotten clearance."

"Why not?" Jonah replied, the vision of Clive's corpse still with him.

"It's too big a trade and too risky to do without approvals. He'd have been asked questions he couldn't answer. I reckon it was for his personal account or for some trading syndicate he's part of."

Jonah thought of the twenty-five million dollars of Allegro Home Finance shares the Baron had asked him to buy. He'd called it a "small punt." The maximum they could lose was twenty-five million dollars. This was in a completely different league. His dad was right. You wouldn't make a massive derivatives trade like this without a very good idea that you were right. The downside was too great. It could be a syndicate? Was that where Amelia came in?

He turned to his father. "Creedence thinks Amelia tipped Scrotycz off that we were meeting in Richmond Park. Does that seem plausible to you?" Jonah threw the question at David, expecting him to be surprised.

He wasn't. "I'd guessed something like that had happened," he said. "That letter to Scrotycz didn't come from Helsby Cattermole."

"Wait, what?" It was Jonah who was surprised.

"Nothing was sent out from the bank. My company insider would have known if it was."

Jonah's eyes narrowed. "So you think it was Amelia who sent that letter to Scrotycz, naming you as the one responsible for losing his money?"

"I think it is very possible." David's expression was blank, impossible to read. "But it's irrelevant at this stage. The problem is that all of this evidence—the Baron's second phone, Clive's working on a Sunday, the fraudulent letter—is circumstantial. The only hard evidence says that I'm the one who's guilty: the trades are on my account; I was online at the time they were made; and I have history."

Jonah shot back, irritated at his father's seeming concession to defeat. "That's pathetic, Dad. The bruising on your face is evidence. Let's go to the police, show them this stuff, and let them handle it," he urged. "Maybe they'll give us protection."

David ran his fingers across the swelling around his eyes and shook his head. "Scrotycz is a very wealthy Russian citizen living in London. Helsby Cattermole is a very successful bank. They have a lot of power. They have a lot of connections. The cops are not going to go charging in and risk upsetting them. They'd have to pussyfoot around, and by the time they got anywhere, if they got anywhere, this will all be over."

Jonah shuddered. None of this was what he wanted to hear.

"Which is why I need the Baron's trading records," David urged. "I have to get some real evidence that directly implicates him and whomever else he's working with: trades, bank accounts, names, addresses."

"Okay . . ." said Jonah slowly, "but why bring me into it?"

David took a deep breath. "Jonah, you are the only person who can get inside the building and extract this information. You know about trading. You know about computers. You know the Baron as well as anybody. And I'm sure your access to the trading floor will be reinstated soon enough."

"I dunno . . ."

David interjected, "He thinks he owns you. He won't suspect you."

"He doesn't own me," Jonah snapped.

David looked at him. "I said he *thinks* he does, like he does all those other people in the Bunker. He's bought their loyalty with money and status. Anybody who doesn't buy into the Baron-Bunker thing disappears pretty rapidly."

Jonah thought of Jammy and Franky. He couldn't speak for the Baron's former assistant, as they'd never actually met, but Franky was loyal—she'd told him so. "What about Franky? She was loyal," he countered.

"Maybe at first, but I'm sure the Baron couldn't have been too happy when she said that she wanted to get married. It would have meant that her allegiances would have been divided."

The knot in Jonah's stomach tightened again.

"Jonah, your life is in danger," David pressed. "One person has been killed over this, and those Russians were for real. *I know.* I've met their kind before." He paused, apparently weighing what he was going to say next. "But I can protect you if you give me the chance," he said slowly.

Jonah almost burst out laughing. "You! Protect me! Biff! The man who doesn't fight back! I was there in the park, Dad. Where was the protection then?"

David stayed composed. "Jonah, give me five more minutes and I'll explain. I should have told you about my past a long time ago. I can only hope that when I've finished, you'll understand why I didn't or, rather, couldn't."

The atmosphere in the car suddenly seemed to have changed. The darkness had closed in around them, isolating them from the outside world. There was something monumental in the tone of his father's voice that wanted to take control of Jonah's being. He felt a shiver go through his body, a goose walking over his grave.

David swallowed hard. "You know I grew up in Africa," he started.

Jonah nodded. That much he did know. Beyond that, though, his father's earlier years were a bit of a mystery. He'd never offered to tell Jonah about them, and, Jonah admitted, he had never thought to ask.

"I was born in Rhodesia, now called Zimbabwe. My father was a tobacco farmer, and we lived an outdoor life." David's eyes lit up. "I could shoot a gun by the time I was ten, skin a buck at about the same time, and fire up a decent barbecue from the age of eight."

Jonah was deadly still. This was the first time in his life that he had had any sense that his father had been a kid too once upon a time. A picture was forming in his mind of his dad in khaki shorts. He was holding a gun and smiling, his parents on either side of him, looking proud.

"But things were getting difficult. Rhodesia was a British colony, and there was a civil war taking place between the whites and the blacks. In the early 1970s things began to really intensify as the black freedom fighters got themselves organized. I left school and headed back to the farm to wait until my eighteenth birthday and the arrival of the drafting papers." David paused, as if summoning all his strength. "Then my parents were murdered."

The picture in Jonah's mind exploded. "What?!" he exclaimed, sweat building at the back of his neck. He knew that his grandparents had died before he was born, but he'd assumed it was from old age. Only now did he appreciate that they were probably younger than his dad was currently.

"I told you they died before you were born."

"Yes. But . . ." Jonah's palms felt clammy.

"I didn't think the details would help you. You really were too young to understand."

"How? What? Who?" Jonah stammered.

"Killed by terrs, short for terrorists—that's what we called the freedom fighters. I was the one who found their bodies."

The car suddenly felt very warm to Jonah, the richness of the leather and wood oppressive. His dad wasn't looking at him anymore. Instead his gaze was focused above him at some spot in the distance. "I'd been into town. It was a Friday night, and I was driving back home after a few beers with the lads. I saw the flames from quite a long way off, lighting up the sky, and when I drove through the gate I could see that the fire was coming from the barn. I saw my father dead in the doorway: shot and chopped. And my mother lay just beyond him."

Jonah's throat constricted as he thought of his grandfather and grandmother's blood drenched bodies dismembered on the ground. He swallowed hard, wincing at the bitterness of the bile that had risen into his mouth, as David's gaze dropped back down to focus on him. Jonah couldn't see any tears in his eyes, but he had the sense that his dad was holding them back. He wanted to say something to comfort his father, even though the pain was decades old, but nothing seemed sufficient, certainly not "I'm sorry."

"I felt so angry. A cold anger. I wanted to hurt something. Kill something. Mutilate it. Hear it scream. Watch it die," David said.

Now Jonah saw emotion in his father's eyes as he recalled the fury he had felt.

"After the funeral I ended up joining the Selous Scouts, an undercover counterterrorism unit within the Rhodesian Defense Forces. We were guerillas. We'd go into an area, dressed and armed as terrs, and hunt them down, infiltrate their groups. We turned the hunters into the hunted."

"*You* joined a counterterrorism unit?" pressed Jonah. Surely this was something a father would be proud to tell his son.

"I did. I was young, but given my tracking ability and fluency in the local language, Shona, I was a candidate. Through my involvement in the Scouts, I learned about weapons and unarmed combat. I also learned to speak Russian."

"In Africa?"

"Yes, the Russians were financing some of the terr groups as part of their efforts to spread Communism. As a whitey speaking Russian, I could pass for one of the soldiers sent there to train the terrs."

Jonah was reeling with shock at everything his dad was telling him. He'd been let down by his father for so long, never understanding how he'd come to be the man he was. But now that he was finally laying it out for him, Jonah could only feel sorrow and regret that he had known such pain.

"I can't remember most of my time with the Scouts. All I know is that we did terrible things in the name of our country. I must have blocked it all out." David took a deep breath, steadying himself. "What I do remember is my last operation. It wasn't 'til then that I woke up."

Jonah leaned forward.

"We'd received orders to raid a village over the border in Botswana. It was a storage dump: guns, missiles, the lot. We were going in first. We were told to gun down anything that moved and to wait for a Botswana Defense Force truck to come and collect the weapons."

*Anything that moved?* Jonah's stomach lurched. Anything meant people. His dad had killed *people*.

"We were dropped by helicopter about twelve miles way and

made our way there overnight. It was still dark when we hit the huts—grenades first and then bullets. Our orders were to sweep the place—no one was to come out alive. That's what we did. When the shooting stopped, I switched on my spotlight and saw the wreckage we'd caused." David's voice caught in his throat, and he placed his right arm against the car door to steady himself. "The hut was strewn with dead children. It wasn't a terrorist camp at all. We'd hit an orphanage or school or something."

Jonah gasped and brought his hands to his face. His father hadn't just killed people—he'd killed *children*, boys and girls younger than himself.

David, who never cried, finally began to tear up. "I thought we must have made a mistake. But the truck arrived and they walked in, cold as anything, and pulled back a tarpaulin in one corner that was covering the cache. That's when we saw what lay beneath: elephant tusks. We hadn't come for weapons. It hadn't been a mistake. We'd come for ivory. And we'd killed children for it." David started visibly shaking. "That was the end for me. I walked into the bush. I was getting out."

This time Jonah couldn't control the bile that welled up into his mouth. He reached for the car door and pushed it open. He couldn't possibly be sick in the Bentley. He leaned out and spat onto the concrete floor. What his father was telling him was worse than anything he could have imagined. He spat again. And again. He breathed deeply, desperate for the cool air as saliva filled his mouth. He was back in control. He wiped his lips with the back of his hand and sat up, turning back to his father, leaving the car door open so that the air flowed in and the lights stayed on.

"You okay?" David asked, peering over at his clearly distressed son.

Jonah nodded, squeezing the handle of the door to steady himself.

David took another deep breath, and Jonah could see the pain in his eyes. "When you were born, it brought back the memories of that hut. The tiny bodies. The terror. The blood," he continued, his voice unsteady. "Every night I would wake up screaming from the dreams that invaded my sleep. I couldn't hold you, couldn't feed you, and eventually couldn't bear to see you. Your mother called it "the darkness" and tried to help me, but I wouldn't listen. Our marriage fell apart, and after the divorce she suffered a nervous breakdown for which she ended up blaming you too. It's why she went to America. I'd driven her close to suicide, she said, and she couldn't have anything to do with either of us anymore." David's head dropped to his chest, and his body began shaking even more vigorously. When he looked up, Jonah could see that tears had started to stream down his cheeks. "I'm so, so sorry Jonah," he said, shaking his head. "So, so sorry. You tried so hard to be loved and I couldn't do it."

Jonah felt his own emotions intensifying, but before he could figure out what to do or how to react, a bright light streamed into the garage.

"Down!" David whispered, pulling Jonah below the windows of the Bentley. Jonah reached for the car door to close it and extinguish the lights, but his father tightened his grip and shook his head.

Jonah heard the sound of high heels clicking across the

concrete floor, coming closer. He caught a flash of blonde hair. His heart beat faster. The heels stopped. *Had she seen the lights and the open door?* He felt his father's grip tighten even more.

Suddenly, the silence was ripped to pieces by the unmistakable roar of a Harley-Davidson engine. The engine revved and moved past them toward the exit. David looked up and out the window as Jonah heard the garage door opening, the engine revving again and finally disappearing out of earshot.

Jonah scrambled back up to the seat, still unsteady over everything his dad had revealed. "That was Amelia."

"Yes," said David, wiping his eyes with the edge of his sleeve. "We've been here too long." He reached into his pocket and took out a cheap cell phone, handing it to Jonah. "Thank you for listening to me, Jonah. I hope I've answered your questions, but if there's anything else you need to know use this rather than your own phone. That way they can't track you."

Jonah took the phone. He couldn't believe it had come to this.

"I'll go out first to check if it's clear. You can find a hiding spot near here, but don't leave until I come back and give the all clear." David placed the envelope into the seat back pocket to be collected by his insider. He opened the door on the driver's side, closed it gently, and disappeared into the darkness.

Jonah followed from the passenger's side, waiting behind the pillar at the bottom of the stairs, as his dad had instructed. His mind was reeling: Selous Scouts, murdered parents, massacred children. It was all too much. He saw the fire escape door open and close. Thirty seconds later the fire escape opened again, and he heard his father whisper, "All clear."

Jonah began to climb the stairs, a new thought occurring to him. If his father had had enough ingenuity to escape the team of special forces that had hunted him in Africa, then maybe he was right that he could protect Jonah.

Jonah needed to find how exactly he had managed to elude capture. He sprinted to the top of the stairs and burst out into the open air, sucking it deep into his lungs, and looked around for his father. Night had fallen, but he could make out an indistinct figure at the end of the deserted lane, walking quickly close to the walls and out of the street lights.

"Dad!" he called in a voice he hoped would carry far enough without alerting anyone else. The figure at the end of the lane stopped, took two steps to the left, and disappeared into the shadows.

Jonah started running. He reached the spot where his father should have been, but there was nobody there. Where was he? Had he ignored Jonah's shout? Jonah looked around in panic. Why would he have disappeared?

A voice behind him made him start. "Jonah. I'm here."

Jonah spun around to see his father step out of the shadows and walk toward him. He must have run right past him.

"What is it?" David asked.

"I need to know more. How did you get away? How do you think you can keep us safe?"

David nodded. "I escaped with the help of an African tracker named Chippy who was a Sangoma, a witch doctor." He paused and in the dim light Jonah saw him lift his chin upward and pull his shoulders back. "If you'll walk with me, I'll tell you the whole story."

Jonah understood that the invitation was to do more than walk to the end of the street. As he considered his answer, his father seemed to grow taller. He seemed solid, trustworthy, reliable. "I'll walk with you," Jonah said, "if you tell me *exactly* how you plan to protect me if this thing really heats up?"

David raised one foot as if about to take a step, but stopped midstride. He tilted his head.

"How exactly will I protect you?" he began, his features assuming a steely expression. "I'll take you back to Africa."

Amelia rode the Harley hard across London. She was late. Late enough to have ignored whoever it had been scrabbling about in the back of the Bentley in the garage. Normally she would have offered to help them find whatever it was they were looking for. It was important for her to keep her traders happy twenty-four hours a day, seven days a week. It was "all part of the service." But nothing and nobody was more important than the Baron, and he needed even more attention than usual at present. Tonight he had demanded three things from her: (1) dinner set up with Scrotycz the following evening, including entertainment afterward; (2) an iPod Touch with a "little something extra"; and (3) for her to be with him when he rang young Mr. Lightbody to ascertain whether it was time for him to return to Hellcat. It would be her job to confirm that Jonah's answers matched the answers Creedence had given her earlier in the day. The girl had fed back what had happened in Richmond Park, and Amelia had checked with the police regarding the assault complaint against Scrotycz. It was time to find out if the boy had completely rejected his father. If he had, the Baron would know that he could be trusted. If he hadn't, well, that was another story. . . .

# CHAPTER 31

**Jonah was sitting** alone in Creedence's flat deep in thought about everything his father had told him when the sound of his phone ringing made him start. It was the Baron; the "Sympathy for the Devil" ringtone left no doubt. He picked up the phone warily, part of him wishing that his father could be there to listen in on the conversation rather than spending another night in Richmond Park. "Hello," he said, the unsteadiness of his voice reflecting his internal uncertainty.

"Are you in bed, iPod? Couple of days off and you're back to your slothful, youthful ways! It's about time you came back to work," boomed the Baron.

Jonah's confusion instantly returned. "What do you mean? I thought I was suspended. What's changed? Has the bank decided that my dad's innocent?"

"Nothing changed there, I'm afraid. Word is that the trades came from your dad's computer."

"They did?" Jonah asked, forcing his tone to remain neutral. He didn't want the Baron knowing that he'd already seen the computer log, courtesy of his father, and that he suspected that the records had been tampered with, possibly at the Baron's request.

"Well, that's the rumor," the Baron said. "But enough of that. I want to talk about you. It's simply that we were all a bit hasty. The boys owe you an apology. I owe you an apology. It was a difficult few days." There was a slight, almost imperceptible pause, before he added, "Have you seen your dad, by the way?"

Jonah was now on full alert. The Baron knew he had seen him this morning if what Creedence had said about Amelia was true. So why was he asking? It could only be to see if Jonah would lie. But what if Amelia had seen them in the Bentley? *Shoot!* He had to answer quickly so as to hide his thoughts. "Yes," he said with forced confidence. "And I won't be doing it again. The client he screwed turned up and beat us up." He decided to only mention the Bentley if the Baron asked him directly.

"Ow! Are you alright?" replied the Baron.

"Yeah. Sore shoulder but that's all." Jonah reasoned that the Baron was testing to see where his allegiances lay.

"Good. You'll need to tell Pistol what your dad said to you. It might be relevant to the inquiry."

Again Jonah answered quickly, easily reading that the Baron was looking for information. "Yeah sure. That won't be difficult. He thanked me for coming to see him, and then this bloke Scrotycz turned up. I didn't hang around after that. I went to the police station and filed an assault complaint against the Russian. The Drizzler was too scared to do it. Some father he is." Jonah held his breath.

"Assault complaint, eh? Nice one!" the Baron breezed on, seemingly amused at this development. "Well, look, you might as well have another day of lounging. It is a bit quiet here for the time being. Why don't you come in on Friday?"

"Friday. Yeah, great," Jonah said with enough enthusiasm to be convincing.

"Excellent," the Baron continued. "Where you staying, by the way? I take it you're not at home?"

"I'm staying with a friend," Jonah replied, keeping things vague.

"A friend, eh? I'd better let you get back to bed then!" the Baron said with a leer. "Make sure you're not too exhausted to come in on Friday. Though you might want to check your bank account before then."

Before Jonah could reply that he wasn't in bed, the Baron had hung up. He was in the clear. The Baron believed him, and it seemed that Amelia hadn't seen them after all.

He slowly put the phone down on to the table, and as it touched the wooden surface, there was a bleep to say he had received a message. He glanced at the screen. It was from the Baron. Jonah's eyes opened as wide as saucers when he saw what it said: "I brought your bonus forward. Don't tell anyone!"

He turned to his computer, logging on to his bank account. The balance flashed up on the screen, causing Jonah to blink once, twice, and then a third time. A deposit of a million pounds had been made by Hellcat.

He stared at it, his father's words ringing in his ears: "He's bought their loyalty with money and status. . . . He thinks he owns you."

Jonah felt sick to his stomach. He could see it now: the suspension, the phone call, the money. Maybe even the last four years! He was no different than Franky or Jammy. There was no special bond between him and the Baron. He was only there if he played by the rules. And the rules were clear: be loyal to the Baron alone and have nothing to do with his dad. Jonah couldn't yet work out why the latter was so important and forty-eight hours ago he wouldn't have thought anything of it. But now it stank. His trust in the Baron had been broken. He was ready to take that walk to Africa.

# Part Three

# *LONDON AND AMSTERDAM*

# CHAPTER 32

## Friday, September 19

**Jonah had phoned** his father immediately after the Baron's call on Wednesday evening. David had come straight around to the flat, and they'd spent the whole of Thursday putting the details of their strategy together. The plan was a simple one: steal the Baron's laptop and run like hell.

Jonah was certain that any hidden trading records would be stored on the servers in Amelia's Boudoir. He knew he wouldn't be able to hack directly in because of the security around the servers, but he might be able to get in through the laptop. The hacking could take time, though, hence the run like hell bit. For the same reason, they had to do it today, Friday. It would buy them a few extra hours because the markets wouldn't be open over the weekend. The hope was that the Baron might not use his laptop until late Saturday, by which time Jonah and David would be long gone.

When Jonah arrived at the Hellcat trading floor on Friday morning, he found the Bunker deserted. The Baron had given the boys the day off as thanks for all the craziness they'd had to put up with lately, though Jonah wondered if perhaps his real motivation was keeping a closer eye on him. Either way, he was full of charm and presented Jonah with a new iPod Touch inside a specially made fluffy blue case. "To show you I'm a soft touch, really," he'd said.

Jonah saw the gift as another bribe, another example of the Baron's duplicity.

His resolve steeled further, and he watched carefully as the Baron took the laptop out of his briefcase and put it on the desk, attaching the cable that would connect it to the bank's network. As the Baron typed in his password, Jonah wheeled his chair back, pretending to answer some e-mails on his phone. In fact, what he'd done was activate his phone's video camera and record the keystrokes of the password. Next, while the Baron was away at meetings, he took out the identical laptop David had bought the previous day and set up the password the same as the Baron's. He would switch this laptop with the Baron's when the time came. Until the Baron actually logged on, it would appear to be his computer. After that, it would freeze thanks to a bug Jonah had installed. It might buy them some extra time.

The real key was to get the Baron away from the desk at the end of the day so that he could make the switch. David was sorting that out, but he wouldn't tell Jonah how, only that his "insider" would help.

The day progressed slowly, Jonah's anticipation of what was to come making it difficult to focus on anything else, but by a quarter past four there was still no sign of the diversion. The Baron had disappeared to yet another meeting, and Jonah had half a mind to go for it and make the switch now.

He resisted the temptation. He knew he had to wait until his father gave him the signal that their escape route was clear.

The laptop plan was risky, but not as risky as the trade he had made in an effort to secure the one hundred million dollars that Scrotycz had demanded. He had put the million pound bonus plus the rest of his savings into an all-or-nothing bet that there would be a massive crash in the stock markets. His dad could only contribute a few thousand pounds because he needed some cash to finance their getaway, and all of his company accounts had been frozen because of the investigation. Jonah knew that there was a chance, and not a small one, that they could lose all their money on this one bet, possibly more. If that happened, their lives would basically be over. Jonah comforted himself with the knowledge that if they didn't get the one hundred million, they'd be dead anyway, according to Scrotycz, so it would be irrelevant.

The light on his direct line flashed, and he punched the screen and answered, "iPod."

A smooth, vaguely familiar voice replied. "Harry Solomons here." It was Pistol. *Shoot.* What did he want?

"Oh, hello," Jonah said, trying to figure the man out. "Is there a problem?"

"No. I am phoning to advise you that I have a meeting with the Baron at five o'clock. It will go on until at least six o'clock."

Jonah couldn't figure out why he was telling him this. The Baron rarely met with the folks in Legal, and even if he did, Jonah wasn't his secretary. Suddenly it clicked: Pistol was the insider! "Oh! Thank you," Jonah said, unable to mask the appreciation in his voice.

"We shall see. Goodbye." Pistol hung up the phone.

Jonah stared at the phone as he placed it back into the base. He couldn't believe it: Pistol, the trader-hater, was the insider! It would have almost been funny if there wasn't so much at stake: Here was the man within the firm who was surreptitiously feeding information to his father, the man who was going to provide a distraction so that Jonah could execute his plan without being observed, and he was the same person whom Jonah had ignored when he'd first started on the desk. Jonah was incredulous. It was crazy to think how much had changed in so little time.

Jonah checked his watch, his mind now focused on the passage of time. There were still forty-five minutes to go until the switch. His nerves began to return. He needed to keep occupied. He stood up and walked across the trading floor, through the doors and down the escalator out of the building, deciding that he'd check the Vespa and get some coffee. The scooter was still there in its parking space on the road. Nobody had blocked him in. He went to the coffee bar at the end of Foster Lane and ordered a cappuccino. He drank it slowly and walked, just as slowly, back toward Hellcat. As he turned onto Gresham Street he came to an abrupt halt. His heart pounded, and fear began to permeate his body. There, outside the office, was a black Audi Q7.

He put his head down to hide his face, walked past the car, into the building, and straight into Scrotycz.

"Lightbody. Junior. How appropriate," came the heavily accented voice. "I have been meeting with your boss. He is a very impressive man."

Jonah said nothing.

"Yes. He will be running my money from now on. I did not know that you worked for him. Maybe this time I have the right Lightbody. Let us hope so. Enjoy your weekend."

Jonah stood aside to let him pass.

*Shoot. Shoot. Shoot.* Now what? It was five to five. The Baron might have returned to the desk to find him. He couldn't risk it. He'd have to wait. He headed to the toilets in reception and locked himself in a stall, where he messaged his father: "Scrotycz here. Met with Baron. What now?"

The reply was quick. "Don't worry. Scrotycz gone. Insider confirms Baron engaged. Collect now. Go!"

*This was it*, thought Jonah. He breathed deeply to slow his heart rate and walked swiftly back to the trading floor. The laptop was still there on the Baron's desk.

Jonah looked around to see if anyone was watching. No one was. He placed his briefcase on the desk and opened it, his fingers thick and immobile. He took out the dummy laptop and made the switch, putting the Baron's computer in his case. Then he moved fast, walking briskly out of the trading floor, down the escalator, across reception, out of the building, and to the Vespa.

He unlocked the pannier and took off his jacket, replacing it with his school coat. His father had advised him that subtle changes of appearance could make a huge difference. He put on his helmet, jammed the briefcase into the pannier, stuffed his jacket on top, closed the lid, and locked it. Once on the bike he gunned the engine and sped off.

The rendezvous point was the Bank of England on Threadneedle Street, about half a mile away. One hundred yards on he saw his father on a trail bike. He was facing the same way, but looking backward, watching the Helsby Cattermole entrance as Jonah passed him. Jonah reached Threadneedle Street, stopping under the bank's solid walls. Thirty seconds later David arrived next to him.

"All clear. Park your bike over there." David was pointing to some bays thirty yards on. "And get on the back of this one. You'll have to hold the case."

Jonah did as he was told, wedging the case between them as he climbed onto his father's bike. They accelerated powerfully away, going east toward Tower Bridge, weaving in and out of the Friday evening traffic and twice mounting the pavement to speed their progress. On past Canary Wharf they burned, Jonah hanging on tight to the briefcase and his father, craning his neck at every opportunity to see if they were being followed, his heart pumping with fear and excitement. The road was clear now, and David opened up the throttle so that Jonah had to tuck his head down until finally they slowed to enter the London City Airport parking area.

"Where are we going?" asked Jonah as they dismounted. He hadn't expected to be leaving the country immediately. He hadn't even said goodbye to Creedence.

"Amsterdam first. I need to collect some new passports." Jonah must have looked confused because David added in explanation, "I've met some *interesting* people while doing business in Russia. Some of them have connections in the underworld. I called in a favor from one of them, and the new passports are waiting in Amsterdam. Short notice job. No time to get them to us in London."

"Oh!" said Jonah. Then he whispered, "It hadn't occurred to

me that they were *those* kind of passports. Fake ones, I mean." He paused, tucking in his shirt, which was hanging out after the ride to the airport. "How long are we going for?"

David handed Jonah a small rucksack from the side panniers of the bike. As he did, Jonah noticed that he was wearing an old watch with an orange strap that had originally belonged to Jonah. He must have picked it up when he'd gone back to the house to collect the clothes in the rucksacks. "Not long," David replied, beginning to march to the check-in area. He motioned for Jonah to follow him. "We'll head to Africa from there. We need to keep moving. They're killers, remember?"

Jonah noticed that his father's eyes were shifting this way and that, scanning for any sign of a pursuer. He did the same, never relaxing until they were on the plane and on their way to Amsterdam.

# CHAPTER 33

**The Baron was** highly irritated after his meeting with Pistol. No surprise there. The man had droned on and on about the new trading controls they would have to put in place, but all the Baron really wanted to do was to check up on the boy.

He swept onto the trading floor to find it deserted. The boy's briefcase was gone as well. He phoned him. The call went straight to voicemail. He was now running late for dinner with Scrotycz. He'd try and find out more then.

He put his laptop in his case and slammed it shut. As he walked toward the doors he pulled out his phone again. "Amelia, it's me," he said as soon as she answered.

"Hello, darling," Amelia purred. "Off to see the nice Russian man, are you? What fun you will have! All that boasting and the vodka and the girls."

"I'd rather put a thistle up my arse," the Baron replied. "More importantly, I need you to get hold of that Clearwater girl."

Amelia's voice became serious. "Is there a problem?"

"I asked iPod to stay, and he's gone. His phone's also off. It shouldn't be. He knows he's on call twenty-four hours a day, seven days a week. I'm guessing he's busy getting loved up, but I want to be sure."

"Hold on, I'll call her on her home line. She's been off since Wednesday, looking after your boy, so to speak." Amelia placed the call on hold, but despite the silence on her end, the Baron carried on walking with his phone to his ear until she came back on line. "No answer on the home number," she said, her tone more declarative than apologetic. "Leave it to me; I'll find them."

It was seven P.M. when the Baron next heard from Amelia. He was in the penthouse suite of the Carstairs Hotel. It was *his* hotel. Not only did he own it, but he also used it as his primary residence. He found living there more efficient than purchasing a house. Everything was on site, and if it wasn't, there was someone to fetch or organize it for him at all hours of the day. Still, tonight the hotel didn't feel as comfortable as usual. The boy's disappearance was nagging at his mind. He had showered and was busy trying to put cufflinks on his shirt when Amelia rang the bell. He let her in.

"Still no answer from the girl," she said, charging into the room, her eyes breathing fire. "Looks like Scrotycz has put the fear of God into young iPod." She produced a pile of photographs similar to the ones David had shown Jonah on Wednesday night and slapped them down onto the dining table. "These are from the closed circuit television cameras in the Hellcat reception area and outside the building," she said.

The Baron surveyed them while continuing to struggle with his cufflinks. The photos documented Jonah's walk, his shock at seeing the Audi, and his meeting with Scrotycz.

"By the look on his face I would surmise that he wasn't very happy at seeing the Russian. The Clearwater girl did say he was terrified after the Richmond Park meeting." She placed five more photos on the table. "You'll notice that he doesn't go straight up the escalator. He goes into the loo first and comes out three minutes later, almost like he was waiting for something or . . . someone."

"Maybe he wanted to be sure Scrotycz had left?" the Baron suggested.

"Maybe," agreed Amelia. Indicating the third photograph, she added, "Then he goes upstairs and comes back almost immediately as if there's a swarm of bees chasing after him. When he leaves the building, he's running." She picked up the final photo, holding it out for the Baron to see. "This last one shows him getting on a moped thingy."

"Bloody Russian," the Baron growled. "I don't want iPod so scared that he does something stupid. He's already filed a complaint with the police, which will complicate things. We need to keep things quiet after Clive's death. Ahhh, bloody cufflinks!" he shouted in frustration as he failed again to insert the left one into his shirt.

Amelia held out her hand. "Here, give them to me."

The Baron dropped the cufflinks into her hands and stuck out his arms toward her, the cuffs now loose and covering his hands. "And what about the GPS tracker in that new iPod I gave him? Is it working? I need to know where he is," he hissed.

Amelia calmly reached toward his left arm, turned his cuff back, and started inserting the link. "The tracker will only function when the iPod is switched on. We'll receive a message as soon as it does."

The Baron grunted. "When did you last hear from the girl?" he asked.

"This morning when she phoned to say she wasn't coming in." Amelia moved to his right arm.

"But iPod *did* come in, so why didn't she? Get someone around to her flat and see if they're there. Deliver them some pizza or something. And do the same with Lightbody's house. My trader radar is saying something's not right here. And I don't like uncertainty at present."

Amelia calmly finished inserting the second cufflink. She stepped back and looked him up and down. "Okay, will do," she said at last in answer to the Baron's directives. "I'll call you if I have any news. You look fabulous by the way." She smiled. "Maybe Scrotycz will let something slip if you get him drunk enough."

In crossing the English Channel to mainland Europe, Jonah and David had gained an hour on UK time. They caught a taxi from Schiphol Airport and into central Amsterdam at what was now eight P.M.

Jonah had visited Amsterdam once before when the Baron had flown him there, by private jet, for lunch to celebrate his exam results at the beginning of the summer. It had been the hottest day of the year, and they had eaten at an expensive restaurant by the side of one of the canals. It had been fantastic, a fitting celebration to the end of a glorious school year: His exam results were in the top three of the school, and he'd shot the lights out of the markets, more than tripling his money to 426,804 pounds. They'd talked about the financial crisis that was developing, the profits the Baron was making, and the bands headlining at the various music festivals during the summer. It was this lunch and discussion that had led Jonah to take a month to travel around Europe. Afterward they'd walked along the canals in the sunshine, jackets over their shoulders, toward the Rembrandt Platz to get a taxi back to the airport.

Jonah peered out of the taxi window as they drove. The sun briefly flashed beneath a canopy of grey clouds before they entered the city, and Jonah tried to identify landmarks from his previous trip. It wasn't until they turned a corner and he saw the prostitutes in the windows that the scene became familiar. They were in the Red Light District. The Baron had insisted that Jonah couldn't come to Amsterdam without seeing this tourist attraction in particular, and he vividly recalled walking these cobblestone streets, gawking at the scene.

It was here that Jonah had had the most memorable part of his trip: meeting the man whom the Baron had said was his mentor: the Flying Dutchman, he'd called him. The man was wearing a heavy dark suit and a tie and, unlike Jonah and the Baron, did not seem to be experiencing any discomfort in the heat.

"The Flying Dutchman! I didn't think you were allowed out of Switzerland. Taxman wouldn't let you," the Baron had roared.

"We came to an agreement," the man had replied solemnly. He'd then turned to Jonah. "And who's this young man? Don't tell me you've procreated!"

Jonah had blushed, but the Baron laughed it off. "No such thing. Though if I had, I would have wanted him to be like this one," he'd said, at which Jonah had swelled with pride. "This is Jonah Lightbody, or iPod as we in the Bunker call him. Jonah, meet the Flying Dutchman. My first ever boss."

The man's hand had been massive, and when he'd shaken it Jonah had felt a large signet ring on his little finger.

They'd had a conversation about the markets and the crisis, and Jonah was surprised to discover that the Flying Dutchman was actually very interested in Jonah's opinion on these issues, making him feel important. Sadly though, the meeting had meant that Jonah's day with the Baron had come to a rapid end, and he ended up traveling back to England alone in the private jet while the two older men repaired to a hotel to catch up on old times.

Back in the present, the taxi pulled up outside a windowless building, and David turned to Jonah. "Sorry, son. The Red Light District's not really appropriate for someone of your age, but it's where I pick up the documents. We'll head to the hotel from here. I hope you're not too shocked by it all."

Jonah decided it was probably best not to tell his dad that he'd been here before. "I'm sure I'll cope," he said.

"Okay. Sit tight. I won't be long." He opened the door and got out, leaving Jonah to gawk just as he had done two and a half months previously.

David returned five minutes later with the passports, a loaded gun, and backup ammunition. He kept the latter two items hidden from his son. "We'll walk from here," he said to the driver, and to Jonah he whispered, "No point in having this taxi connecting us with the airport and the hotel."

Jonah clambered out of the car, the few belongings they'd come with in hand, and hurried along after his father. It was dark, and they walked quickly. Jonah was very conscious of the laptop in his brief-case and held it close to his body, fearing that someone might snatch it. In the background he could hear David blabbering away trying to relieve the tension. "Did you know that Amsterdam was at the center of one of the world's first financial bubbles? Yes, it was tulips back in the 1600s. It was the Dutch who created the first derivatives."

Jonah wasn't in the mood to talk.

At the hotel Jonah hung back while David checked in. He looked around the seedy lobby with its nicotine-stained walls, worn carpet, and cheap furniture. When David finished, they headed for the elevator, which was small and old, with an inner and outer door. "We're on the top floor," his father informed him, pressing the buttons. "Room 835. Can you time how long it takes to get to the top?"

"Why?"

"Might come in useful." David shrugged, and they reverted to silence until the elevator shuddered to a halt.

"Forty-eight seconds," said Jonah. "I could have run up the stairs quicker."

"Well, there they are," said David, pointing to the fire escape at the end of the corridor as he unlocked their room door. David went in first, and Jonah followed.

"I see you're keeping costs down, Dad," he said. The room was very basic, with two beds, a wardrobe, a desk, and a bathroom. It looked old and tired, in keeping with the rest of the hotel.

"I chose the hotel for its location, not its quality," David answered. "It's built in the middle of a single block, which means there will be at least four possible ways out should we have visitors. It also has a fast, free Internet connection." David paused. "And besides, you know as well as I do where most of our money is right now."

Jonah nodded. It was strange to him that he'd been given a million pounds and yet in a way he was poorer than he'd been previously due to the Scrotycz bet. "What about food?" he asked, throwing his bag on the bed. He wasn't trying to be indignant, but his stomach was growling. He hadn't eaten on the plane. "It doesn't look like the type of place that does room service."

"I'm going to go out and check all the exits in a minute. There's a Hard Rock Cafe nearby. I could get takeout."

"That'll do. Double cheeseburger with chips, please. I'll get started on the laptop."

David left the room, and Jonah took the laptop out from the case and placed it on the desk. He opened it, pressed the "start" button, input the password he'd memorized, and waited for computer to fire up. When it did, the desktop was blank, and the dock at the bottom displayed only the usual programs—Word, Excel, PowerPoint, iTunes, Firefox, Bloomberg, and the Hellcat system link.

He went into Finder and clicked on "applications." Again, all the usual suspects, but nothing that indicated a link into the servers in Amelia's Boudoir. He looked in the documents folder, but that was empty. He checked the contacts. That was empty as well. The calendar offered the same story. Jonah knew that it was possible that the link was through the Hellcat system, but he didn't want to go in there yet in case it alerted someone. And anyway, the trades had to be *outside* the Hellcat interface. Hellcat had already investigated those trades and come up with nothing.

*Okay, Baron,* thought Jonah, *I am going to take your laptop to pieces bit by bit. I will find it if it is there. And it is here. I know it is. We'll start at A for address book.*

When David came back with the burgers and coffee, Jonah explained the situation. Upon hearing of his son's lack of progress, David opened his hands. "I can be of no help, I'm afraid. I wouldn't even have gotten as far as you have. Do you mind if I get some sleep?"

Jonah was fine with that. Having someone sitting on his shoulder would be irritating anyway. "Okay by me. You stick to your hotel floorplans and elevators; I'll do the clever work."

# CHAPTER 34

**The Baron and** Scrotycz had finished their dinner and were in a private club in Soho that provided "company" in the form of young ladies without many clothes on. There was a bar and a dance floor with a series of dark, secluded booths located around its perimeter. If you saw a girl you liked, you asked her to join you for a drink. She would request champagne at hugely inflated prices and give the buyer her undivided attention. Depending on the buyer and the quality of the champagne, the level of that undivided attention would vary.

For the Baron and Scrotycz it was now *mano a mano*—one on one—two alpha males competing over their capacity for alcohol and their attractiveness to women. Of course, the game was loaded. The three stunning Eastern European girls draping themselves over Scrotycz had been prepaid for by Hellcat.

The Baron was in the company of a striking Chinese girl. She was also on the Hellcat payroll, but the company's arrangement with her was different from the way that it usually hired strippers. Her job was to flirt with Scrotycz, or whomever the Baron happened to be wining and dining, and keep the vodka and champagne flowing, to make it a party. She had worked with the Baron for nearly a year now, specially selected by Amelia, and was a genuine courtesan—beautiful, witty, and intelligent. In the morning when Scrotycz woke up with his hangover and his one, two, or three blonde bimbettes, he would be a happy man. But still he would think of Kim, the girl who he'd believe had gone home with the Baron. Of course she wouldn't have—the Baron didn't do hookers—but Scrotycz would be hung over and jealous enough to think otherwise. It was a straight power game, convincing him that the Baron had something he couldn't have.

That was some time hence though. For now it was a game of who could drink the most vodka. Scrotycz had to win this one. That was the only way that the Baron could extract the information he wanted from him. But he had to believe he had won it fair and square. Again, normally this was fairly easy to engineer. After a bottle of vodka even the most hardened drinkers would struggle to have any grip on reality. Scrotycz, however, was a whole other level of drinker, and the Baron was struggling, despite the fact that Kim had arranged for every other shot of his to be water. His phone rang as Scrotycz called for the third bottle of ice-cold alcohol.

The Baron staggered to his feet. "I must take this call. New York office," he lied and went out to the street and its relative silence.

"There is nobody at the girl's flat or at Lightbody's house," Amelia said bluntly.

"So where the hell are they?" This was not what he wanted to hear.

"I don't know. Yet. What news from Scrotycz?" she asked, deftly moving the issue away from her own lack of success.

"Scrotycz is an animal, and as far as his dealings with Lightbody or the boy are concerned he's been as tight as a gnat's arse. I can't seem to get anything out of him. I'm beginning to wonder if we need Kim to go above and beyond her normal duties. It might, at the very least, get me out of the third bottle of that rocket fuel you imported." Amelia had seen to it that the vodka Scrotycz had been given was his most favored brand from his homeland in a remote valley in the Ural Mountains.

"My God, darling, I only have three behind the bar, you poor, poor dear. I'm sure Kim will oblige. I will solve."

The Baron went back inside and stood at the table, swaying slightly, feigning total inebriation. "Scrot . . . itch, I must depart. It has been a most magnifishent evening," he slurred, going for maximum effect. "But I must . . . bid you . . . adieu. I have an issue in the USh that needs my attention."

Scrotycz remained seated, a blonde on either side and one on his knee. "My dear Baron, magnifishent is an under . . . statement. I have never . . . ordered a third bottle . . . before. I would get up if I could . . . but I am not sure it will be posshible."

"Shcrot. Kim here"—she tucked herself under the Baron's arm—"can help anyone up. I shuggesht that you enlisht her help." He winked theatrically, and Scrotycz's eyes lit up despite the effects of the vodka. "She fanshies you more anyway." He lifted his arm up to release her.

"I feel that we will . . . work well together," slurred Scrotycz. He raised his glass, saying something that sounded to the Baron like "ypa."

"Ypa to you too, Scrot mate," said the Baron raising only his hand. He turned and made his way to his waiting car and slumped into the back seat, one thought raging in his mind: *Where the hell was that boy?*

# CHAPTER 35
## Saturday, September 20

**"That boy" had** finally staggered into bed, exhausted, at about three in the morning, no wiser as to the link that would take him into the Baron's private files. He was woken by his father at eight with coffee and croissants and was immediately back at the laptop. His dad was visibly very tense, and it wasn't helping. Jonah could hear him in the background, keeping himself busy by organizing the car and flights for the afternoon. Still, every five minutes he would ask for a progress update. It had been better when he'd been asleep. Jonah decided to shut him out with music. He extracted the new iPod Touch from his briefcase, discarding the fluffy blue casing, and plugged noise-reducing headphones into his ears.

In London the Baron and Amelia both received a message at the same time. It was the one they'd been waiting for, from the Global Positioning control center in Greenwich. They now knew that Jonah was in Amsterdam. They even had the address of the hotel.

The Baron was practically salivating as he ushered Amelia and Kim the stripper into his study—they were there to update him on Scrotycz—and dispatched Jez from IT to the sitting room to sort out his laptop, which had crashed when he'd switched it on this morning. He sat himself down at his desk across from the two women. "So what's the story with Scrotycz and the boy?" he asked Kim, leaving all pleasantries aside. Part of him wondered whether she actually had any clothing on under her mid-thigh-length fur coat. There was no visible evidence to suggest this was the case.

"The boy is in a tough spot. Probably scared witless," Kim said as if reporting some minor change in the weather. "Scrotycz has told him and his father that he will kill them if they don't give him one hundred million dollars in thirty days."

*Well, that would explain the boy's disappearance*, thought the Baron. One hundred million dollars in thirty days was an impossible ask. No wonder the boy was on the run. The big question was whether this was the only thing he was running from. "Do you think he *would* kill them?" he asked.

"Definitely," came the instant reply. "He is not a nice man. He likes to hurt people." Kim shook her head as if remembering a detail from the night before that was too painful to discuss. Amelia leaned over and placed her hand on the girl's knee to comfort her, and Kim hurriedly added, "No, no not me. He was nice to me. He wants me to go to a football match with him today. It was the other girls he was not so nice to."

"He wants to spend time with you, does he?" The Baron ran his fingers thoughtfully through his mustache. "Has he said for how long?"

"No, but it will be as long as I want it to be. It always is." She smiled sweetly.

"Naturally." The Baron grinned. "Stay with him if you would be so kind, and feed back anything else you find out." He turned to Amelia. "Make sure Kim is properly rewarded for her troubles, will you?" He didn't want to run the risk that Scrotycz might somehow start paying her more and therefore cause her to switch allegiances.

"Of course," said Amelia. "Thank you, Kim. Let me show you out. Ask the concierge for a car to take you to wherever you want to go." She stood up and escorted Kim out of the study while the Baron formulated his next move.

When she returned, the Baron began barking orders her way before she had even sat down. "We need someone watching that hotel *now*. We need to find out why he is there and who he is with. If Scrotycz finds out he's run, he might go after him. And we can't have him being killed." The Baron paused as he thought about how attached he'd grown to the boy over the years. He took a deep breath. He couldn't let his personal feelings impact the mission. There was too much at stake. He resumed his tirade. "If his death comes so quickly on the heels of Clive's, we are going to have the police crawling all over us."

"Yes, darling," Amelia said with a sigh. "I already have some muscle organized. They'll be at the hotel in"—she looked at her watch—"the next . . ."

There was a timid knock on the door. The Baron put his finger to his lips, signaling for Amelia to be quiet. "Come in," he called, and the man from IT pushed himself through the door, holding the laptop. "All sorted?" asked the Baron brightly.

"This isn't your laptop," the man replied.

The Baron's face froze for a second, and Amelia swung around in her chair. "What do you mean?" he demanded.

"It's not your laptop," Jez repeated. "The serial number is different. I checked. This is a brand new computer. There's nothing on it except a bug that makes it crash as soon as it's switched on." As an afterthought he added, "And if you used your password to get into it, then whoever's got your laptop also has your log-in."

The Baron sat impassively at his desk, trying to keep his anger in check: *The boy wasn't just on the run from Scrotycz; he had stolen the laptop! He had turned!*

"What can they do with that information?" he snapped.

"They can get into the Hellcat trading system pretty easily. And they could theoretically get into your personal servers, although the security on that is rather imaginative, so it's less likely," Jez replied.

The Baron grunted. "Well, you'd better change my access to the trading system immediately, and we'll need to do the same with my personal files. Can you do it from here?"

"I can do the Hellcat changes from here, but not the personal ones," said Jez. "I'll need to go back to the office for that. I can only do it by plugging a laptop straight into the servers." He looked at Amelia. "I'll need you to let me into your office."

Amelia nodded. "Why don't you sort out the Hellcat issues while the Baron and I finish off? We won't be long."

"Okay," said Jez, and he closed the door.

The Baron waited a couple of seconds for Jez to be completely out of earshot and then snarled through clenched teeth. "They're

together. We've been outsmarted by a Drizzler, a boy, and a bimbo."
He channeled his anger into single-minded focus, still in shock that
*he* of all people had been so clearly betrayed—and by a child. "Everything is on those servers. You and I are going to Amsterdam to bring
them back. Get a plane and do it fast and put a rocket up the arse
of that muscle in Amsterdam. They must not lose them."

"Yes, dar . . ." Amelia started, but the Baron cut in, pointing his
finger at her.

"And Kloot doesn't need to know. Okay? He'll only get over-
excited and complicate things. We can sort this out on our own."
The last thing the Baron wanted was for the Flying Dutchman to
discover that the boy *he* recruited had morphed into Apollyon's
greatest liability.

"Of course, darling. Let me go and let that Jez boy into your
servers, and I will call you with flight details. Stay calm. We'll have
this all cleared up by this evening." She stood up, blew him a kiss,
and marched out of the study. By the time she had reached the
car, she had a private aircraft organized to depart from Northolt
Jet Center, only twelve miles away from the Carstairs Hotel. They
would be in the air in half an hour and on the ground in Amsterdam
fifty minutes after that.

# CHAPTER 36

"**iTunes! It must** be iTunes!" Jonah exclaimed, suddenly remembering something Amelia had told him that day in her Boudoir: *The Baron's hard drive . . . he likes me to look after it for him.* She had said that on it was the Baron's complete music collection *amongst other things.* What other reason could there be for her to manage it?

David jumped up from the bed in surprise. "What's going on?" he asked.

Jonah twisted and looked around at him, pulling the earphones out of his ears. "The link's in iTunes. It has to be. He downloads music from the servers in Amelia's office to his laptop. iTunes is the access route."

"Go on then," David urged, "look."

Jonah opened up the music library on the laptop again. He had marveled at the extent of it last night, even though he knew it only represented a fraction of the Baron's holdings. *Where was the link hidden?* He scrolled down the menu.

There were fourteen thousand songs on the library taking up sixty-six gigs of memory, one hundred videos taking up forty gigs, and one app taking up a whole gig of memory. Jonah paused, his hand hovering above the track pad. *That couldn't be right!* Apps took up megabytes not gigabytes.

He clicked on the app. It was a relatively simple music trivia quiz. Why did that require so much memory? "This app is supposed to be a music quiz, but it's too big for that," he said to his father. "There must be something behind it." He moved the cursor over the app icon.

"Click on it! Click on it!" David exclaimed impatiently.

"No. Wait," said Jonah, looking up. "We need to connect to the Internet. If this goes straight through, we'll need to be ready or we might get shut out." He cleared the iPod and headphones off the table and put them in the briefcase. Then he plugged in the hotel Ethernet cable. "Ready?"

"Ready," said David.

Jonah clicked on the app and a new window opened.

*YOU HAVE TEN SECONDS TO ANSWER THE FOLLOW-ING QUESTIONS.*

"No Googling. Smart," said Jonah.

Question One: Who was God?

"I thought this was a music quiz, not a test of religious philosophy," said David, as Jonah typed in CLAPTON.

*CORRECT*, the system replied.

"Dad, you need to shut it unless you've got the answer. It's a famous piece of graffiti from the 1960s—Clapton is God."

Question Two: Which band is worth fifteen pounds?

Again Jonah was straight on it: COMMODORES

*CORRECT*

There was complete quiet now in the hotel room. Jonah focused on the laptop with David on his shoulder.

Question Three: Who were losing their religion?

REM

*CORRECT*

The window dissolved to say *WELL DONE*.

"Well, that was easy," said David.

*NOW ON TO LEVEL TWO*

"No. There's more," said Jonah before rapidly answering three more questions correctly.

The window dissolved again, coming back with: *YOU COULD BE ME BUT I'M NOT SURE. WHY DON'T YOU TRY THREE QUESTIONS MORE?*

Once again Jonah managed to answer the questions correctly. Jonah's music education at the hands of the Baron had backfired on his teacher.

The window disappeared completely, leaving the desktop image of a blank screen and the toolbar below. "What's happened? We got them all right," said David, worried.

"Relax, Dad. Look at the toolbar at the bottom. There's a new icon." Jonah put his finger on a shield with a red triplane—the same image he'd seen on the Baron's stationery and as part of the training tool the Baron had given him so many moons ago. "That's the link!" said Jonah excitedly. "That's the access point."

"Let's go! Let's go!" yelled David.

"Patience, Dad. I'm going to change the security settings first so that anyone else who attempts to enter is blocked. I'll also be able to see if someone else is trying to get in."

"Do it, Jonah. Just do it." His father was now highly agitated.

Jonah's fingers clattered across the keyboard as he put a new layer over the Baron's trivia quiz. When he finished he immediately clicked on the shield, holding his breath as a window came up saying, "Connecting to server." The screen went blank for a moment and came back as a universe-like image of stars and space. In the middle was a new window with a whole new set of files.

Jonah's breath quickened. They were into the Baron's servers.

"All right!" David exclaimed. He slapped his son five, grinning. Getting a hold of himself, he said, "Right. Find those files. I'm going to go downstairs to sort out the car. Ring me if there is any sign of anything strange."

"Hold on," Jonah replied. He took an envelope out of the briefcase and handed it to his father. "It has the Vespa keys inside. Can you mail it to Creedence? I've asked her to pick it up." The envelope included a more personal letter as well, but that was private and not worth mentioning to his dad. David hesitated, and for a moment Jonah thought he was going to say he should maintain his silence with her. "It doesn't say where we're going next," he added.

His father nodded and took the envelope. "Understood," he said and headed out of the room.

The Baron was in the back of a chauffeured Mercedes, speeding toward the Northolt Jet Center along the A40. Jez the IT man was on the other end of the phone.

"What do you mean password? There is no password. You know that."

"Well, there is now. Which means someone's altered the security."

"How could they have done that?"

Jez gave a nervous cough. "By cracking the original defense mechanisms."

The Baron jerked the phone away from his ear as if it had burned him. This was now getting very serious. There was another level of security to be broken before anyone could reach his trading records, but nobody was supposed to be able to get this far. "Can you shut the whole thing down? Pull the plug or something?" he said, trying to stay composed.

"Won't work. Do you remember how you wanted this set up? Bombproof, hurricane proof, the lot. It's a sealed unit with its own backup power and wireless telecom system. I can pull the plug, but the thing will still run for three more days. The only way is to go in and remove the files directly."

"Well pull the bloody plug and find the password," the Baron commanded. He then killed the call and dialed Amelia. "Where are you? I'm nearly there," he barked. "Looks like they're into the first level of the files. Tell those goons of yours not to let them leave that hotel." He was about to hang up when he added, "And I'm going to need a gun."

David identified the first of Amelia's "muscle" as soon as he stepped out of the elevator. He was a big man in a black leather jacket, sitting in the lobby pretending to read a newspaper. When David walked past him, the man stood up and followed him outside, confirming David's assessment: They had been found. He became conscious of the gun in the waistband of his trousers, pressing against his back. He walked left and left again around the hotel toward the street of shops that bordered the block to the south.

The man followed.

*This was good*, David thought. It meant that he was an observer—here to follow, not approach. The question was: How many more were there?

David passed a parked car, a dark blue Mercedes, its driver wearing sunglasses despite the fact that the sun was nowhere to be seen. *Observer number two*, thought David. He walked on without stopping, finding a small supermarket on the corner. He went in and bought a newspaper and stamps for Jonah's letter, which he also mailed. The big man loitered outside, and David decided that he couldn't risk collecting the car. He'd have to do that just before they went to the airport. He'd call the rental company when he was back in the room and tell them he was going to be in a rush. He exited the shop and carried on his stroll around the building, endeavoring to maintain a casual air so that the men who'd been assigned to watch them didn't notice that *he* was now scoping *them* out. At the next corner the leather-jacketed man turned back, but up ahead David spied another man, standing by the rear entrance of the hotel: *observer number three*. David walked past him, and sure enough he picked up the tail and followed along the east side of the hotel until David turned the final corner. There, leather-jacket man was waiting to shepherd him back into the main entrance of the hotel.

*So there were three of them*, David thought, one of whom was in a vehicle. They would have to escape through the east fire escape and would need a backup plan in case they didn't manage a clean getaway. He called the elevator and headed up to the eighth floor.

Jonah's anxiety levels were high now. He had hoped to see a big file saying "Trading Records" or something similar. Instead there were thousands of files with only a vague system to organize them. He'd tried searching files by date to see if anything came up from the last few days. Nothing. He'd tried searching the name "Allegro Home Finance." Again nothing. He was trying "Lightbody" when a red light started flashing in the top right hand corner of his screen and his father returned. He swung around. "They've found out about the laptop, Dad."

"How do you know?" said David, coming over to look at the computer screen.

"See the light? Someone else is trying to get in."

"Well, I guess we knew that would happen at some point. Good thing you reset the security," he said, an air of calmness about him that helped soothe Jonah's nerves. "Anyway, how are you getting on?"

"Nothing yet," Jonah answered.

"Well, keep plugging away. I need to call the car company and my contact in Africa, Once I've done that we'll decide when to move on."

Jonah jerked his head up. "We can't leave until we've found the files, Dad. My security won't last forever, and once they get through, we'll be shut out."

"Oh," said David, still calm. "I see. Well, I know you'll find it. Now let me make those calls." He started walking to the other side of the room to give each of them a modicum of privacy when he hesitated and turned back to Jonah. "Can I borrow your corporate credit card? I reckon it could speed up our progress through the airport when we get there, and even if the Baron traces it, he won't work out where we are going."

Jonah handed David his Black American Express card, noting his father's raised eyebrows and thinking about how weird it was that at long last his dad was showing confidence in him. It only took a false accusation, a scary bunch of Russians, and being forced to run for their lives. Jonah snorted. So that was all he had needed to forge the beginnings of a relationship with his father: the prospect of death!

After another half an hour of searching, Jonah still hadn't found anything. He could hear that his father had finished on the phone, so he called him over. "Dad," Jonah said, "I need a new set of eyes on this. Maybe you can see something that I can't?"

David came over and took Jonah's place in front of the screen while Jonah poured himself another cup of coffee and stretched.

"What am I looking for?"

"I'm not entirely sure," said Jonah. "Where would you put something you didn't want found?" He took a sip of his coffee.

"I'd put it in the safe in my study," David reasoned aloud. "No, I wouldn't. I'd put it in a bank's safe. One of those Swiss banks that are famed for their privacy." He stared at the screen. "Is there a digital equivalent of a Swiss bank safety deposit box?"

Jonah took another sip of coffee. "There are places that will host your servers, but I don't think there's a specific high-security hosting service. Unless you count the military or the Secret Service, but

I doubt they rent out space to people somehow. . . ." As he said it, an idea sparked in his brain: *The military? The Baron. Baron von Richthofen. That could be it!* "Here, let me sit down again," he said, putting his coffee cup on the desk and pushing his father out of the seat.

"What is it? What is it?" demanded David impatiently.

In the dock at the bottom of the screen was an icon of a red triplane. Jonah had seen it many times before. It was the icon for the Baron's personally designed video game, the one that he'd given him in the case with the letter "A" on it. Over the last four years Jonah had played it hundreds of times, but never managed to beat the Baron. He'd always thought that it was fixed in some way.

"What are you doing?" David inquired.

"I'm going to see if his files are protected by the military. The iTunes quiz was set up with answers only the Baron would know, theoretically. I think he's put the files somewhere where only he, as his avatar Baron von Richthofen, can fly."

The game appeared on the screen, providing the usual choices of: "New recruit," "English Dumkompf," or "Manfred Albrecht Freiherr von Richthofen." This time Jonah chose von Richthofen. The screen rotated and came up with a list of missions. This was new. He scrolled down, weighing his options: "Champagne Charlie Carnage," "Eton Rifle Ruckus," "Hooray Henry Horror," the list went on. It was basic stuff, but the theme was clear, save for one: "Prophet and Schloss." *Was it a play on profit and loss?* Jonah hit the button quickly, reckoning he had to behave like the Baron, which meant minimal hesitation. The screen faded out and came back with a scene of pilots running toward various planes parked in a field, the red Fokker at the front.

The game began.

Jonah went into a zone of complete focus as he maneuvered the Fokker and shot his opponents out of the sky, one by one. He was flying the Baron's plane and using the skills the Baron taught him to literally beat him at his own game. It felt bittersweet. It didn't take long for him to eliminate all of the opposing pilots, except one, who was standing on the ground waving his hands in supplication; his plane had been winged and forced to crash land. But somehow Jonah's screen started to fade, his life draining away. *Why was he dying? What had he missed?* He took a deep breath. He couldn't simply think like the Baron; he had to *be* the Baron. His mind raced. *What would he do?* He would take no prisoners.

*That was it!* The pilot on the ground had to die! Jonah turned the plane around and bore down on the figure below, who started to run.

The pilot might as well have stayed in place. Any attempts at escape were too little, too late; Jonah had him in his sights. He fired and the pilot was ripped to pieces by the force of the bullets from the machine gun. Jonah held his breath. *Was he right?* The screen strengthened again, and the plane began to fly on its own, low toward some heavily forested hills where Jonah could see a castle. The plane circled the massive structure once and then landed on a grass runway and came to a halt. The von Richthofen character stepped out and removed his leather helmet as he walked toward the huge door. He pushed the door open, and the image before Jonah faded back to the regular desktop.

Jonah's eyes flicked across the screen. There, on the right, was a new hard disk icon named "Schloss," the German word for castle. He breathed deeply, in through his nose and out through his mouth, suddenly aware of his father leaning over his shoulder.

"You've done it, my boy. You've cracked it, you bloody genius!" He banged Jonah on the back in excitement.

Jonah breathed out even more deeply. This was no time for self-congratulation; he had to keep going. "Do you want to look at it first or download it straight away?" he asked his dad as the intruder alert began flashing up in the top right hand corner once again.

"Download it, don't you think? How long will it take?"

Jonah clicked the icon, revealing a single unnamed folder. He dragged the folder onto the desktop and the download window popped up. "Fourteen minutes," he answered and stood up to stretch.

His father came over to him and put his hands on his shoulders, looking him in the eye. "That was great work there, Jonah. Great work. I'm going to go and bring the car round to the east exit. As soon as the download is complete, we're going to run again."

Jonah nodded. None of this came as a surprise.

"There's more," continued David. "The hotel is being watched. When I went for a walk, I saw three heavies."

Jonah tensed up.

"That's why we're using the east exit. It's not covered. I'm going to go out of the fire escape so that they don't see me. If they believe that we are still in the room, they won't move. However"—he dropped his hands from Jonah's shoulders and reached behind his back—"there is a small chance that someone will come up while I am out."

Jonah's eyes widened with horror at what he saw next: his father reaching behind his back and producing a gun that must have been tucked into his trousers.

"I'm going to give you this," he said, holding the gun flat in the palm of his hand. "It came with the passports. They won't expect you to be armed, so it will give you an advantage. All you do is release the safety catch"—he flicked it across with his thumb, and then back again—"pull the trigger, and aim for the chest. Head shots are only for the movies."

Jonah stood stock still.

"Take it, Jonah," said David, his voice low, "for your protection."

Jonah reached out and took the gun. The reality of their situation returned. They were on the run, hunted by killers. He felt his father's thumbs dig into his flesh.

"Do you understand, Jonah?"

# CHAPTER 37

**A few minutes** after David Lightbody exited the hotel via the east side fire escape, a taxi drew up at the main entrance. Inside were the Baron and Amelia. Amelia paid the driver, and the two of them walked casually around the corner to where the blue Mercedes was parked. The Baron climbed into the front passenger seat. Amelia sat directly behind the driver.

"Good afternoon," said the driver politely.

"Do you have the gun?" the Baron replied, this being no time for small talk.

The man handed over a Heckler & Koch pistol with a silencer that the Baron put straight into the pocket of his leather coat.

"And the bike?" Again, it was the Baron speaking.

"It is in front of the hotel," said the driver, handing over the keys.

"Give them to her," said the Baron.

Amelia's slender fingers reached forward between the two seats.

"Any movement?"

"Only the father this morning. The boy has not left the room."

"You are sure it is them?" asked the Baron. He wanted to be certain that there were no mistakes.

"Quite sure. The concierge matched the photographs. Room 835."

"Okay. I am going straight in. I will bring the boy out of the fire escape there?" He pointed to the exit next to them on the west wall of the hotel.

"Correct," said the driver.

"And you have the address to meet afterward?"

"I do."

"Good. Tell your man at the front to come up to the room if I am not down in five minutes." He turned to Amelia. "Go to the bike and get it ready to go."

The Baron and Amelia stepped out of the car—the Baron striding into the hotel through the west fire escape; Amelia heading back around to the main entrance. The driver followed her rear view keenly until she disappeared around the corner. He radioed through the Baron's instructions to the big man in reception. As he did, a small, grey car drew up behind him. He watched in his mirror as a man wearing a baseball cap got out of the car and walked toward him. He was holding a map. *A lost tourist*, thought the driver. The man knocked on his window, and the driver lowered it, ready to provide directions. *Probably wanting to know about how to get to the Rijksmuseum*, he thought.

As the window came down, David Lightbody's left hand flashed inside and grabbed the driver by the throat, pinning him back against the seat. The driver tore at the hand, trying to pull it away, but the grip was too strong. David brought his right hand onto the driver's face, covering his mouth as he squeezed hard on the carotid artery in his neck. The driver struggled for a moment and then fell limp, unconscious. David withdrew from the window and removed his baseball cap, placing it on the driver's head, bill pulled down so that the driver looked asleep. He returned to his car and drove on to the end of the street and around to the front of the building.

A flash of blonde hair caught his eye. He did a double take. It was Amelia, standing next to a motorbike and sidecar, putting on a helmet. *What?* If she was here, then . . .

David put his foot down on the accelerator and turned quickly onto the road running up the east side of the building. He parked the car illegally and sprinted to the fire exit and up the stairs. He could hear the sound of running feet reverberating through the enclosed space: one set fast and light, another set much slower and heavier. He pushed harder up the stairs. The lighter set of feet suddenly stopped to be replaced by a series of heavy thumps. He turned the corner of the stairs and saw Jonah on his knees above him. "Go, go, go!" he mouthed at his son as he ran past him.

"Gun!" shouted Jonah.

David looked up again. There was a man on the landing above: the big man from reception, and he had a gun in his hand! David bent his legs and propelled himself toward the man, his right arm outstretched, his hand aiming for the man's throat. He felt his fingers crash into the man's windpipe, and he rolled his shoulder so that his momentum brought the man down and the gun spilled to the floor. He was now on top of the man, his hand around his throat. Without thinking, he brought his head down hard into the man's face, feeling the cheekbone collapse under the impact. He rolled off the man, who lay unconscious on the floor, leaped back up to his feet, and ran back down the stairs, sweeping up the fallen gun and propelling Jonah downward toward the fire exit and out onto the street. He unlocked the car as he ran, directing Jonah toward the passenger door. Once they were both inside and the engine was started, he drove hard to the end of the road, through the red traffic light, and into the rush of cars heading east.

Jonah sat shaking in the passenger seat, unable to speak. He'd just watched his father smash another man's face, possibly killing him. But that was nothing compared to what he'd done: He had shot *the Baron*. He'd seen the mustache and the familiar eyes, and he'd shot him—the man who had been his mentor—as his father had told him to do.

Jonah's senses were in complete overload: his ears roaring, his eyes seeing only the flash of color as they weaved in and out of the traffic, his nose full of the smell of the gunshot, his mouth tasting of vomit. He felt his father's hand touch his arm and heard his voice somewhere in the background.

"You've got to hold it together, Jonah. We're not out of this yet." David's tone was surprisingly calm and assuring. "Tell me what happened up there. Was it the Baron?"

Jonah tried to breathe deeply, gasping at first but slowly bringing himself back under control. "Yyess," he stuttered. "He bbbroke down the door. I shot him. I tthought I killed him, but I waited for the ddddownload before running aaand he woke up." He looked across at his father, expecting to be reprimanded for not running immediately.

For a moment David took his eye off the road and looked straight at his son. "You did well, Jonah," he said comfortingly. "You did very well." He focused back on the traffic around him. "Now, we're going to have to dump this car."

"What! Why?" exclaimed Jonah. The Honda Civic felt like a security blanket to him after the events of the last few minutes—small, mobile. With his father driving, it felt safe.

"If we take the car, we'll have to park it in a garage at the airport," David continued. "I saw Amelia back there with a motorbike and sidecar. If they're still on us, we'll be dead bait with how long that would take." He took a deep breath. "There is a taxi-only drop-off area at the airport, guarded by the antiterrorism police. It'll offer us protection. Now put the laptop in the briefcase. It's in the backseat."

David took a sharp left and began a series of evasive turns and changes of speed that would reveal any pursuer. Satisfied, he swung the car into an underground parking lot. "Have you got the gun?" he asked Jonah when he had parked the sedan. "We need to get rid of it too. We can't exactly take guns on the plane."

Jonah took the weapon out of his coat pocket and handed it over. His father wiped it clean of fingerprints and wrapped it in a plastic bag, adding in the gun he had been carrying in his own pocket. They made their way on foot to the street, and David dropped the guns in a garbage bin at the lot's exit. Once above ground he hailed a taxi to Schiphol Airport.

The taxi pulled away, and Jonah put the briefcase on his lap and opened it up. He wanted to see if the download had been successful. He ran his hand over the track pad, aware that his father was watching his every movement intently. The screen came to life. "Download completed," read Jonah. "Looks like we got it all," he said and heard his father exhale with relief.

"Well done. Very well done. Okay. Shut it down and put it away."

Jonah pressed the button to shut the laptop down properly. As he waited for the computer to complete the process, he saw that the new iPod was still playing. He switched it off and shut the case.

Less than 500 yards back, hidden behind a white transit van, the dot on the Baron's telephone disappeared. "Too late, lad," he said. "I have visual."

# CHAPTER 38

**The taxi climbed** the approach road to Schiphol Airport, over one of the runways, where a KLM Boeing 747 was parked on the right, and swung left and down toward the terminal buildings. "Which airline, sir?" asked the driver.

"British Airways," replied David. "Can you do me a favor though? There's been a problem with the booking, so can you drop us at the first door and then drive to the end and wait? We might have to switch to a charter. Here's a hundred euros. If we're not out within three minutes it means everything is fine, in which case keep the change and have a Heineken on me." David handed over two fifty-euro notes to the driver, who nodded.

They were now at the barrier leading to the taxi slipway. A policeman stood by, his machine gun pointed downward. The barrier opened for them, and they drove through.

Jonah was once more impressed at his father's foresight. It seemed that he had covered every possible detail in planning their escape. All other vehicles had to drop off on the road set back from the terminal entrances. He was about to say something to this effect, when David leaned over and started talking quietly in his ear. "Get out of the car on my side and follow me. They may have someone inside the airport. When we get inside, we're going to turn immediately left to reach some stairs. We are going down those stairs. Try and keep the same pace as the other people inside. Anybody watching will be looking for unusual movement."

Jonah nodded and climbed out of the taxi after his father, walking with him toward the revolving doors. A car horn suddenly blasted behind them. Jonah turned without thinking and saw a motorbike and sidecar weaving through the cars, trying to find a parking place. His pulse began to race. The blonde hair of the driver and the hefty build of the helmeted figure in the side car left no doubt as to the identity of the newcomers. "It's them," he gasped. He felt his father grab his hand and squeeze it tight, almost hurting him.

"Don't run," David hissed. "They haven't seen us yet. If we run, they will." They entered the terminal building, a maze of check-in desks in front of them, and ducked left, walking briskly to meld in with the crowd. A sign above indicated stairs downward to terminals one and two and the railway station. They reached the stairs, and Jonah glanced behind to see the Baron and Amelia burst into the hall, instantly confused by the mass of people and desks.

"Now run," said David. "Run!" And down the stairs they flew, out of the Baron's sight and into a long straight corridor about one hundred yards long. Jonah pulled slightly ahead and heard his father shout, "Go up the stairs on the left. Our taxi should be waiting outside."

Jonah sprinted up the stairs, three at a time, sidestepping a woman carrying a baby, and pushed through another revolving door and back out into the open, his father right behind him. He saw the taxi, ran toward it, and climbed into the backseat. David climbed in after him, causing him to have to shift along the seat. The taxi driver turned, bemused and awaiting further instructions.

"What a cockup," David said to the driver, panting. "We're going to have to take a private charter. Can you whip us around to the charter terminal as quickly as possible? How far is it?"

"Ten minutes," replied the driver.

"Should be okay. The quicker the better."

Jonah looked out of the rear windshield as the taxi pulled away. The Baron never appeared.

Within twenty-five minutes Jonah and David were in the air onboard a Beechcraft King Air bound for Frankfurt, Germany. The booking was in the name of a company called "Pathways to the Sun," paid for with Jonah's Black American Express card, and the only two passengers on the flight were South Africans by the names of Harry Swanepoel and Eric Botha, according to their passports. But of course, that wasn't who they were, not in the slightest.

From Frankfurt they would be going to Namibia in Africa—and safety. Or at least that was the hope. . . .

# Part Four

# *NAMIBIA AND ZURICH*

# CHAPTER 39
## Sunday, September 21

**Air Namibia flight** 286 to Windhoek from Frankfurt landed four minutes late at eight forty-four A.M. on Sunday, September 21. Jonah still couldn't believe that they'd come to Namibia of all places to escape. To think that a place where his dad had known such violence could actually offer safe refuge, that it could be safer than their home in London, was mind blowing to Jonah.

Upon arriving, Jonah and his father filed into a Toyota HiLux Twin Cab on their way to meet with Chippy, the Shona tracker who had helped David escape from Rhodesia after the slaughter of the children. He, too, had left the country when the war ended and now used his tracking and military skills on a conservation farm in Namibia.

At the beginning of the drive Jonah had been awake and alert, taking in their new surroundings. But the lack of sleep on the plane and the monotonous straightness of the road soon led him to close his eyes. He only woke once they left the smooth tarmac after a further two hundred and forty miles of driving. Blinking quickly to clear the sleep from his eyes, he saw that they were now maneuvering along a wide, red sand road flanked on both sides by a high wire fence. Behind the fence was a landscape of grass and bushes, patchworked with low, flat-topped trees and occasional kopjes of rock. Everything was tinged with the red of the sand.

"Are we nearly there?" he asked his father, who, despite having the air conditioning on full blast, had the window rolled down and seemed to be enjoying the heat and dust coming through the opening.

"Not far now," David replied and pointed out the window. "This fence marks the perimeter of the game conservation farm we're going to. I'm looking for the gate. Here, let's ask—aha!" David's face brightened.

Jonah looked ahead to see who or what had caught his father's attention. There was a black man squatting by the side of the road. He got to his feet as they drew up next to him, and Jonah could see that he was tall, dressed in khaki shorts and a short-sleeved shirt. He had a light beard around his chin and two parallel scars across his nose and left cheek. The most distinguishing feature was the man's eyes. They were yellow. Like a leopard's.

David stuck his head out the window, but before he could speak, the man greeted him with, "Masikati, David."

*Huh? The man knew his father's name?*

David replied with, "Masikati, Chippy." Now Jonah understood: This was Chippy, the man they had come to see.

He watched silently as the two men completed an elaborate handshake through the open window. First they gripped each other's palms in the normal way, then they angled their hands upward to grip the thumbs, and finally they hooked their fingers against each other before pulling away with a flourish. Huge smiles lit up both their faces, an expression Jonah had not seen on his father's face for many years, or at least not to this extent.

"How did you know it was us?" David asked.

"Your spirit remains strong, David," said Chippy solemnly and mysteriously, reminding Jonah that he was supposed to be a witch doctor, a Sangoma, although he didn't look or sound like one. He spoke perfect English.

"And there is another, younger, forceful presence about you," Chippy said, looking across at Jonah for the first time.

Jonah felt as if the yellow eyes were penetrating his very soul. "You could see our spirits coming?" he asked, mesmerized.

"I could." Chippy nodded. But then the witch doctor grinned and held up a cell phone. "Plus, I have a friend who works in customs at the airport, and he sent me a message when you came through."

David laughed and flicked his head to indicate the passenger seat. "This is my son, Jonah."

"Of course. Good to meet you, Jonah. Welcome to Africa," said Chippy, reaching through the window to shake hands.

"Hi," said Jonah. "You too." And he repeated the handshake his dad had done.

"Ya! You are African already!" cried Chippy, making Jonah chuckle. His face was so alive, so obviously ready to laugh at every opportunity, that Jonah instantly liked and trusted him.

"Jump in and show us the way," said David, and Chippy climbed into the backseat and stuck his head between Jonah and his father.

Once they were through the gate, the road was reduced to two single sandy tracks, one for each set of wheels, with grass in between. The tracks were rough, and the car bucked and rolled as they drove on toward the camp. "Keep your eyes peeled for animals," said Chippy. "There were quite a lot about when I came down earlier."

Jonah scanned the thorn trees and grass, figuring that if he couldn't spend time with Creedence or live his normal life in England, he could at least see lions, elephants, or any other of the many animals he associated with the African bush. But he didn't get a good glimpse of anything exotic until suddenly David jammed on the brakes and Jonah was thrown forward in his seat. In front of the car, a massive antelope stood arrogantly on the track, a huge dewlap hanging from his neck. It had to be at least nine feet tall, and on top of its head, which was higher than the car, was a mass of fur below two scimitar-like horns. It stood and gazed at the car, unconcerned by its presence. "Phwor! What is that?" exclaimed Jonah in amazement. "It's huge!"

"Eland," answered Chippy. "They are the biggest antelope in the world."

*Wow*, thought Jonah. He'd never seen anything like it.

They lurched on for another twenty minutes, seeing a family of warthogs, some smaller antelope, and a Land Rover circling a muddy lake before Chippy directed them off the main track and into a natural garage within the thorn trees. When Jonah stepped out of the car, he felt the full force of the heat. It must have been well over one hundred degrees, and it was only eleven thirty in the morning. Jonah pulled at his jeans. His dad had said it would only get hotter as the day progressed.

David handed him the briefcase and signaled for him to follow Chippy, who was carrying the rest of the bags, along a narrow path that was completely shaded by the density of the vegetation and the ancient, black trunks of the thorn trees. Many of the trees seemed dead, suffocated by the lack of light and strangled by the lichens that clung to the branches. As they walked, a bird cried above them, giving the path an eerie, sinister feel. "Grey Lourie," said David behind him, causing Jonah to turn his head.

"What?"

"That bird screeching is called a Grey Lourie. Doesn't it sound like it's telling us to 'go away'?"

Jonah shivered. It seemed all too apt. "Oh. Thanks, *Doctor* Light-body," he said, trying to play it off. He turned back. "I'll . . . ahhh!" he screamed and stopped dead in his tracks. In front of him was a bleached skull with two spiraling horns growing out of the top. It looked down from above a gateway in a corral type fence of black, pointed staves, its eye sockets empty yet seeing at the same time. "What is that?!"

"Kudu skull," answered Chippy in a low, reverential voice. "It offers protection against evil spirits. The kudu is a great animal. Evil spirits will never dare to challenge him." He bowed his head to it before stepping through the gateway. "Welcome to Main Camp," he said when he was through.

Jonah followed as recollections of the previous three days careered through his head once more. The camp was in a clearing in which there was a long table, shaded by a wooden, slatted roof. The table and the chairs around it were rugged, and a dying fire burned to the right, the smoke hanging in the windless atmosphere, catching the sunlight that broke through the tree canopy above.

"Dining area and kitchen. There's food and drink here for your lunch," Chippy informed them before leading them back into the trees, along an even narrower, darker path until they reached a tent. It was a big tent, permanently fixed to a manmade concrete base. Chippy pulled open the flaps at the front to reveal two beds, covered with mosquito nets. "The presidential suite. Hot showers available through the back; star gazing included," he announced with a big smile, putting the bags down. "And no telephone reception to disturb your peace and quiet. Make yourselves comfortable."

"It looks great," said David, but Jonah wasn't so sure. He walked inside. It was hot and dark and smelled of dust. There was a toilet and sink through the back, which was open to the skies and buzzed with insects. Jonah wanted to flop on the bed to continue the nap he'd begun earlier, but there was a spider climbing up the mosquito net. He walked back outside. There he found Chippy talking to his father to about rhinoceroses.

"You have rhinos here? Aren't they really endangered?" Jonah exclaimed.

Chippy nodded. "We have eight of them in all and yes they are endangered. But thanks to them, you two should be safe. We have twenty-four-hour security in the form of heavily armed anti-poaching squads."

Jonah's eyes widened. Those must have been the men in the Land Rover they saw on the way in. "Do they use crossbows?" he asked, pointing at the weapon in Chippy's hands.

Chippy shook his head solemnly. "No, I left this here earlier. For the poachers we have to fight fire with fire, so it's assault rifles, machine guns, and grenades. Rhino poaching is big business." He stood up. "Why don't you two settle in? I will be back in about an hour," he announced, melting away into the dark woodland before there could be any further discussion.

Jonah turned to his dad. "Well it puts a new perspective on getting away from it all," he said drily and gestured at the tent. "It's a bit rough, isn't it? Presidential suite?"

"Welcome to Africa," said David, chuckling.

"Well, I suppose it's better than being hunted down and killed," Jonah deadpanned.

"I'd say so." David pulled some clothes out of a holdall and threw them at Jonah. "Now have a shower and put some shorts on. Then we'll get some food before hitting those trading records."

Jonah did as he was instructed and was pleased to discover that he felt a lot better after the shower, the change of clothes, and the food—he'd calculated that he hadn't washed since Friday morning. He was ready to turn his attention to the laptop, which was on the dining table inside the briefcase. He removed the laptop and locked the briefcase lid in the open position. Then he pressed a small button on the inside, causing three solar panels to emerge from the sides. The larger one was a double panel that Jonah manually folded back so that it covered the lid. Next, he unrolled a thin cable from the inside of the case. "Can you get this up on the roof?" he said to his father. There was no electricity in the camp. Lighting came from candles and paraffin lamps, and the fridge was powered by gas.

"Sure," David replied and climbed onto the back of one of the chairs, where Jonah passed the case to him. He placed it on the roof, and Jonah plugged the cable into the power port on the laptop and switched it on. The desktop appeared, and in the top right hand corner it said "charging."

"We have power!" he said and held up the iPod Touch. "Before we start I'm going to make a backup of the files, just in case something goes wrong."

The Baron and Amelia were in Kloot's house in Zurich when the tracker again went live. They had traveled there overnight from Amsterdam, despite the Baron's aversion to getting his mentor involved, in order for the Baron to see Kloot's private doctor: He would ask no questions about the gunshot wound.

Kloot had gone ballistic when he'd been told that the Apollyon files were now in the open. He had flown immediately from his home in South Africa, landing that morning, to take over the operation. He wanted the Lightbodys dead. No Drizzler and certainly no kid was going to jeopardize Apollyon's plans. There could be no more mistakes.

Kloot addressed the Baron, who was twisting uncomfortably in his seat. "You will fly to Namibia immediately. The younger Lightbody was your recruit. Under the code of Apollyon, he and his father are your responsibility."

The Baron nodded dumbly. Painkillers had dulled his senses.

"I have a man who will act as your guide." Kloot pulled up an image of a burly-looking man on his computer. "His name is Klaasens. He is a professional hunter, amongst other things. I use him primarily as my chief bodyguard. He will find these people and ensure that your job is completed even if you are unable to do it yourself. He will also be able to extract from them how much information they have managed to acquire from the files and what they have done with it."

The Baron nodded again, seeing through the fog of medication enough to comprehend that Kloot was protecting himself by having this man Klaasens run the hunt. If the Baron failed, Kloot's own position would be in jeopardy.

"I will arrange for him to meet you at Windhoek airport in Namibia. He will come prepared. Once the job is done you will come to Johannesburg. You cannot go back to London." Kloot turned to his daughter. "Amelia, you will come back to Johannesburg with me today on the private jet. We will smuggle you on so that there is no record of your departure."

Amelia nodded demurely. She never argued with her father. She'd learned that lesson at a very early age.

# CHAPTER 40

**Once the backup** had completed, Jonah called his father over, wondering how he was feeling. David's freedom sat somewhere inside these files. Or possibly it didn't. Jonah watched as his dad walked around the table to stand behind him.

David was visibly tense, his face stern and his mouth firmly shut. He put a hand on Jonah's shoulder. "Go on then. Let's find out, shall we?" It seemed as if they'd been waiting their whole lives to discover the information hidden in this folder, though in actuality it had only been a few days.

Jonah ran the cursor over to the folder and pressed down on the trackpad. The whole desktop went black except for two short lines of text: "Red Baron A Fund" and "Apollyon Two."

David read them out loud.

"What or who is Apollyon?" said Jonah. "It sounds like a space mission."

"No idea," replied David. "Google it."

"I can't. There's no cell phone coverage here, remember?"

"Oh, yes. Well, it doesn't really matter anyway. Start with the Red Baron one. It must be his personal account."

Jonah clicked again. A list of years going back to 1992 came up on the screen.

"This year," David whispered. The only other sounds were the buzzing of a fly and the faint hiss from the wood on the fire.

Jonah clicked again. A list of months appeared. "September," he said, clicking once more.

The screen filled with a complicated combination of graphs, numbers, and letters. Jonah could see immediately that it was the trading records of some sort of investment fund. It was the same as the layout they had in the Bunker, showing performance, trades, dates, and times. Jonah scanned the page quickly, looking at the individual trades.

"Do you recognize any of this?" David asked.

Jonah nodded. "Yeah. It's close to what we were doing in the Bunker, shorting the financial stocks, but the numbers are different, not as big. It also continues up to Friday, and Hellcat pretty much shut down on Wednesday." He pointed to some of the trades. "There are a few Allegro Home Finance trades there, but they're all sells. No one hundred million dollar buys." Jonah thought it best not to add that the Baron had made eighty million dollars in profits so far this month; it wasn't exactly the news he suspected his father wanted to hear.

"Look at some of the other months," said David, the disappointment clear in his voice. "See if the trades are in there."

Jonah scanned back through a year, but nowhere were there

any more Allegro trades. He also saw that the Baron wasn't completely infallible either. In some months he had made a loss. Jonah felt almost disappointed by this fact. Not even the Baron got it right every time.

"Okay. Let's try the Apollyon file," said David.

Jonah exited the Red Baron A Fund and entered the Apollyon Two records for September. He had been quite calm when he had opened the first set of records, but this time his hand quivered slightly. This was all or nothing: *If the proof wasn't in here, then what?* Jonah was acutely aware of his father's presence behind his right shoulder. He could hear his breathing—short and shallow. He pressed down on the trackpad, and the screen seemed to change in slow motion so that for a moment Jonah thought it had crashed. When it finally loaded, he gasped. "Bloody hell!"

Jonah couldn't believe what he was seeing. The numbers in front of him were enormous: bets of hundreds of millions of dollars on single trades; profits in the billions.

Suddenly he was aware of his father's breath quickening,

"It's there, Jonah. It's there. Look, look!" His voice was rising, and his finger was moving toward the screen. "There. See it?"

Jonah looked. There were five buy trades in Allegro Home Finance stock, one out of London, one out of New York, one from Zurich, one from Hong Kong, and one from Chicago. The one from London was for one hundred million dollars. It was the exact same trade as the one David Lightbody was being investigated for—same amount, same time, same day.

"But this says the trade was made by Apollyon," said Jonah, utterly confused.

"No, look at the bottom." David moved his finger downward to a window headlined "Balancing Items." He exclaimed, "Look, there it is again, going out this time!"

Jonah followed his finger. The one hundred million had been "sold" to Hellcat account number JL4193 on the evening of Sunday, September 14. The date rang in Jonah's mind—*it was right after the U.S. government announced that it did not intend to bail out Allegro Home Finance!*

"That's my Scrotycz account," David cried. "He transferred the trade to me. It's there, Jonah. It's there!" David spun away from the table, fists pumping. "Gotcha! You bastards!" he shouted in triumph. "Gotcha!"

Jonah meanwhile was urgently scanning through the previous months, running numbers in his head, shocked at the scale of what he was seeing. "Yep. We've got him, Dad, but this thing is huge. Do you know how much money they're playing with?" he said. "It's more than a hundred *billion* dollars."

David spun back. "But that can't be right. We figured that the Baron wasn't working alone, but that's more than a syndicate. That would make this Apollyon thing the biggest hedge fund in the world!" he exclaimed. Then he shook his head. "Which isn't possible. I'd have heard of it if it was. It would be in the league tables."

"It's correct, Dad," said Jonah. "I've double-checked. And what's more, Allegro is the first time Apollyon—whatever it is—has ever got it wrong." Jonah brought up the profits for every month since the records started. He motioned for his dad to peer over his shoulder. "Look, in one hundred and ninety-two months, there has never been a loss-making month. That's statistically impossible."

"Unless you're using inside information!" David exclaimed. "I knew it!"

Jonah was now scrolling at high speed through the records month by month, his photographic memory absorbing every trade. "It's global too," he said. "The Baron must be one cog in a colossal machine. There are trades here from London, New York, Zurich, Hong Kong, Chicago, Frankfurt, Paris, Johannesburg, Toronto, Dubai, Mumbai, Moscow, you name it." He continued to scroll. He could see a pattern in the trades. "Do you know what I think?" he asked. He didn't wait for his father to respond. "It feeds off crises."

"What do you mean it feeds off crises?" said David, now squatting next to Jonah.

"Every time there's a disaster in the markets, it makes enormous profits. It's been creaming it over the past months up until Allegro, and it's done it before." Jonah opened up the records from 1998. "Look at this: the Russian crisis, when you dropped thirty million. You didn't stand a chance if they had the inside track."

On the screen were a series of massive trades against the market.

"It's a monster," said David.

"And what about this one?" Jonah had brought up the records for September 2001. "On the day al-Qaeda flew their planes into the Twin Towers, Apollyon Two made more than a billion dollars and another billion in the following week. The Baron once told me that this had been a good trading day, but this is more than that: It's as if they knew it was going to happen!"

The two of them stared at each other, and David said what Jonah was thinking. "Do you think that's because they *made* it happen?"

Jonah could feel the fear rising again inside of him. A fund that engineered events such as 9/11 for its own financial benefit? A fund that had enough financial clout to bring the world's banking system to the brink of collapse? What type of people were behind this behemoth?

But before Jonah could turn back to the computer to find out, the sound of an engine in high revs cut through the quiet of the camp, followed by the pitter-patter of running feet. They both turned toward the noise as Chippy burst into the clearing. "Where's the rhino?" he shouted, his crossbow in one hand and a small radio-like device in the other.

"A rhino?" Jonah exclaimed as he looked around in panic and began climbing onto the table.

"Here. Right here. There is a rhino here," repeated Chippy.

"Where?" David and Jonah shouted together this time. Surely it would be easy to spot a ton of armored animal flesh crashing about.

"The automated rhino tracker says it's within fifteen feet of us," said Chippy, looking at the device in his hand. He held it up in explanation. "We use GPS transmitters drilled into the rhinos' horns so that we know where they are. A signal appeared ten minutes ago, right in the middle of the camp. Control radioed me to check it out."

"There's no rhino here, Chippy," said David in an amused tone.

"Well, something is transmitting a signal. Have you got any GPS devices with you?"

"GPS? Not that we're aware of," David replied, shaking his head. "How accurate is that thing?"

"To a few feet," said Chippy. He started walking toward them. "The signal is coming frommmm . . . here." He stopped right next to Jonah.

Jonah looked at the laptop at his feet. "When did you say you first got the signal?" he asked.

"About ten minutes ago."

Jonah looked at David. "That's when we switched the Baron's laptop on!"

"Shit," said David. "It's got a tracker inside it. Of course it has. No wonder he managed to find us so quickly in Amsterdam."

"And follow us to the airport," added Jonah.

"Quickly, switch it off," said David, and Jonah jumped down from the table and powered down the laptop.

Chippy shook his head, his eyes on the receiver. "Nope. I've still got a signal," he said. "Anything else?"

Jonah reached across the table and picked up the new iPod. Despite the heat, he felt cold. "He's not tracking the laptop. He's tracking me," he said in a hush. "He gave me this on Friday as a present." Jonah felt a pit in his stomach. Sure, he'd had to shoot the Baron, and sure, he understood the man was part of some evil, world-defiling operation. But the idea that their relationship was so meaningless that the last gift he'd ever given him was actually a GPS tracker still managed to crush him further. He pressed down on the button to turn it off and watched as the screen went blank.

There was silence in the camp as Jonah and David looked at Chippy, hoping that this would be enough. It took a couple of seconds before Chippy raised his head. "The signal's gone," he said, and the silence returned.

Jonah threw the iPod onto the table in disgust. He felt anger and hatred welling up inside. Why had the Baron even paid him any attention in the first place? The Baron had put a tracker on him, so he could hunt him down; the Baron was part of this Apollyon thing. Jonah couldn't figure it out . . . unless . . . unless . . . *the Baron was grooming him to be part of Apollyon!*

The notion made more and more sense the longer he thought about it. And now that it had occurred to him, the mysteries of the past began to fall into place—why the Baron had sought him out that day his father took him to work, why the training game the Baron had given him had the initial "A" on its case, why he'd taken him to Amsterdam and they'd just so happened to run into the Baron's own mentor.

"We must make plans," his father said, interrupting his thoughts. "What do you think, Chippy?"

"They know," Chippy answered enigmatically. "And they will come. Maybe as soon as tomorrow."

"Is there another camp?" David inquired.

Jonah jerked his head up. "No! No way!" he burst out. "We're not running again. They'll keep finding us." He could see the surprise in David's and Chippy's faces at his reaction. "The point of this place wasn't only that they wouldn't find us, Dad. We also have protection. We have the poaching squads, and we have you and Chippy." An idea formed in his mind. *What was it his dad had said the Selous Scouts had done?* "We could do the opposite," said Jonah.

"What do you mean?" said David with a puzzled expression on his face.

"He means: bring them here," Chippy clarified, his leopard eyes afire.

"Yes," said Jonah, feeling strength from Chippy's understanding. "They think they are the hunters. We ran from Hellcat, and we ran from Amsterdam. They'll expect us to run again. So let's do the opposite. Let's turn the hunters into the hunted. Isn't that what you guys did when you were in the Selous Scouts?" He looked to Chippy, who lifted his hand to his chin and started stroking it. Then he glanced at his father, whose expression had switched from puzzled to thoughtful.

"The Baron is a city man," Jonah continued. "This isn't the city. We have the advantage here. You know this world. He doesn't. Let's get Chippy's man at the airport to watch out for him; and when he arrives, we follow him. When he gets here we . . ."

"Take him," continued Chippy.

"And interrogate him," finished David, nodding.

It wasn't quite what Jonah was thinking. "I was going to say that we capture him so he can't escape now that we have proof he set you up," said Jonah. "Then we can get him into court."

"No," said David, now excited. "We have to get to him before he can hide behind expensive lawyers. We want him to talk. We have to find out what's behind this Apollyon thing before it ever gets near a court. The trading files will clear my name, but they don't tell us the whole story." David's eyes lit up as the implications of what they were about to do took hold. "You're right, Jonah! You're right!" He turned to Chippy again. "Will you put your man at customs on alert?"

"I will call him immediately," Chippy answered.

"And is there somewhere secure we can keep the Baron once we have him?" David asked.

Chippy nodded. "There are some caves not far from here. They will make a very good place for an interrogation."

"That should do the job," said David grimly. "A few days in a cave with only rats for company, and the Baron will be desperate to talk." As an afterthought he added, "Although we may have to make it quicker than a few days."

Jonah didn't like the sound of the word "interrogation"—or "rats" for that matter. "Will you hurt him?" Jonah asked, worried that his idea had morphed into something more violent than he had envisioned.

The question hung in the air for some seconds before David answered. "No. I will do what is necessary to make him talk, but I'm not talking about physical torture if that's what you mean." He turned to Chippy. "You never told us why you carry a crossbow?"

"I was culling some antelope," Chippy replied, as if this was no big deal. "It's important to control the size of the herd so that there's no overpopulation." He looked at Jonah. "The crossbow is more humane than a gun. There is no noise, and generally they don't even know they have been shot."

"Interesting," said David. "Another one of those might come in handy in the next couple of days." He began pacing around the table, deep in thought, counting off something on his fingers, very alert and very alive. He stopped and addressed Chippy. "We'll need some other hardware. Can you put together an inventory of what you've got in your stores so that we can decide what we need?"

"Sure," said Chippy. "Give me a couple of hours."

David started his pacing again. "And then you'll show us the caves, yes?"

Chippy nodded as Jonah looked on. He wasn't entirely satisfied with his father's answer about physical torture, but he was pacified enough to accept his dad's next instruction without further discussion. "Jonah, you carry on going through the files. I've got some planning to do."

It ended up taking three hours for Chippy to return, but for Jonah it felt like mere minutes, such was his absorption in the Apollyon files. Having been torn from the computer, his mind was still racing as they made their way to the caves. Jonah had suggested that he stay behind while David and Chippy checked out the caves, largely so he could research Apollyon further, but his father would have none of it.

"No, you must come," he'd said. "I'm not leaving you alone, and Chippy says that there's a hill near the caves where we can get cell phone reception. I want to e-mail a copy of the September records to Harry Solomons, and I need your help. I'd probably delete all the files if I tried to do it myself."

Jonah backed down. If he could e-mail Pistol, it meant he could also e-mail Creedence and research Apollyon online to see if he could find anything on them. He followed Chippy and his father out of the camp, eager to reestablish communication with the outside world.

It quickly became clear that his father and Chippy were using this walk as an opportunity to discuss possible interrogation techniques, so Jonah consumed himself in his own reflections, a strategy which also helped him ignore the discomfort of the heat and the grass and thorns scratching his bare legs as they walked.

His thoughts were only broken by Chippy coming to a halt. "Here we are," he said.

Jonah looked around. They were in front of a low rocky cliff riddled with fissures and ledges. The trees and bushes were greener and thicker than back at Main Camp, and a muddy water hole suggested to Jonah that this must be a river when the rains came. He chuckled to himself: *So geography class had been useful after all!* Another huge antelope was drinking at the water hole, which Jonah identified from its horns. He'd seen the same spiraling horns above the entrance to the camp. It was a kudu.

"Look at these," said Chippy, gesturing at the ground. "They are fossilized dinosaur footprints. We've had them verified."

Jonah bent down to see what Chippy was pointing at. They looked like nothing more than scratches in the rock, but were somehow weirdly enthralling all the same. The footprints, his memory of the kudu skull, the long shadows being thrown by the falling sun, and Chippy's comment about evil spirits gave this place a very ancient and mystical aura.

Jonah stood up and followed Chippy up to the cliff and to the edge of a large fissure in the rock face. "Stamp your feet when you walk inside," Chippy instructed. "There may be a few snakes around."

"Snakes!" screamed Jonah, now really convinced that he should have stayed behind. "Poisonous ones?"

"Don't worry," said David behind him. "They'll be long gone if you stamp."

Chippy took a flashlight out of his rucksack, switched it on, and led them into the fissure. He kept the light fixed on the ground. As they progressed, complete blackness enveloped them, the pinpoint of light becoming their only guide. The floor was strewn with rocks and dirt, and the air was stale and fetid. Suddenly Chippy flicked the light upward, and Jonah gasped. The chamber they were in was huge, and Jonah could make out magnificent formations of stalactites and stalagmites, royal boxes and stages, nooks and crannies.

"Wow," said Jonah. "It's even bigger than the trading floor."

"Man has used this place for thousands of years," Chippy explained, fixing the light on what looked like paintings of stick men hunting stick animals. "These rock paintings are more than four thousand years old, and we've found arrowheads made from stone, bronze, and iron."

"It'll certainly make a good place to keep the Baron," said David. Chippy answered in Shona, and the two of them went back to whatever they were talking about on the walk over, leaving Jonah alone in the dim light, feeling the darkness closing in around him and the precipitous drop in temperature now that they were out of the sunshine.

After a while David switched back to English. "Let's go and send that e-mail. Tomorrow's going to be a big day."

# CHAPTER 41

## Monday, September 22

**The Baron's plane** from Zurich landed in Namibia at seven twenty-five on Monday morning. He was stopped at Windhoek Airport customs, but only briefly. A friendly official looked at his passport, asked him his reason for entering the country, and wished him a good holiday. Soon after, Kristoff Klaasens, big game hunter and sadist, introduced himself to the Baron in the arrivals hall. He had driven from Johannesburg overnight, entering Namibia along a dry river bed before returning to the highway. He didn't want customs looking at the contents of his Land Cruiser.

Klaasens would have been somewhat pleased to know that his fears were justified. He and the Baron *were* being watched. When the Baron had left customs, wearing his usual shirt and tie, the official he had dealt with had phoned one of the attendants at the small parking lot outside. In turn, that attendant noted the registration details of the Land Cruiser (when Klaasens returned to the vehicle with the Baron) and phoned them through to Chippy.

It was just as Jonah had predicted—the hunter was becoming the hunted.

When Jonah made his way to Main Camp's dining area soon after eight o'clock in the morning, he was greeted by the smell of cooking bacon and a table strewn with guns, knives, crossbows, wires, ropes, and clothing. David and Chippy were at the far end, deep in conversation.

"Is he here?" Jonah asked, all of the previous nights' concerns flooding back.

David nodded grimly. "He is. Chippy's man at customs says he landed about half an hour ago and is on the road. He was met by a big South African guy dressed in hunting gear. Chippy will meet up with them about sixty miles from here and tail them."

"There's only one road and not much traffic, so it won't be difficult," Chippy explained. "I'll follow them and find out what they are up to, and we'll make plans from there."

"Are they coming by tank?" Jonah asked drily, indicating the armory on the table.

Neither David nor Chippy laughed. "We can't be too careful after last time," said David. "Plus, you know what we found yesterday. We must be fully prepared."

Jonah surveyed the guns on the table, his stomach churning. He'd already shot a gun once. He didn't want to have to do it again.

"Right," said David, moving toward the fire and changing the subject. "Let's get you some bacon and eggs, and after that you can help us get ready for tonight."

*Bacon and eggs?* His dad had never cooked him breakfast in his life. He sat down at an empty space at the table and watched David busying himself with pans and food while Chippy stripped down an assault rifle. It was a strange sight to say the least. "How did I get to bed last night?" he asked. The last thing he remembered was sitting by the fire in the camp following dinner as Chippy played on a harmonica he'd brought along.

"I carried you," David answered simply, as if this was no big deal and not the first time in as long as Jonah could remember that he'd done something so attentive. "You passed out. One minute you were awake, and the next you were gone." He threw some rashers of bacon into a frying pan.

"Oh," said Jonah. "Thanks."

Chippy was now cleaning the gun's parts with a rag, and Jonah remembered what else he had discovered while they had had Internet reception on the hill the previous night. "So," he said to his father, "I didn't tell you what I learned while you and Chippy were enjoying the sunset on the hill last night."

"No," said David. "What is it?"

"I found out where the word 'Apollyon' comes from." He paused for effect. He wanted to ensure he had his dad's full attention for what he was about to tell him. "I didn't tell you then because it seemed like you two were really enjoying yourselves."

"Oh?" David raised his eyebrows.

"Yeah. It's from the Bible, the Book of Revelation. Apollyon is basically another name for the devil. He is 'the Destroyer' and 'the Angel of Death.' It's supposed to be Apollyon who brings about the Apocalypse, the end of the world." He watched carefully to see David's reaction, but all he did was break an egg into the pan.

"Oh, I wouldn't read too much into that. Lots of hedge funds get their names from the Bible or Greek and Roman history. They think it shows intelligence and aggression." He turned to face Jonah and held up a silver packet. "Do you want coffee?"

Jonah was surprised at the lack of reaction. He thought it was a big deal: a massive fund named after the Angel of Death that fed off crises and that was supposed to bring about the end of the world!

"Coffee, Jonah?" David repeated.

"Uh . . . yes, please," he answered and looked again at the armory on the table. "Well, if you don't think the name's anything to worry about, how about explaining the interrogation plan?"

"We'll get to that," David replied, obviously not wishing to be distracted from his culinary efforts.

Jonah grunted with frustration. Here he was with killers hunting him, killers backed by more money than a decent sized country and named after the Angel of Death, and his dad cared more about cooking bacon and eggs! *He* might have been to war before, but Jonah hadn't. *He* might feel comfortable surrounded by assault rifles, but Jonah wasn't. And *he* might consider an interrogation as perfectly normal, but Jonah didn't. If Jonah had been forced to trade on the information he had at present, he would be buying "Apollyon," not "Lightbody." He wanted something more than breakfast to change the odds that appeared heavily stacked against them.

# CHAPTER 42

**After three and** a half hours of driving, Klaasens pulled off the road into a rest stop. There was a concrete table and chairs under the shade of a couple of acacia trees.

"Come, let us stretch our legs, and I will show you where we are going from here," he said in a guttural South African accent. He spread out a map on the table and showed the Baron the Lightbodys' last known location on the farm and the access point he planned to use: a hunting reserve called Luipaard. Kloot had it all arranged in advance, ensuring complete privacy except for a local tracker who was being paid handsomely to keep his mouth shut. They would set up their base near the perimeter fence, and Klaasens and the tracker would explore the area once darkness fell. When the Lightbodys were asleep, Klaasens, the tracker, and the Baron would go in and enable the Baron to do what he had come to do.

The Baron gave his assent, and they returned to the Land Cruiser and continued their journey, turning off the road some twelve miles short of where David had turned the day before.

For all the precaution they took, it was not enough. Chippy watched them turn from some way back and drove on another five hundred yards. He parked his open-backed vehicle and entered the reserve by scaling the game fence that surrounded it. From there he proceeded on foot, silent and invisible. He watched, as still as a praying mantis, as they set up their camp. It was very basic: two small tents still to be erected, a cooking fire, and two chairs. Everything else stayed in the Land Cruiser. Chippy couldn't see anyone else, and it was obvious that this set-up was short term and not meant for a hunting trip, or at least not of the animal kind.

Less than a mile away on the game farm, Jonah was learning how to use a crossbow. They were nothing like the ones he had seen in history books. These were high-performance weapons made of carbon fiber and with telescopic and thermal sights. Once David had fired a few bolts and found a feel for the weapon, he handed it over to Jonah. "Here. Have a go." Jonah took the bow, immediately surprised by its lightness. David showed him how to activate the self-cocking mechanism and how to load the bolts, which were aerodynamically designed and made of high tensile steel. "From there it's point and fire like you would a gun."

Jonah looked down the crosshairs of the sight at a target set up twenty yards away on a tree. When he squeezed the trigger, there was only the faintest "whoosh" as the bolt sped on its way and thudded into the target: silent and deadly.

•   •   •

"There are only two of them," Chippy said, panting upon his return. "They are on the reserve next door, camped very near the perimeter. I think their plan is to strike tonight. We should go as soon as we can."

Silence fell over Main Camp, dispelling any joviality that remained from the crossbow practice. "Okay," said David, almost standing to attention. "Let's get this done. What do we need? Are we driving or walking?"

"We'll take the tranquilizer gun and a crossbow, plus some cord. We'll walk in. It will be quieter, and we can drive out in their vehicle."

"Tranquilizer gun?" asked Jonah.

"Yes. They're designed to bring down a rhino. They'll knock a person out instantaneously," answered Chippy.

Jonah was relieved. That meant they didn't plan to kill anyone.

"It sounds simple enough," David replied. "I'll get ready." He picked up a handgun in a holster and started attaching it to his belt.

"Do I stay here?" asked Jonah. It struck him that while he was mentally prepared for almost anything on the trading floor, there was no way to prepare for this.

"Yes," said David. "Stay where it's safe."

"No, David," said Chippy. "Jonah comes with us."

"You must be joking!" snapped David, testing the mechanism of the automatic pistol. "Those men are here to kill us. I'm not taking my son out there. He's not trained for this kind of thing."

Jonah's pulse started to race. It wasn't the excited racing of running cross-country or participating in a killer trade. This felt different. It felt fuelled by mortal terror.

"No," repeated Chippy. "He must come. He will be good for us." Jonah could see that his leopard eyes were ablaze again and recalled what David had said about Chippy being a Sangoma and having a sixth sense for danger. He looked back at his father, and for a moment he thought he saw fear flick across his face, to be replaced by acknowledgment that Chippy hadn't steered him wrong before.

"Okay," said David slowly, shoving the pistol back into its holster. "But only if Jonah is all right with this." He turned to his son. "How do feel about it, Jonah?"

Jonah was struck by the oddity of it all—he'd always wanted his father to seek out his opinion more often, and now that he was, it was only after their world had imploded.

"What would you have me do?" asked Jonah, his stomach twisting at the thought of seeing the Baron again.

"You watch. Hidden. The third set of eyes. You don't enter the extraction zone," said Chippy as if reading his thoughts.

"If you see anything that threatens the extraction, you shout," added David. "And get out immediately. We'll follow."

"And it would be a good idea if you carried a gun," said Chippy, handing him the one he was currently holding.

Jonah took the gun. It was a nine-millimeter automatic, the same as the gun he'd fired in Amsterdam. It didn't feel so heavy this time.

They followed the game paths, avoiding the main track. Chippy led, a crossbow strapped to his back, with Jonah thirty yards behind and David bringing up the rear, a tranquilizer gun in hand. It was the hottest time of the day, and they were the only things moving. They hiked in silence, and Jonah concentrated on lifting his feet high to avoid stumbling and walking around bushes even if it meant stepping off the path, as Chippy had shown him to do. Soon he began to find a kind of rhythm.

After half an hour Chippy moved off the track and into a clump of thorn trees, stopping and squatting on his haunches. Jonah and David followed and squatted next to him. He pointed forward, and Jonah followed the direction of his arm to the sight of the Baron, a hundred yards away, sitting in a chair in the shade. It was the first time he had set eyes on his former mentor since Amsterdam. His arm was in a sling, and he looked much smaller than Jonah remembered. He wore a standard business shirt with cufflinks plus a tie loosened around his neck—an odd choice for Africa, Jonah mused—and appeared uncomfortable and ill at ease, saying nothing as the big South African man tended to a fire. A light breeze carried the sounds and smells of the man's activities to Jonah. He was making lunch.

"You stay here," whispered David, "and keep your eyes peeled. We might be a while." Chippy gave him a thumbs-up, and the two men peeled off to the right to take a wide circle toward the camp. Jonah looked tentatively for somewhere comfortable to wait and settled on a sandy clearing in the shade. The grass and shadows would cover him, and he had a clear view of the camp. He lay down on his stomach, keeping his eyes on the camp. It was hot, even in the shade, and flies soon gathered to drink the sweat from his face. He swatted at them at first but soon gave up and let them settle.

He watched the Baron and the other man eat their lunch, tidy it away, and put up two tents. Once the tents were up, the other man looked at his watch and said something, leading the Baron to nod. Soon after two P.M. both men retired to their separate tents, presumably for an afternoon nap. There was some movement for ten minutes and then complete stillness; even the breeze seemed to have gone to sleep. Jonah watched carefully, trying to pick up any sign of his father or Chippy.

Suddenly he caught movement behind the Baron's tent. He heard the faint rip of canvas followed by the pop of a tranquilizer gun. *They were doing it!* His father and Chippy were going after the Baron. Now he could see Chippy crawling toward the second tent. A glint of unnatural light in the trees to the left grabbed Jonah's attention. *It was a person! Had David and Chippy seen him too?* The person was standing stock still. He was black and wearing dark khaki clothing, almost invisible in the dappled shadows of the tree. Only the movement had given away his presence.

Jonah relaxed. *No, they hadn't seen him. They were concentrating on the tents.* But then the man began raising something slowly up from his waist.

A gun!

Jonah shouted, ripping the silence to pieces and causing an unseen animal nearby to bolt. The man in the trees swung his gun around toward the noise as David and Chippy split and dove to the ground. Jonah prayed that his cover would hold and lay rigidly still. He could see Chippy aiming the crossbow as the man began to swing his gun back toward the tents. In mid-movement he jerked backward with his arm pinned against the tree he had been leaning against. The gun fell to the ground. There was a pop, and the man slumped awkwardly, still attached to the tree. Chippy was now putting another bolt into the crossbow as the first tent erupted and the big South African catapulted out of its front. David stood up behind the second tent with the tranquilizer gun in his hand. There was another pop. The man fell still, and everything was quiet again.

Jonah saw his father take his pistol out and walk toward the tall South African, the gun held out in front of him. He stood over him and bent down, putting the gun against the back of his head. Jonah gagged, but David dropped his left hand off the butt to remove the tranquilizer dart from the man's neck and check his pulse. He walked over to the third man and reached down to his thigh to pull out the tranquilizer dart, again checking his pulse. Meanwhile, Chippy was dragging the Baron out of his tent.

David turned toward Jonah and called out, "All clear, Jonah. Where are you?"

Jonah stood up, his nerves still firing a mile a minute. "Over here," he called back and ran over to the perimeter fence where David met him.

"Good thing you came," said David. "I don't know how we missed that guy. He must have joined after Chippy left this morning. I assume he's their tracker."

"Yeah. Nice work, Jonah," called Chippy from the tent, smiling. "I told you you would be good for us."

Jonah tossed his head in acknowledgment. "Would he have shot you?" he asked his dad.

"I doubt it. He looks as if he's a local lad. But I'm glad we didn't get to find out. Now, do you reckon you can get over this fence and give us a hand? Otherwise it's about a mile walk to the next gap."

Jonah looked upward. The fence was about fifteen feet high, but without any barbed wire at the top. He put his hands into the hexagonal holes of the wire, shifting his weight to the fence. It supported him easily with only the slightest of give, but he couldn't get his feet into the holes, or at least not with his shoes on. He bent down, took his trainers off, tied the laces together, and hung them around his neck. "Should be able to do it now," he said. He gripped the fence once more and scaled it with ease, heaving himself up and over the top, and back down the other side.

"Ya, this boy is definitely African," shouted Chippy, laughing.

Jonah dropped from about six feet and took the impact with his knees. "That was fun," he said, wiping the sweat from his forehead. He was surprised that after so many months spent trading, he could still find hopping a fence so exhilarating. He would have to tell Creedence when he saw her next. "What do you want me to do now?"

"Can you go over to the vehicle there?" David pointed toward the Land Cruiser in the shade behind the camp. "And clear out the back so that we can get the Baron and his friend inside. I think we'll leave the watchman behind. No need to get him involved."

"Okay." Jonah walked over to the truck and tried the rear door. It was unlocked. He lifted it up. Inside, the Land Cruiser was packed with boxes and supplies, and he hauled these out one by one as his father and Chippy dragged the drugged bodies over to the vehicle. The last thing to come out was a knapsack, and as he heaved it toward him, it fell open. Jonah's mouth dropped. Inside were guns! Serious guns! "Hey, Dad! Chippy! Come and look at this!"

David ran over, and Jonah showed him the contents of the bag. On the top were two genuine hunting rifles, but below that were a sniper's rifle, two assault rifles, and an assortment of automatic handguns as well as some evil-looking knives and an axe.

"Mmm. Not very pleasant," said David. "Chippy, have a look in this guy's pockets, will you, and find out who he is. I think we've got ourselves a rhino poacher. Now that's someone whom the police can take care of, even without our help."

"Kristoff Klaasens," Chippy called back after finding the man's wallet.

"Well, Kristoff, I hope you like Namibian jails," David said quietly. "I wouldn't." He turned back to Jonah. "Put the guns in the backseat, please—and do be careful about it—and let's get these two inside the car."

Jonah did as he was told and then helped David and Chippy haul the two unconscious men into the trunk. Everything seemed to be going according to plan. They would transfer the Baron to the caves first, and then Chippy would take Klaasens to the police station.

David slammed the back door shut.

Kloot received the phone call from Klaasens at three thirty P.M. He had somehow ended up in police custody and was about to be charged with attempted rhino poaching. He didn't know what had happened to the Baron.

Kloot crashed his massive fist down on his desk with such force that there was an audible crack as something gave way. Now they had the trading records *and* they had the Baron. The records wouldn't talk. The Baron might. "Say nothing," he barked into the phone. "I will have you out of there, but you must complete the job." He slammed the phone down. It was time to call on the network once more. He opened an old black leather diary and searched for the phone number of a senior member of the South African government.

He snatched the phone up and dialed the number. When he gave his name, he was put straight through. Quietly, he explained that a South African national had been detained by the Namibian police. He wanted him to be released. The minister said he would do what he could. Kloot explained that that wasn't enough. His man needed to be out of custody this afternoon. If he wasn't, Kloot told him, the minister might find life a bit more difficult in the future. This time the minister understood.

Kloot hung up the phone, sighing. He couldn't leave Klaasens to finish the job alone. He would have to send Amelia in there. The Baron might have been a great trader, but he wasn't as resourceful as his daughter. After all, she was willing to use *all* of her natural assets to her advantage. He stood up from his desk and went to find her. She would not fail.

# CHAPTER 43

**Inside the cave,** the Baron had been alone and awake for ten minutes when he felt a hand on his face. He recoiled and cried out through the thick rope gag in his mouth. He felt fingers undoing the rope and then a cup being pushed against his lips. The liquid was warm and sweet, some kind of tea. He drank it greedily and gratefully. It wasn't enough to quench his burning thirst, but it seemed to confirm that he was alive. He had been concerned that he wasn't. He had no idea where he was nor how he had got there. His last memory had been lying in the tent waiting to go to sleep. There were things crawling on him and flying past him. Was this the holding room for hell?

"Where am I?" he asked but received no reply, only the rope being shoved back into his mouth and then nothingness once more. He heard no footsteps and no breathing except his own. Had it been a ghost?

• • •

Chippy repeated the process every half hour for the next four hours, never speaking and never removing the blindfold. By now the Baron was murmuring to himself, dreaming things he didn't want to dream. The tea had seen to that. It was a powerful psychotropic mix of herbs laced with honey to sweeten it, one of the tools of a witch doctor's trade. The Baron was now ready for the interrogation.

Chippy returned to Main Camp to collect Jonah and David.

Klaasens walked out of the police station at five thirty, all charges dropped; pressure had been applied from someone very high up. There was a car waiting to take him back to the Luipaard Hunting Reserve so that he could rendezvous with Amelia. She arrived at six thirty, bringing sophisticated heat- and sound-detecting equipment along with her. They drove straight to the fence and from there headed to the hill by the cave. It was time to show the Lightbody family that Apollyon was not to be trifled with.

The sun had dropped behind the hill when Jonah, David, and Chippy approached the cave. Chippy was wearing the clothing of a traditional witch doctor: beads and bones around his ankles and neck, rings of fur below his knees, a kilt of goatskin and mongoose pelts, more skins and pelts around his shoulders and upper arms, and a headdress of feathers and plaited grasses that matched the color of his ochre face paint. In his hand was a long throwing spear, and around his neck hung a small flask and a pouch that contained herbs. David, meanwhile, was wearing dark trousers and an old overcoat borrowed from Chippy. Around his neck was a scarf, and on his head was a flattish cap with a small peak. Pinned to the scarf was a cross, fashioned out of tin foil and cardboard to resemble the Prussian Blue Max, the highest medal of valor in the World War I–era German air force. Jonah considered himself dressed normally relative to these two, in black jeans and a black T-shirt. However, his face and arms had also been blacked up with mud from the water hole. He was carrying a bundle of firewood and two African drums. In his belt was the gun, and in his pocket was Chippy's harmonica. David also had a gun in the pocket of his overcoat. Jonah reckoned that—had the circumstances been different—they would have been well prepared for trick-or-treating.

As they entered the cave, Chippy put his fingers to his lips and took the firewood from Jonah. He switched on a pencil flashlight, illuminating the scene in front of them. There lay the Baron on the ground looking more like a filthy, mumbling tramp than the king of Hellcat. Jonah's hand went inadvertently to his mouth. David had explained that the interrogation would involve a combination of hooding and sensory deprivation, with the addition of psychotropic drugs to speed up the process. But it was still all very difficult for Jonah to process. Two rats were gnawing at the Baron's boots and only scuttled off when Chippy approached. Jonah looked at him and back at the Baron. He'd seen the Baron sprawled on the floor two days ago, after he'd shot him, but this was far, far worse.

At about the same time as Jonah, his father, and Chippy entered the cave, Amelia and Klaasens reached the summit of the hill nearby. Up there, the sun was about to set, but they had no interest in the beauty of the scene. The hill's dominance of the surrounding land provided the ideal location to set up Amelia's surveillance cameras.

They erected the tripod, attached the scanner—which resembled a small movie camera—and plugged the device into the battery unit. There were two portable screens and two pairs of headphones. The screens also held the directional controls. Amelia focused the lens on Main Camp. It was empty, although the screen showed the remains of a fire. She set the camera to "automatic scan," and it began to pan slowly across the land below, highlighting the clear shapes of animals, including two rhinos, preparing for the night, but no human beings. She listened carefully through the headphones, but again there was nothing that resembled human voices. The two of them sat down on canvas stools and watched and listened and waited. The sun had set now, and the temperature had dropped.

Chippy placed the wood on the floor near the Baron and approached him, speaking aloud for the first time, though not in English. The effect on the Baron was electric. He immediately tried to sit up and, when the gag was removed, called out, "Who is it? Who are you? Speak to me!"

Chippy pushed the flask to this lips and made him drink, talking all the time in a low incanted voice. When the flask was empty, he began to make a fire. He started with dry grass and used a flint to light it. As the flames grew, he added twigs and finally the wood. In the growing light Jonah could now see the Baron clearly. He was carrying his head in a way that indicated considerable pain in the shoulder where Jonah had shot him. His once lustrous mustache was a mess of dirt and droppings. Even his neck tie, formerly so prominent and stylish, was now a muddied, wrinkled mess. He continued to call out, "Who are you? What are you doing?"

and move his head, desperate for some sight or sign of what was happening.

For a brief moment Jonah felt the urge to help him, but it didn't last long as he reminded himself that the man was a crook, a liar, and a cheat.

As the fire gained strength, its light threw shadows from the rock formations inside the cavern, flickering phantoms that danced and leaped around the walls and roof. Chippy came over to Jonah and took one of the drums, motioning for him to move into a dark cleft in the shadows with the other one. Jonah walked carefully and silently into the darkness, his black clothing and makeup rendering him invisible. Chippy sat himself down by the fire and began to drum softly, continually muttering his incantations and throwing herbs from the pouch onto the fire so that the cavern began to fill with a smoky, misty haze. Jonah looked for his father, but he, too, had disappeared into the gloom. There was only Chippy and his hypnotic drumming and the Baron writhing on the ground, sinking deeper and deeper into his drug-fuelled hell.

Chippy continued his drumming and chanting for more than half an hour before Jonah heard the pace and volume increase. This was his cue to join in. As the drumming rose in volume, it echoed and bounced around the cave so that it was as if there was a whole army of drummers beating away, surrounding the Baron in noise. Jonah put Chippy's harmonica to his lips and drew a haunting chord. He saw his father move behind a pillar of limestone and Chippy stand up and resituate himself in front of the Baron. His drumming stopped, but his chanting intensified, distorted by the acoustics of the cavern into many different voices, and joining the howling of Jonah's harmonica and its spectral accompanists. *The effect on the Baron must be terrifying,* Jonah thought, as he watched him curl into a fetal position, his knees pulled up to his chest, rolling on the ground, moaning and whimpering.

Suddenly Chippy reached forward and grabbed the Baron by the hair, yanking him upward so that he was kneeling, and with an ear-splitting cackle he pulled the blindfold off. The Baron screamed as he was greeted by Chippy's orange face and hair inches in front of his own. Chippy leapt upward, spinning in the air and throwing something on the fire that made the flames roar toward the roof of the cave. For a moment he seemed to hang within the flames before landing and facing the Baron once more, and began to dance around him, shaking his spear in his face, shouting, and cackling. Jonah drew one last note on the harmonica and grabbed the drum. He settled the instrument between his legs and began to pound with all the passion he possessed. The shadows danced, the noise reverberated, and the Baron twisted and turned to avoid the jabbing spear. Jonah had never seen so much fear in someone's face. He was in a deep, deep trance: somewhere very dark and very evil.

Chippy stopped in front of him again, his arms out wide, lowering them as a signal to Jonah to slow the drumming down. As Jonah did so, Chippy descended into a squatting position, his face no more than a foot away from the Baron's. This was Jonah's second cue, and he began to thump out a very familiar rhythm: the opening beats to the Baron's favorite record—"Sympathy for the Devil."

Dum dum de de dum dum de dum dum. Dum dum de de dum dum de dum dum.

There was recognition in the Baron's eyes, and Chippy started speaking, in English this time. "Please allow me to introduce myself," he said, and the recognition grew. "I am"—here he paused, before imbuing his voice with an air of dark desperation—"*Apollyon.*"

The Baron jerked and tried to move away. But Chippy held up a hand, and he froze, rigid. "I am Apollyon, the Angel of Death. I am the Devastator. I am the Destroyer!" he cried. Jonah began to increase the volume of his drumming. "You"—Chippy now had the point of the spear under the Baron's chin—"you have belittled me. How dare you use the name of Apollyon?" The Baron crumpled as if the bones in his body had been dissolved.

Up on the hillside Amelia was straining to pick up a new sound on her headphones. She had heard the earlier drumming when it had reached its peak, but without any visual image she and Klaasens had put it down to some of the farm workers. Now it was different. This was familiar. Amelia had heard it hundreds, maybe thousands of times. This could not be a coincidence. She panned the camera, but still there was no heat image.

"That's them," she said to Klaasens. "We're going down." She removed the camera from its tripod and disconnected it from the power pack, allowing it to run on the portable battery. Klaasens picked up the bag, and they moved swiftly down the hill, tracing the location of the sound through the headphones.

# CHAPTER 44

**Jonah slammed the** drum with all the force he could muster as Chippy reached a crescendo, pulling the Baron by his hair into a kneeling position. "You have belittled others too," he screeched. "Who are you to take the name of the Angel of Death? Who are you to use the name of Apollyon?" he screamed in the Baron's face, throwing some more herbs into the fire. The flames rose and billowed smoke, Jonah beat the drums, and the Baron collapsed again, convulsing on the ground.

When the flames died down, Chippy was gone, replaced by a second figure, ethereal within the swirling smoke: a man in an overcoat and a Jagdstaffel cap, a man with the Blue Max at his throat. Jonah quieted his drumming to allow the full effect of the vision that faced the Baron to take hold.

Dum dum de de dum dum de dum dum. Dum dum de de dum dum de dum dum.

David Lightbody spoke in English with a German accent.

"Please allow me to introduce myself," he said coldly. "I am Baron." He stopped. "Manfred." He stopped again. "Albrecht." And again. "Von Richthofen." He took two strides forward so that he now stood looking down at the Baron. "And you dare to take my name in vain, you dog," he snarled, kicking the Baron as he said it. "Why? Why?" he shouted.

The Baron didn't answer. He just shook his head, his body shaking, trying to slither away from the ghostly figure.

"No answer. This does not surprise me," said David arrogantly. "Many have talked bravely of the Red Baron, but when faced with his reality they have come to appreciate their mortality. Let me try another question. Perhaps you can redeem yourself in my eyes. What is Apollyon Two?"

The Baron ceased his writhing and lifted his head toward David. He tried to speak, but broke out in a coughing fit.

"Answer me, you imbecile," said David in his German accent.

"Apo . . . Apollyon Two is a, uh, machine," the Baron stammered. "An infallible money-making machine." Jonah could hear the desperation in his voice.

"Who invented it?"

"I did. I invented it. It was my idea. Nobody else could have done it."

"That is good," said David. "Maybe you are worthy of the name Baron." The Baron's chest puffed out at this compliment, but only barely.

"How does it make money?" David demanded.

"Crises and information. Apollyon drives the market, knowing that others will follow their lead."

"Where does the money come from?" David demanded.

"The money comes from the League."

"The League?"

"The League of Apollo."

The fire had died down now; only the embers glowed, giving the smoke an orange glow.

"What is the League of Apollo? Who is behind it?"

The Baron looked confused. "I do not know all their names."

David tried a different approach. "What does it do?"

"It protects the interests of capitalism. It has members in industry and finance, in government, in universities, in the military. They are men of influence able to mold the future of the world."

It was beginning to make sense to Jonah. This was a network of powerful individuals with access to all kinds of inside information; and when there was fear and panic in the markets, Apollyon used its financial muscle to expand the fear and panic knowing that everyone would get in line—"the herd mentality."

David's voice hardened further. "Who runs the League of Apollo?"

"The Group of Five."

"Who are they?"

"I only know Kloot. Nobody but the G5 knows all the identities."

"Who is Kloot?" David demanded.

"Kloot has the best information. That is why Apollyon is infallible."

"Not always infallible," David spat back. "What happened with Allegro Home Finance?"

"Uh," the Baron frowned, and coughed again. "The Allegro trade was"—he paused, his voice full of fear—"bad information."

He shook his head, steadying himself. "The facts were wrong. But it has been corrected."

Jonah picked up the pace of his drumming, sensing the full truth was about to be revealed.

"It was corrected? How was it corrected?"

"It was offloaded. The informer was silenced. Others silenced too. They had to be."

"Who were these people who were silenced? Did you silence them?" David pressed.

"I only know Clive. I didn't kill them. Kloot arranged it." He coughed once more. This time Jonah could see blood dribble out of the corner of his mouth.

David Lightbody reached into his pocket and pulled out his gun. The Baron's eyes locked on it as David lifted it up and pointed it at the Baron's face.

"Tell me who Kloot is!" he growled from between gritted teeth.

"I, I can't. He would kill me," spluttered the Baron.

David Lightbody stepped forward and shoved the gun between the Baron's eyes. "Tell me who Kloot is or you will die anyway," he shouted.

Suddenly the air in the cavern exploded. Seeing lights sparking to his right, Jonah stopped drumming, thinking that his father had shot the Baron. *But no, that wasn't it. . . .* He heard a noise and saw his father fall, dropping the gun; saw Chippy leap out of the smoke and hurl his spear at the oncoming light; saw the spear leave his hand; saw bullets rip into his body, sending him backward with their force; saw the flesh exploding with each impact; saw the side of his head blown away; saw him crumple as he fell.

The shooting stopped, but the echoes continued for several seconds until finally they ceased as well and there was quiet. Jonah moved his knees to his chest, his heart racing. Chippy and David were both prone on the ground—Chippy silent; his father groaning. The looming light narrowed into a single beam, flicking over the bodies and pointing downward to highlight a third body with a long spear in its chest. The body belonged to the man Jonah had seen at the Baron's camp, the man Chippy had brought to the police station. He should have been there now, not lying dead in front of Jonah.

The flashlight flicked around the cavern, and Jonah withdrew further into the shadows in terror. The beam moved toward the Baron, and suddenly a familiar form appeared in what was left of the firelight. Amelia. She held a gun in her hand.

Jonah saw his father moving, trying to drag himself along the ground away from Amelia and toward where his gun lay. Amelia passed the Baron, who was in some other world, and proceeded toward David Lightbody's helpless, scrabbling body.

It was only now that Jonah began to move, something in the core of his being urging him on, telling him his father would die if he so much as hesitated. He pulled the pistol from his belt, his hands shaking. Although he knew he couldn't guarantee hitting Amelia from where he was, about thirty yards away from her, he had to try. He would use the Baron as bait.

He moved silently into a crouch and exploded into a spring across the cavern floor, racing toward the Baron. He fired his pistol in the vague direction of Amelia, and she fell to the ground. *Had he hit her?* "One more step and he dies," he shouted. He was still three yards from the Baron, but his momentum carried him all the way in the time it took Amelia to stand up and turn around.

His bullet had missed. She'd only fallen to the ground so as to avoid the bullet's path. Now she stood straight up and put her gun to David's head. "Jonah, darling," she said, almost brightly, "what did you say? I missed it in all the excitement." They were ten yards apart, her gun to David's head, Jonah's to the Baron's. "And there I was wondering where you'd gone off to. And you were here all the time. It makes my job so much easier." She had moved around so that she was now facing him. Her eyes fixed on his, her voice dropping to its most seductive purr as she stared at him. "Put the gun down, Jonah. This isn't some playground game."

Jonah glared back. No, it wasn't a playground game; it was a trade, a very grown-up trade, a trade of lives.

He held her gaze for a few seconds more before he spoke. "You kill my father, I kill the Baron," he said coldly.

He saw her plucked eyebrows rise, and her hand rise too, aiming the gun at him. "I think the Baron is rather irrelevant now, don't you? Lost his mojo, eh, darling? I don't really care if you kill him. And given your father's state, I've changed my mind as to where this thing should be pointing," she purred.

Jonah thought fast and flicked his wrist so that his gun was now aiming at her. "You won't shoot me, Amelia. I'm just a kid," he said. "And you do need the Baron alive. He is the only one who can unwind the trades I have set up. They'll rip your Apollyon game to pieces. You are nothing without him." It was all a bluff, but he had a hunch that she didn't understand enough to know that there was no way he could have set up trades for the Apollyon funds.

"I don't believe you," she said, a trace of hesitancy now audible in her voice.

"You don't believe what?" Jonah sneered. "You don't believe that I shot the Baron? That *was me* in case you were wondering. You don't believe that I stole his laptop? Me again. You don't believe that I broke into your servers and kept you out of them? Yup, I did that. You don't believe that I have seen all of your trading records? Me as well. You don't believe that I have put trading bombs in there?" He stood with his feet spread apart, challenging her. "Which bit don't you believe, Amelia?"

His father groaned, and both sets of eyes focused briefly on him. Jonah knew he had to push on, had to get the trade done. "My offer is your only way out. A life for a life. You walk out of here, and I get my father to a hospital. If not, the bombs will go off tomorrow morning when the London market opens. That's how long you've got before the program kicks in." He turned the gun back toward the Baron, leaving himself open to her shooting him. "You have three seconds before I kill him. If you shoot me, you'll have to kill me outright with a single bullet. I won't miss from here."

Amelia lifted her gun upward a fraction, readying to shoot.

"One!" shouted Jonah. He could sense her indecision. The smile had become a grimace; she was biting on her bottom lip. *Come on, Amelia*, willed Jonah, *come on*.

"Two!"

She took a deep breath and put a second hand on the gun to steady her aim. Jonah prepared himself to dive.

"Thr . . ."

"I accept," she said quickly, the gun still trained on him. "But you will put your gun down first. You can trust me, Jonah." She raised her right eyebrow. "My word is my bond."

Jonah laughed. "That phrase lost all value some time ago," he sneered, glaring at her with every ounce of attitude he could muster, willing her to back down. "Put your gun on the floor and I will let *you* go. You will have to trust *me*. It will not be the other way around." He was surprised at how calm he sounded, how in control he was.

Her eyes dropped. She couldn't hold his stare any longer. She knew he was the one in control. The trade had been done. Amelia transferred the gun to the index finger and thumb of her other hand, bent her knees so that she could reach the floor while still watching Jonah, and put the gun down. She stood up, tossed her hair proudly, and strode toward him.

There was almost no light at all now as Jonah moved away from the Baron and toward his father. He kept his gun trained on Amelia the whole time. She pulled the Baron to his feet. There was some sense of reality returning to his eyes, a sign that the drugs were wearing off, but it would be quite some time before he was fully compos mentis. Jonah picked up the other gun so that he now had one in each hand as she put the Baron's arm over her shoulder and led him toward the exit. The second man's body—Klaasens, his license had read—was spotlighted once more by the flashlight, and she halted and turned back toward Jonah.

Jonah tensed.

"How do I know you won't follow us once we are out?" she said.

"I will follow you," he said as menacingly as he could. "But not until my father is safe. You have as long as that takes. I suggest you hurry."

She turned again and disappeared into the darkness.

As soon as the flashlight disappeared, Jonah ran and placed more logs on the fire to provide some light and went back to his father. His eyes were open, but even in the orange glow of the firelight his face was grey.

"Can't . . . feel . . . my . . . legs," he gasped. Jonah could now see the damage. He had taken a bullet in the hip and another in the side of his chest and was bleeding heavily. It would be reckless to move him; Jonah would have to leave him there and get help. He took his father's hand, his throat closing, tears welling in his eyes. "I'll get you out, Dad. I'll get you out. Hold on. Don't die. I'll get you out."

"I . . . know . . . go . . . go . . . now." Jonah felt David's hand tighten around his own.

He squeezed back.

And then he ran. He ran for his father's life. Out of the cave and through the bush, running, hurdling, falling, rising, jumping, swerving, scratched, cut, bruised, breathless, gasping, until he reached the camp and found Chippy's radio on the table. He snatched it up and pressed the communication button on the side. "Come in! Come in! Come in!" he shouted and released the button.

There was a crackling of static, and a voice came back. "Squad Two reading you. Who is this? Confirm please. Over." The voice was African, professional, calm, and clear.

"My name is, umm, Eric Botha," Jonah said, giving the name from his doctored passport. "My father has been shot. Chippy is dead." He racked his brain, searching for some easily explainable justification. *Rhino poachers! That was the only credible answer.* "Poachers are escaping. Come quickly. Over," he begged.

"Okay, Mr. Botha. Stay calm. What is your location? Over."

"I am at Main Camp. They are at the cave. Over."

"Stay put. We are on our way. ETA less than two minutes. Over and out."

Within a minute Jonah heard the sound of an engine at full throttle. He grabbed a flashlight and ran out of the camp, pointing it upward so that the beam provided a fix on his position. He could see three beams of light bouncing into the night about half a mile away. He stayed put. The lights swung around a corner along the main track several hundred yards away and then swung away again as the track wound its way toward him. Five hundred yards. Three hundred yards. One hundred yards. The Land Rover came around the bend flat out, and Jonah was caught in the lights, dazzled. He stood still as the vehicle drew up.

"Jump in the back," said the same voice from the radio, and Jonah grabbed the arm that reached out to pull him in, almost without the vehicle stopping. The engine roared again, and they sped toward the cave, bouncing and lurching over the rough terrain. Jonah counted four men in the open-topped Landy, two in the back, two in the front. They were all in camouflage, and the two in the back held assault rifles. The one in the passenger seat held a powerful spotlight that he swept across the bush as the driver fought to keep control. It was pointless trying to speak; the noise was too great.

They reached the cave. The driver barked something in an African language, and two of the men began searching the surrounding bush with the spotlight while the fourth man grabbed a folded stretcher and a rucksack marked with a red cross. "They will follow the trail. There is another team driving to the perimeter fence. They have dogs," the driver said to Jonah in explanation. "Now show us the way."

At the cave, Jonah led the driver and the medic inside, where the fire had all but died. He ran to his father, whose eyes were now closed. "I'm back, Dad. I've brought you help. You have to keep going."

The driver peeled off to assess Chippy and Klaasens while the kneeled down and felt David's pulse. "Keep talking to him," he ordered Jonah.

Jonah held on to David's hand. his own slick with sweat. "Dad, it's me, Jonah. I've got the medics here. They're going to get you to the hospital." Jonah watched the medic rip open the rucksack and get to work, narrating the steps he was taking. "He's staunching the blood. Now he's injecting you with morphine. It'll take the pain away." He squeezed his dad's hand, trying to get a reaction, and David's eyelids flickered open for a second. "That's it, Dad! Hold on!"

The driver came over from inspecting the other two bodies "Nothing you can do for them. What about this one?"

"We need the chopper," said the medic. "Pulse is weak, and he's losing a lot of blood."

The driver nodded and ran out of the cave. The medic now spoke to Jonah. "Your father was hit twice. The bullet here," he pointed to the hip wound, "may have touched his spinal cord, which could cause paralysis of his legs. The other bullet looks as if it has pierced a lung and possibly touched an artery. We're going to bring in a medical rescue chopper from Tsumeb. It will take fifteen minutes. They will fly him to Windhoek."

Jonah looked down at his father. "Will he live?" he asked.

The man raised his eyebrows and shook his head. "I don't know," he said.

Jonah knelt down and put his mouth close to David's ear. "Don't die, Dad. Not now. I need you. Don't die." He squeezed his hand again. His father's eyes opened, and his lips moved silently. "What, Dad? What is it?" Jonah asked urgently, lowering his head again. "Tell me, what can I do?"

The words were faint but clear. "Make them pay, Jonah. Find Kloot. Make them pay." And then his eyes closed again, and he slipped back out of consciousness.

Outside, the driver was in radio contact with the helicopter dispatcher, giving them details of David's injuries and the GPS co-ordinates of their location. The chopper was in the air within five minutes, heading south toward the cave. The driver placed four lanterns on the ground to mark a landing area and returned to the cave to help transfer David to the stretcher.

Jonah and the two men had brought David down to the flat ground of the old riverbed. He had not regained consciousness despite his son's best efforts. Jonah waited for the helicopter in a thick sweat, praying that his father would live; that the chopper would come to take him to the hospital in enough time to save him; that the two of them would return to London and he would be greeted by Creedence's warm embrace; that they had found enough evidence to exonerate his father and incriminate the Baron and the Apollyon network.

He watched the helicopter coming in from the north, low and fast, visible by the spotlight on the nose that panned across the ground below. It began to slow, rising slightly. The spotlight locked onto Jonah, and he had to turn away from its brightness. The driver motioned for Jonah to squat down. The downdraft from the rotor blades blasted him with air and debris as the pilot brought the helicopter gently down onto the rock. The rotor blades slowed but didn't stop.

Two men came out and ran over to where David lay. They inserted a drip into his wrist and put an oxygen mask on his face before checking the straps that bound him to the stretcher. Satisfied, they lifted up the stretcher and carried it to the waiting helicopter. Jonah followed. The stretcher was placed inside and secured, and the men beckoned for Jonah to step in. They strapped him into a jump seat and put a set of headphones over his ears. The driver and the medic gave him the thumbs-up and retreated. As the chopper's doors were pulled closed, the volume and pitch of the engine began to rise, and the helicopter lifted into the air, tilted slightly forward, and headed for the hospital in Windhoek.

They had been in the air twenty-three minutes when Jonah saw the paramedic start pumping David's chest. His impassive voice came over the headphones, "Patient has gone into cardiac arrest! Am performing CPR. Activate the defibrillators." The second paramedic pushed past Jonah and pulled a box out from under the stretcher, flicking a switch on it and holding up the two defibrillator pads.

"Charging," Jonah heard over the headphones. "Charged!"

The first paramedic moved away to allow the second access to David. He placed the pads on his chest, and Jonah saw his father spasm as the electricity shot through his body, attempting to restart his heart. Jonah could feel his throat tightening and the tears begin to stream down his face.

"Nothing!" The first paramedic was pumping his chest again.

"Charging! Charged!" David's body went into spasm again.

"Still nothing! Again!"

Jonah was helpless, strapped into his seat, shaking, and praying to a god that, save for a few minutes earlier, he had not prayed to since he had gone to boarding school. "Please, God, let him live. Please, God."

"Nothing."

Jonah waited for the second paramedic to shout "Charged!" again. But it didn't come. He gripped the edge of his seat. *Why weren't they doing it again?!*

"Do it again! Don't stop!" he shouted. "Why aren't you doing it again?" he begged, but as the words came out his mouth, he already knew the answer. *He was gone. His father was gone.* Jonah could see the two paramedics still working, pumping his chest, trying to re-suscitate him, but Jonah knew that the life had left his body. Jonah looked on, thinking how he'd gotten his dad back only to have him taken away again. David's final words echoed inside Jonah's head. "Make them pay. Make them pay."

"I will, Dad. I will," Jonah said to himself, the words seeming to extinguish his desire to cry and instead give him strength. "I will make them pay," he said again and again, feeling stronger every time. He heard the poacher team call in on the radio that they'd caught one of the escapees, but not the other.

"I will make them pay," Jonah repeated to himself once more.

**To be continued ...**

# Acknowledgments

I would like to thank all those people who have played a part in this book, in particular my parents; my wife Jo; Andy and Carlie; the Colonel; Slash; Tommo; Charles Curtis; Robyn Beer; Mike Cordy; Bruno Nebe at Mundulea; Jackie, Catherine, and Caroline at Felicity Bryan; Gillian and the team at Razorbill; plus all of the friends, family, and colleagues who have shown their enthusiasm and interest throughout its writing.

Finally, an apology to the jinxed generation who will carry the costs of the 2008 financial crisis in higher taxes and fewer jobs. Sorry, kids. Gekko was wrong. Greed wasn't good.